Summer's RUNAWAY

A Princess Island novel

Rebecca L. Marsh

Visit the author's website: rebeccalmarsh.com

Cover design by Rebecca L. Marsh

Cover photos by Kanosky at IStock

And Inside Creative House at IStock

ISBN: 978-1-949498-09-7

1Thessalonians 5:11
"Therefore encourage one another and build one another up,
just as you are doing."

For Joe
my husband and best friend

Praise for Summer's Runaway

"*Summer's Runaway* is an emotional, heart-wrenching read, but it is also an uplifting story of forgiveness, fixing broken relationships and opening your heart to new possibilities." – **A Quintillion Words**

"This is heartwarming, uplifting but emotional all at the same time. Marsh has pulled me in from the beginning and kept me captive throughout." – **Little Miss Book Lover**

"Summer's Runaway is filled with love and hope with the power of family and friendship shining through. The characters are strong and loveable, each still have their own back story and good level of continuity is maintained with the first book of the series. Some difficult subjects are covered sensitively but Rebecca manages to capture the emotions perfectly." – **Good Books Come To Those Who Read**

"This story hooked me during the first few lines and I could not put it down. I read it in just a couple of evenings and I couldn't wait to get back to it." – **Author Angela Scavone**

"Heart-wrenching, but ultimately hopeful, this is another warmly heartfelt contemporary drama from this author" – **Bookshine and Readbows**

Other books by Rebecca L. Marsh

Princess Island series

Where Hope is Found

Beyond the Broken Shore

Standalone novels

When the Storm Ends

The Rift Between Us

Remember the Butterfly

Short Stories collection

The Santa Hat

Chapter 1

Hurrying from the ferry dock, Hallie made her way through Harper's Town with her head down. She hadn't been to the island in three years and didn't think anyone would recognize her, but she wanted to be sure. It was most likely overkill as she'd grown about a foot since her last visit. She was twelve now and had been barely nine the last time anyone here laid eyes on her. The baby face she used to have was gone and so were the braids she once wore in her kinky, black hair. Her mother never had time to braid her hair anymore, so now she didn't know what to do with it except pull it into puffy ponytails on either side of her brown face.

Once she was through town, Hallie slowed her pace to search the residential area for the right street. She couldn't remember the street name, but she figured she would know it when she saw it. The daylight was waning and gave the sky ribbons of pink as Hallie strode down the sidewalk. When she heard voices, she stopped cold. Darting behind a bush, she spotted two ladies talking in front of a house on the other side of the street. She squinted to see their faces. *Do I remember them? Do they remember me?* Since she couldn't be sure, she waited behind the bush until they went back inside their houses.

Stepping back out on the sidewalk, Hallie brushed leaves off her t-shirt and shorts. The sun was almost gone, and she really needed to find the house she was looking for. She came to the end of the street and turned left. Halfway down the new street, she saw the house she sought: a cedar-shingled Cape Cod.

Hallie watched the house for a few minutes. There were lights on inside, but she didn't see anyone outside. After a few beats, she took a deep breath and ran toward the side of the house. She hoped the small window in the garage wasn't locked.

Trying the window, Hallie smiled. It slid up easily, and just as she remembered, there was no screen. She tossed her backpack into the garage, then wiggled her way through the opening, struggling a bit. She was bigger now than the last time she and Charlie had gone through this window.

Once inside, Hallie straightened her clothes and dusted off before sliding the window back down.

She let her eyes roam over the garage. Owen's drum set sat on one side. That was new. He used to keep it inside the house. On the other side, there were some boxes stacked up near the wall. *That would work.* Hallie walked over to the boxes and began pushing the heavy stacks around to make a space between them and the wall where no one would see her.

When the work was done, she wiped sweat from her forehead with the back of her hand before dropping to the floor in her new hiding place. She rummaged through her backpack and retrieved a bottle of water. It wasn't cold anymore, but it still felt good as it washed down her parched throat. She had to be careful though. There were only two more bottles of water in her pack, and she wasn't sure how long they'd have to last.

Glancing around the now dark garage, she pulled two blankets from her pack. Arranging one on the floor, Hallie wished she had room to bring something with a little padding. She sighed as she lay down on the hard floor and pulled the other blanket over her. Hopefully by tomorrow night she would have something more comfortable to sleep on, but even if she didn't, it was better than staying at home this summer—anything would be.

Chapter 2

Owen washed a plate and handed it to his son, Charlie, who gave a small huff before grabbing the plate and drying it. Owen restrained a sigh, and for a split second missed the days when his son was younger and enjoyed their time together doing simple things. Now eleven-years-old, soon to be twelve, Charlie was beginning to develop the traits of a teenager.

"Why don't we just get a dishwasher, Dad?" Charlie asked.

"And lose this special time together?" Owen's voice held some sarcasm, but he did consider it special time. And these days, Charlie was getting busier with his friends and activities. Their time together was less and less.

Charlie took another dish from Owen. "Can't anything ever change?"

"Things are always changing. That's why I want some things to stay the same." He peered out the octagonal window over the sink at the last bit of color from the sunset. They usually ate dinner a lot earlier, but they'd been at Charlie's school for an end-of-the-year academic awards presentation. Charlie, who had struggled for a long time with math, earned a certificate this year.

Charlie stopped drying and turned to face his father. "Is that why you don't want to marry Carrie Ann?"

Owen's eyebrows shot up. "Whether or not I want to marry someone is for me to decide."

Charlie shrugged and began drying again. "I know that's why she broke up with you."

"Do you?" Owen was a bit uncomfortable with the direction this conversation was taking. However, Charlie had been through some hard things in his young life and Owen

3

knew his breakup with Carrie Ann affected his son. Charlie and Carrie Ann had grown close over the last couple of years. In their time as a couple, Carrie Ann became something of a mother figure to Charlie. His actual mother, Casey, had abandoned him at the age of five and went on to continue her life as a drug addict. She'd shown up with Charlie, stayed one night, then left him with Owen the following morning along with a note saying that Owen may or may not be Charlie's father and informing him that he was listed as the father on the boy's birth certificate.

When a strange man began lurking around the island watching them, Owen decided to get a DNA test, fearing the man might believe *he* was Charlie's father. It turned out Owen wasn't Charlie's biological father. But Travis, the lurker, had only come to check on Charlie for Casey and to deliver a letter to Owen. In the letter, Casey let Owen know that the other man who *might* be Charlie's father had died of an overdose. Owen was free to raise Charlie without any fear that another man would come to claim him.

His voice insolent, Charlie said, "Yes, and I think it's stupid for you to let her go. I miss her and so do you."

Owen took a deep breath and tried to keep his emotions even. "Yeah, I miss her. But that doesn't mean I should jump into marrying her."

Finishing the last dish, Charlie put it away and stared at his father. "Jump into it? You guys were dating for over two years. Aunt Marissa and Howard got married and had a baby already in practically the same amount of time."

"All right, Charlie, I think this conversation has gone about as far as it needs to. Not all relationships should follow the same map and they don't always lead to marriage."

Charlie's shoulders slumped. "Fine. Whatever. I'm going to my room now."

"Hang on. Did you bring that frozen pie in from the freezer in the garage like I asked you to? I need it to thaw out by dinner time tomorrow night."

4

Charlie sighed elaborately and changed direction to head for the garage door.

"Hey, Charlie," Owen called to him, and the boy turned and made eye contact. "Great job on the math this year."

One corner of Charlie's mouth turned up for a split second before he remembered he was mad at his father. He headed to the garage.

Owen went to the refrigerator and pulled a package of chicken out to thaw for tomorrow's dinner. Marissa and Howard were coming over along with his two nieces. He was looking through recipes when Charlie returned, tossed the frozen pie onto the counter, and turned to leave. Owen knew Charlie was upset with him, but his son's behavior seemed a little odd like he wanted to get away before any questions could be asked. Owen furrowed a brow at Charlie's back and decided to let it go.

Hallie waited anxiously in the corner of the garage behind the boxes. The hard concrete floor made her body ache, and the summer heat caused her chocolate-brown skin to grow damp with sweat. Thank goodness Charlie was going to come back soon and bring her a sleeping bag to lie on. There were a number of things she didn't think through before deciding to come here.

When Charlie had come into the garage earlier that evening to get a pie from the freezer, Hallie was sprawled on her blanket staring at her bottle of water. She desperately wanted to guzzle the rest of it down, but then she'd have to pee. Hallie was so glad to see her old friend come in. She'd crept to the edge of the boxes and whispered, "Charlie."

Charlie jumped and whirled around, his eyes searching the dimly lit garage. "Who's there?"

"Charlie, it's me—Hallie."

Charlie stepped closer and peered through the gloom. "Hallie? Is that really you?"

Hallie took a step closer. "It's me."

"You're so tall now. And you look different—your hair." Charlie pointed to the puffball-like ponytails on either side of Hallie's head, and she self-conscientiously lifted a hand to touch one of them. She hated them and missed the braids she used to wear.

"Yeah, you look different too," she said, taking in his long, lanky frame.

You haven't visited the island in three years. Why are you here now? Why are you in my garage?"

"I ran away from home." Hallie hugged herself as the words came out. She was already getting a little homesick. She missed her mom. She missed her little brothers and maybe even Dustin—a bit. But she couldn't go back, not until the end of summer.

"Ran away? Why?" Charlie shuffled a little closer.

Shrugging her shoulders and straightening her back, Hallie hoped her body language would show rebellion rather than fear. "'Cause my mom doesn't listen. She only cares about the twins now."

Charlie's face crinkled. "Your mom was nice before … and who are the twins?"

Of course, Charlie wouldn't know about her mother's *new* children. "My little brothers. Mom got remarried two years ago. She and Dustin have their own kids now. The twins keep them busy. It's like I'm not even there anymore."

"I bet she's worried about you. We should go talk to my dad," Charlie said.

"No!" Hallie grabbed Charlie's arm before he could turn to walk away. Her heart raced with fear.

He cocked his head to one side. "Why? Hallie, what's going on?"

6

"I told you, my mom doesn't listen. She doesn't care about me. She probably doesn't even know I'm gone." Hallie let go of Charlie's arm and stepped back from him.

Charlie put a hand on his hip as his brow furrowed in disbelief. "I know she loves you. I remember that much." He glanced around. "And you can't stay *here* forever."

"Not forever, just till the end of summer."

"Till the end of summer! You can't hide here that long."

Hallie's stomach knotted with desperation. "I have to! Please."

"I don't get it, why do you need to stay here for the summer?"

"You don't need to know everything, Charlie. Just trust me." She heard the frustration in the snap of her tone. Taking a deep breath, she looked down at her feet, then back up to meet his eyes. "We're still friends, aren't we?"

He folded his arms across his chest. "I don't know, are we? I haven't seen you in so long … and you never answered the letter I sent you. Besides, friends tell each other things and keep each other's secrets."

Hallie frowned as her anxiety threw acid up from her stomach. Getting Charlie to help her was turning out to be more difficult than she anticipated. And this *had* to work. Still, she was *not* going to tell him the reason. She didn't want to tell anyone about that. "You wouldn't understand. Can't you just trust me?"

He glared at her. When he spoke, his voice wavered with emotion. "No, I guess I wouldn't understand running away from a mother who loves you."

Regret stabbed Hallie's heart. It *would* be hard for him to understand since his mother had run away from him when he was only five years old. Even as young as they were the last time she was on the island, the pain he felt over his mother's abandonment hadn't escaped her.

Hallie reached out and gently touched Charlie's arm. "I'm sorry. I want to tell you, but I can't … not yet. I really

7

need you to trust me." She lowered her voice to a near whisper. "I need you to be my friend right now, Charlie, and help me."

He exhaled loudly as his posture relaxed. "Help you how?"

Hallie's mouth turned up a bit, relief washing over her. "Well, for starters, don't tell your dad or anyone else I'm out here."

"That's going to be hard. Dad gives drum lessons out here twice a week."

Hallie's eyes moved back to the drum set. "Didn't he do that in the house before?"

Charlie nodded. "He moved them out here when my aunt and cousin moved in. I guess that must have been just a few months after the last time you were here."

"Your aunt and cousin live here too?" *Great, this is getting more complicated by the minute.*

"Not anymore."

Hallie sighed with relief. "Okay, will your dad notice that I moved these boxes?"

Charlie examined the stacks of boxes. "Probably not."

"Good. Then just let me know when the lessons are, and I'll go hide outside." She tipped her head to the window.

"Okay, what else?"

She looked at the sleeping area she made on the floor. "I couldn't bring much with me. I could use something soft to sleep on, maybe a pillow, and I don't have a lot of water or food."

One side of Charlie's mouth raised as he thought. "I can bring out a sleeping bag and pillow." He pointed to the refrigerator on the wall near the door to the house. "There are bottles of water in there."

Hallie nodded. *Why didn't I think to check that out?*

"I could bring you some granola bars," Charlie said.

Hallie grinned. "That would be great! Thanks, Charlie."

"What about using the bathroom and stuff?"

She tapped her chin, considering that. "I know, I'll sneak out the window and go in that little patch of woods on the other side of Mrs. Mitchell's yard."

Charlie's face darkened. "I go to a day camp during summer, but Dad is usually still working when it's over. Now that I'm almost twelve, he lets me come home and stay by myself for a while. I can sneak you in the house tomorrow so you can wash up. But you'll have to be quick."

Hallie nodded. "I can be really fast." She lunged forward and hugged him. "Thanks for being a friend."

Rebecca L. Marsh

Chapter 3

Marissa pulled her car into a parking space in front of the pharmacy and cut the engine. Instinctively, she glanced at the backseat. But, of course, the infant car seat along with her tiny new baby was not there. It was her first day back at work and Owen's neighbor, Betty, was taking care of the baby.

She slid out of her car and smiled as she opened the pharmacy door.

"I should have known that brother of yours was going to be a mistake," Carrie Ann, Marissa's boss, said the minute Marissa walked inside. "He really is like a monk or something."

"I've been gone on maternity leave for two months and that's the first thing you have to say to me the day I come back?" Marissa asked, raising an eyebrow.

Carrie Ann waved her complaints away and continued to rearrange the candy selection at the register—something Marissa had noticed her boss did when she was frazzled. "It's not like we haven't talked or seen each other while you were out with the baby—who is adorable by the way."

Marissa smiled at the compliment to her new little daughter. "She is awfully cute. I'm hoping she'll keep Howard's blue eyes."

Carrie Ann waited for Marissa to say more about the baby, even letting her attention drop from the candy, but it was clear she wanted to talk about Owen and their breakup. Marissa decided that was fine, even if it was a little strange to have her best friend and boss vent to her about her brother. Aside from Howard, who was now her husband, Carrie Ann had been the most helpful, non-related person for Marissa when she first moved to Princess Island more than two years before. Back then, Marissa was struggling to recover from the terrible loss of her first husband, Kevin, and her oldest daughter, Kyla, after they'd drowned during a family vacation.

Marissa sighed at the thought of her lost husband and child, then recovering, asked, "Okay, what do you want to tell me about Owen?"

"I *had* to dump him. I didn't want to, but he refuses to move forward." Carrie Ann spewed the words out in a fast string and sucked in a breath. She went back to the candy and continued to talk. "We've been *just dating* for two years, but he's not ready for anything more. I don't think he'll ever be ready." Carrie Ann turned her eyes on Marissa. They were filled with sadness. "I need more."

Marissa stepped in close to her friend and put a hand on her shoulder. "You deserve more. I wish I knew what to tell you about Owen, but I don't understand myself. I know he cares about you."

Carrie Ann turned her eyes away and sniffed. "But maybe he doesn't love me the way I love him."

Marissa shook her head. "I didn't say that."

Pushing her light brown hair back which was now streaked with purple in a few places, Carrie Ann said, "I know you didn't. But if he loved me, wouldn't he want to move forward?"

Marissa was at a loss for anything helpful to say. Everything she saw in Owen when he was with Carrie Ann told her that he did love her, but she didn't have any idea why he wanted to keep their relationship at a standstill. She shrugged. "I don't know. I wish I did."

Carrie Ann regarded her for a moment with tight lips. "Yeah, me too." She began her work again with the candy display. "I need you to stock shelves in the snack food aisle. There are some boxes waiting for you."

Marissa nodded, accepting the fact that Carrie Ann was ready to end the conversation, and headed for the snack food aisle. Despite her sorrow for what Carrie Ann was going through, she smiled when she heard Cory, the pharmacist, humming in the back corner of the store. He was the happiest person she knew. When she'd first taken this job, she thought he must be a rare person with no problems in his life. But during one of her grief support group meetings, Cory showed up with his wife, Doreen, and they talked about losing their son. He was in the army and had died in an explosion. Cory lost his only child and managed to keep a happy demeanor even after such a great loss. He was one of the reasons Marissa had grown to love this job. She was going to miss her baby after spending every day of the last two months with her, but it was good to be back.

Rebecca L. Marsh

Chapter 4

Hallie sighed with relief when the door into the house opened and Charlie called out to her. She had little to do all day and was sick of being alone. Staying in this garage all summer was not going to be easy. But every time she thought about letting her mom or her grandparents know where she was, she remembered why she'd come in the first place. She would have to deal with the boredom for a few weeks.

She hurried to the door with her backpack and hugged Charlie again. "You're a good friend."

He smiled shyly and his cheeks pinked. "C'mon, I'll show you to the bathroom."

"The one upstairs?" she asked, and Charlie nodded. "I remember where it is."

Hallie knew she had to be fast, so she didn't waste any time looking around the house on her way to the bathroom. When she got there, she brushed her teeth before undressing and jumping in the shower. The warm water felt great on her skin after staying in a dirty garage for twenty-four hours. She wished she could linger but that wasn't an option.

Once out of the shower, Hallie pulled her extra outfit from her pack and put it on. She stared at the clothes she had taken off. She was going to have to figure out some way to wash them. For the time being, she gathered them up and stuffed them in the backpack.

After hastily putting her hair back up in the two ponytails, she hurried back downstairs and found Charlie in the living room with a book in his hand.

"Your dad still doesn't have a TV, huh?" she asked.

Charlie looked up. "Nope, but sometimes I get to watch when I go to my aunt's house."

He got up and set his book on the couch cushion. "You were really fast."

"Yeah, I tried to be." She looked down, hating to ask for any more favors. "Charlie, thanks for everything, but, um, do you think I could get something to eat before your dad gets home? I'm getting tired of the granola bars."

Charlie's lips pushed to one side as he thought. "There's some left-over hamburger helper in the fridge. I can heat it up for you."

Hallie beamed and her stomach rumbled at the thought of some real food. "That would be so great! Thank you!"

Charlie led her into the kitchen, and she sat down at the table and waited for him. He brought a steaming bowl over and put it in front of her.

Hallie blew on the hot mixture before taking a bite of the cheesy noodles and meat. "This is the best food ever!"

Charlie laughed. "It's only hamburger helper."

She took another bite, burning her mouth a little in her haste. "It tastes great!" Looking at her friend, she said, "I'm trying to figure out how to wash my clothes."

"If you'd just let me tell Dad you're here, I'm sure he would help you," Charlie insisted.

She looked at him with pleading eyes. "We can't do that. Please, Charlie."

He frowned with a huff. "Okay. I do my own laundry now. If you give the clothes to me, I'll wash them with mine, but I only do laundry once a week."

Hallie hesitated before answering. There were some things she didn't want him to wash. "That could work, but can I go back in the bathroom? There's something I want to wash myself."

Charlie looked confused but nodded.

"And I guess I'll have to make these clothes last until you can wash my other ones," Hallie added. Focusing on her food, she began to shovel it into her mouth fast as it cooled.

Charlie drummed his fingers on the table, filling the silence while she ate, then he said, "I like your new hairstyle."

Hallie self-consciously ran her hands over the ponytails. "I hate it, but my mom never has time to do the braids anymore." She remembered the last time her mom had tried. The boys were down for a nap, but Tyler woke up when the braids were only half-way done. Mom had settled him down with a bottle and tried to get the rest of Hallie's hair done, but minutes later, Tyson woke up and that was the end of it. Hallie ended up taking the braids back out because she couldn't finish them herself.

"So," Charlie said, "you have brothers now?"

"Yeah," she said keeping her attention on her bowl of food.

"I've always wondered what it would be like to have a little brother or sister."

Hallie rolled her eyes at him. "It's not that great."

"You don't like them?"

Scraping the last of the noodles and meat onto her spoon, Hallie thought about the question. "I like them. They're pretty cute and sometimes fun ... but they take all my mom's time." She pointed to her hair. "She doesn't have time for me anymore."

"Sorry," Charlie said.

Hallie could see he was trying to make conversation and didn't know what else to say. Studying him, she said, "You had your cousin here for a while. That must have been like having a sister."

He cocked his head to the side, considering the thought. "I guess it was in a way. But she was going through a bad time then and sometimes she took it out on me. She's nicer now."

"Brothers and sisters do that too, ya know." When he looked confused, she added, "Take things out on each other."

17

"Yeah, I guess. I did like having her here sometimes." His face clouded with a thoughtful look. "You and Maisy actually have a lot in common."

"Your cousin? Really?" This seemed hard for Hallie to imagine. She didn't feel like anyone could possibly understand her and how she felt lately. "Like what?"

"Her dad died too ... and her big sister—that part's not like you. That was what she was dealing with when she came here to live. And now her mom is married again and just had a baby." Charlie's eyes got big. "Hey, guess who her mom married."

Hallie furrowed her brow and shrugged. "I was only here in the summertime, Charlie. It's not like I know everyone."

"You know this person. Remember Mr. Paxton?"

She thought about it. "Your math tutor?"

Charlie nodded emphatically.

"So, now your math tutor is your uncle?"

Charlie grinned. "Yeah, but he's not my tutor anymore. I even got a certificate for my math grades this year."

Hallie didn't think that was terribly exciting, but she could see her friend did and he deserved her support after all he was doing for her. She mustered up a big smile. "That's awesome!"

"Yeah, thanks." He took her bowl and washed it. "My dad will be home soon."

She hated the idea of going back to the garage, but there was no other choice. "You got any books you're not reading? I don't have a lot to do out there all day."

"Stay here and I'll get you some."

Charlie ran upstairs and Hallie took the moment to walk around the living space in the house. She looked at the pictures on the wall, zoning in on one of a young girl who she thought might be the cousin Charlie told her about.

"Here's some stuff for you," Charlie said coming back downstairs. He handed her a bag.

She peered into the bag and saw a couple of books to read as well as some books of crossword puzzles. This would be better than staring at a wall all day. "Thanks."

As they walked through the kitchen on the way back to the garage, Charlie grabbed an apple and handed it to her. She smiled and accepted it.

When they got to the garage door, Charlie said, "My dad will be home earlier tomorrow, so I won't be able to bring you inside. He has drum lessons from two o'clock until five. I'll try to bring you out something to eat in the morning before I go to day camp and then later if I can."

"Okay, I'll make sure I'm outside before the drum lessons start." She looked at the watch on her wrist as she went back to her hiding place behind the boxes. Her dad gave the watch to her before his last deployment, the one he didn't come home from. She usually only wore it because it was from him, but now she was glad to have it for other reasons.

Rebecca L. Marsh

Chapter 5

Owen tossed a pinch of his own concoction of spices onto the chicken he was cooking in a large skillet. Satisfied with the seasoning, he checked on the biscuits in the oven, and seeing they were nicely browned, he pulled them out and put them in a basket, then covered them with a towel to keep them warm. He took a peek out the window and smiled at the seagulls flying by before returning his attention to the chicken in the skillet. It was time to flip each piece over, so he grabbed the tongs, flipped them, and added seasoning to the other side.

"Ouch!" Owen said when the doorbell startled him and caused him to burn his finger on the skillet. He waved his hand back and forth, trying to cool it as he headed to the front door.

"Come on in," he said, opening the door for his sister, Howard, and his two nieces.

As they all stepped into the house, Owen peered into the infant carrier his sister held. "There's my new little niece," He cooed. Then he glanced at his older niece, Maisy, and said, "And there's my other lovely niece."

"It's okay, Uncle Owen. I'm ten now. I know everyone wants to drool over the baby," Maisy said.

Owen snickered at Maisy's response. She was working hard to be grown up these days, but he knew having a new baby sister was a big adjustment for her.

Owen shook his hand again, feeling the pain in his finger.

Marissa scrunched up her face. "What's wrong?"

"I burned my finger when you rang the bell. It'll be fine. I just need to get it under some cold water." He headed back into the kitchen with his visitors following behind.

Turning on the faucet, he sighed when the cold water rushed over the burn.

"Can I help?" Marissa asked after setting baby Sylvie's carrier on the floor.

Owen nodded toward the stove. "The chicken is almost done and everything else is ready." He turned his eyes on Maisy. "You could help by going upstairs and telling Charlie it's time for dinner."

Maisy hurried off to do as he asked, and with his finger feeling better, Owen turned off the water and went back to the cooking chicken. He was just in time to save it from overcooking.

"Looks like we're ready," Owen said.

Marissa's stomach rumbled loudly with the news.

Owen raised his eyebrows. "None too soon, I guess."

Howard, Marissa's husband, and Owen's long-time friend, laughed. "She's always ready to eat."

Marissa shoved him playfully. "I'm feeding a baby. And I've already lost ten pounds of the baby weight," she added defensively.

"It wasn't a put-down," Howard said. He pulled Marissa into his arms. "You're beautiful—always have been and always will be."

Marissa kissed him before he let his arms drop. "I'll feel better when I can get back into my pre-baby clothes," she said.

"You can eat all the food you want here, and I won't say a word about it," Owen told her.

Charlie and Maisy ran into the room. "Does that mean there won't be any left-overs?" Charlie asked.

Owen furrowed his brow in his son's direction. "I guess we won't know until we're done. What's with the concern for left-overs?"

Charlie shrugged, but there was something off in his manner. "No reason."

Owen's gaze lingered on Charlie for a moment. *Was something going on with him?* But what could be going on that would relate to him asking about left-over food?

He let it go and put the chicken on a plate and took it to the table. When everyone was seated, Owen said a blessing, and they started to pass the food around.

"Awards night went well this year," Howard said once they all dug into their meal.

"It did. Maisy, congrats on your reading certificate," Owen said.

The girl smiled. "Thanks. And congrats to Charlie for getting one in math."

Everyone turned their attention to Charlie, but he was, for some reason, staring at the door to the garage.

"Charlie," Owen said, "your cousin gave you a compliment."

The boy's head whipped around. "Huh?" He looked at Maisy. "Oh, thanks."

Owen eyed his son suspiciously. "Is there something in the garage that needs your attention?"

"No!" Charlie's eyes widened and the word snapped out in a clipped, high voice. Then, seeing all the eyes on him, Charlie took on a placid demeanor and said, "I was just thinking about ice cream for dessert, that's all."

"Ooookay," Owen responded, unsure what to make of his son's odd behavior.

"Ice cream sounds great to me," Marissa said, breaking the awkwardness of the moment.

The conversation turned back to the awards night and the fact that it had been Charlie's last year at the elementary school. When the baby began to fuss, Marissa took her to the other room to feed her, and ended up missing the ice cream.

Coming back into the kitchen, she handed the baby to Owen. "How about you have some quality time with Miss Sylvie? Howard and I can take care of the dishes."

"You don't have to do that," Owen said. "You're my guests."

Marissa waved a hand. "We're family and I lived here for more than a year."

Owen gazed down at the tiny baby in his arms and shrugged. "You don't have to twist my arm. Sylvie and I will be in the living room."

Marissa headed to the sink and started the water running, squirting in some soap.

"Can I go over to Mrs. Mitchel's yard and play with Max?" Maisy asked, referring to the dog that belonged to Owen's neighbor.

"Sure, I imagine Betty would love to have someone run a little energy out of him," Marissa said before rolling up her sleeves and plunging the first dish into the soapy water.

As Maisy hurried out the back door, Howard joined Marissa with a towel, ready to do the drying, and Charlie started clearing the table.

When the dishes were done, Howard kissed Marissa's cheek and said, "I think I'll join Owen in the other room. What about you?"

She smiled at him, amazed at how happy she was. Less than three years ago, she didn't think it was possible to ever be truly happy again. She'd suffered a great loss when her first husband, Kevin, and their oldest daughter, Kyla, had drowned in the ocean during a family vacation. Back then, she felt like her life had been ripped apart. Had it not been for Maisy, she probably would not have survived. She certainly didn't think it possible then that she would find love again and have another child.

"I'll be there in a few minutes," Marissa said.

Howard headed to the other room and Marissa went to the window and looked out. Expecting to see Maisy playing with the dog, Marissa was surprised to see her daughter standing alone near the tree swing while Max ran around the yard on his own. Marissa moved in closer to the window curiously.

When Owen stepped in behind her and touched her shoulder, Marissa jumped. Glancing back at him with an irritated expression, she said, "I thought we talked about you not sneaking up on me."

"There was no sneaking intended. I was just wondering what you're up to in here," Owen said innocently.

Marissa pointed to Maisy in the neighbor's yard. "What do you suppose she's doing?"

Owen looked out the window where she pointed and they both watched as Maisy stood staring at the empty swing. Then her lips began to move.

"Who's she talking to?" Owen asked.

"No idea. You don't think she's developed an imaginary friend, do you?" Marissa's chest tightened with worry. She thought her daughter was in a good place now.

"I guess that's possible, but that usually happens with younger kids. I would think Maisy a little too old for that."

"Yeah, me too. But then, what is she doing?"

Maisy stopped talking and sat down on the swing.

"I'm sure it's nothing," Owen said. "But if you're worried, maybe you should ask her about it."

Still staring at her child, Marissa nodded. Then she turned to her brother, cocked her head to one side, and said, "Aren't you going to ask?"

Though Marissa knew her brother knew exactly what she was talking about, he did his best to turn his face into a mask of indifference. With a shrug of one shoulder, he said, "Ask what?"

"How my first day back at work was." Marissa fixed her gaze on him. She could see the effect in the waver of resolve in his eyes. But he managed to keep the look of indifference solid otherwise.

"So, how was it, then?"

She walked to the table and picked up the water glass she'd left there, taking a sip before turning back to him. "It was good to be back. I missed it and there's nothing like Cory's humming to put a smile on my face."

Owen faltered by allowing relief to wash over his face, but Marissa wasn't done.

"It was a little awkward, though, having my boss, who is also my best friend, grill me about my brother's apparent lack of feeling for her." Marissa leaned against the counter and crossed her arms.

"She was the one who dumped me," Owen said defensively, his body straightening up.

"Yeah, I know. But we both know why."

Running a hand through his blond curls, Owen exhaled loudly. "Not you too, Rissa."

She raised an eyebrow at him.

"I just had this conversation with Charlie yesterday," he explained.

"Probably because none of us can understand." She gave a little shake of her head. "Owen, I know your feelings for her are deeper than you're letting on. I know you."

"She wants more than I can give right now." Owen looked away.

His obvious discomfort was painful for Marissa, but she pressed on, lowering her voice to a more compassionate tone. "I don't understand. What's holding you back? Charlie's doing well. What's standing in the way?"

"I'm just not ready, Marissa. Now, please, let it go."

It was rare for Owen to call her anything other than Rissa, so she knew it was time to give up the questions. With a sigh, she closed the distance between them and patted his arm. "When you're ready to talk about it, I'm here. And I sure hope you figure out what's holding you back soon because she loves you. But eventually, she's going to get tired of waiting for you to come to your senses. She'll move on and find someone else. That'd be a shame because I'm pretty sure you love her too."

Rebecca L. Marsh

Chapter 6

Hallie sprang up from the sleeping bag, gasping. With fuzzy eyes, she glanced around at the boxes that surrounded her. *Oh, yeah, I'm in Charlie's garage.* She rubbed her eyes and looked at the watch on her wrist. It was only four in the morning. Despite the nightmare she had, she needed to sleep for a while longer, at least until the sun came up. Then she could read one of the books Charlie gave her.

She laid back down and tried to relax. Her heart began to race again when she heard a scraping sound. "It's nothing," she told herself, speaking the words out loud for good measure. "I'm on the island. Nothing will hurt me here."

The noise came again: *scrape, scrape.* Hallie pulled her blanket over her head and tried to ignore it. When she heard it a third time, she hesitantly crawled out from under her blanket and inched her way to the window. Glancing out, she sighed in relief, realizing the sound was just a tree branch hitting the side of the garage.

Hallie went back to her sleeping bag and closed her eyes. She didn't think she would be able to sleep and was surprised when she woke to Charlie shaking her shoulder. She blinked a few times, trying to wake up.

"Hallie," Charlie said in a soft voice. "I need to hurry. I woke up a little late today and my dad is almost ready to leave."

She shook her head to wake herself up and pushed into a sitting position. "Okay. I'm awake."

He handed her a paper bag and she peered inside. There was a sandwich, some grapes, and more granola bars. "Thanks," she said.

"Don't forget, Dad has drum lessons today."

Hallie nodded. "I remember. I'll get outside before two o'clock."

"Great! Gotta go."

As Charlie turned to leave, Hallie thought about the nightmare she had during the night and the fear she'd felt hearing a strange sound—until she realized it was just a branch—and she was flooded with gratefulness. Her fear was unnecessary. There was no real threat, but if she were at home right now, there would be. "Charlie," she called to his back.

When he turned and looked at her with curiosity, she hopped up and hurried over to him. Wrapping her arms around him, she said, "Thank you for helping me stay here."

Hallie pulled back, her eyes moist, and looked at her friend. His cheeks were pink, and his mouth turned up in a shy half-smile. "No problem," he said. "That's what friends are for."

"And you're a good one." She smiled at him and he grinned in response before turning to leave.

When Charlie was gone, Hallie reached into the paper bag and pulled out a granola bar and some grapes to eat for breakfast. She made a face at the bar. Granola wasn't a favorite of hers and she was sick of it already. But she had to eat, and beggars can't be choosers; that's what her mom always said.

Finished with her breakfast, she crawled through the window and hurried into the nearby wooded area to relieve her bladder. Then she took a short walk to stretch her legs before returning to the garage where she kept busy reading and doing crossword puzzles until she grew too sleepy to keep her eyes open.

She glanced at her watch. It was almost noon. She grabbed the paper bag again and pulled the sandwich out along with the rest of the grapes.

After eating, she laid down on her sleeping bag and closed her eyes. To her surprise, she fell asleep quickly and when she woke, it was almost two o'clock. "Oh no!" she gasped. Grabbing the book she'd been reading earlier, she rushed to crawl out the window again and get into the woods before anyone saw her.

As she passed Mrs. Mitchel's yard, Hallie noticed the tree swing and wished she could sit there to read her book. As it was, she'd have to find a rock to sit on or just plant her butt on the ground. She left the garage in such a hurry; she didn't take the time to grab something to sit on. But she had a book and a bottle of water, so she'd be all right.

Owen was tired after several hours of work as a handyman followed by three hours of drum lessons. On the plus side, his last lesson of the day had been with Harvey Slone, a sixty-five-year-old who was on a mission to learn to play as many instruments as he possibly could with the years he had left. He'd told Owen it was the first thing on his bucket list. When Owen told him he was too young for a bucket list, Harvey laughed. "It's never too early to start a bucket list," the man had said, "The sooner you start the more you can accomplish." It was hard to argue with that.

Owen enjoyed having Harvey as a student because he didn't have the mentality that hitting the drums harder made you better. As much as he loved all his much younger students, they often left him with a desperate need for a Tylenol.

Today his head was okay, but he didn't feel much like cooking. He opened the refrigerator and searched its contents. After closing the door, he scratched his head and called out, "Charlie, can you come here, please?"

While Owen waited for his son to appear, he opened the door to the pantry and found himself scratching his head again.

"What is it, Dad?" Charlie asked, coming up behind Owen.

Turning to face his son, Owen asked, "Do you know where all the granola bars went and the left-over Hamburger Helper?"

Owen didn't miss the way Charlie's face paled at the question. "I ate them," Charlie said quickly.

Owen raised his eyebrows. "You ate all of that? Two servings of Hamburger Helper and five granola bars in the last two days plus all your regular meals?"

Charlie nodded.

It wasn't unheard of for a boy Charlie's age to have a ravenous appetite, but if that was the case, it was new. Owen probably would believe it without question if it were not for the odd way his son was behaving. He kept his eyes on Charlie's for a few seconds to see if his story might change under pressure.

Charlie said nothing more but looked like he'd been caught with his hand in the cookie jar. Owen thought about asking if Charlie might have had a friend or two over while he was home alone after day camp, but before he had the chance, his phone rang.

Owen picked up the phone. "Hello?"

"Someone just ran out of the woods and behind my yard. Did you see?" said his neighbor, Betty.

He went to the kitchen window but didn't see anything out of the ordinary. "No, I didn't see anyone. Maybe it was one of the Thatcher boys," Owen suggested. The Thatcher family lived down the road and had three young boys. They weren't allowed to play this far from home, but maybe one of them decided to break the rules.

"It looked like a girl to me," Betty said. "But I didn't get a good look. She—or he—was moving fast. Looked to be headed for your house."

"Well, no one is out there now. I'll keep my eyes open. But it's probably just a kid running around."

"Probably," Betty said, not sounding convinced. "I read an article about dog thieves. I hope I don't have to worry about my little Max."

"I haven't heard of any of that on the island and I doubt anyone would come here just to steal dogs. I'm sure Max will be fine," Owen assured her before saying goodbye and hanging up.

He turned back to Charlie, who was still standing nearby. "Mrs. Mitchel says she saw someone run out of the woods and toward our house. Do you know any kids in the area that might be playing in those woods? She said it looked like a girl."

"No," Charlie spat the word out with a vigorous head shake.

Owen's forehead crinkled. "Okay," he said. "Well, I was going to heat up that Hamburger Helper for dinner, and now I can't, so we need to figure something out for dinner. Got any ideas for me that don't require much energy?"

"Hot dogs and fruit salad? I'll take care of the fruit and all you'd have to do is grill the hot dogs."

Charlie was being unusually accommodating, which made Owen suspicious. But he was tired and decided accepting help was the best choice.

By the time Charlie came out to the garage that evening, Hallie's stomach was growling. She thought she might have to sleep on an empty stomach that night. When Charlie handed her a banana and a bag of cheese crackers, she greedily accepted them and tore into the banana right away.

Charlie sat behind the boxes with her and watched her eat. "Sorry it took me so long, but my dad is asking questions about where the food is going." He stopped and gave her an uneasy look. "There's another problem too."

Hallie made eye contact with him for a moment before opening the bag of crackers and stuffing two in her mouth. "What?" she asked.

"Mrs. Mitchel saw you coming back today. She called my dad and was worried about it. I don't think we're going to be able to keep you out here secretly much longer. We should just tell my dad. He'll help you."

Hallie's eyes met his, a sharp look in them. "No, Charlie. He'll want to call my grandparents."

"Why is that so bad?"

She stared at him. A part of her wanted to tell him why she'd come, but she didn't think he would understand. Even if he did, he'd probably want her to tell the adults and she didn't trust any of them to help her. "Because they would tell my mom. Then *she* would make me come home and I can't do that." That wasn't the only reason she didn't want to see her grandparents, but she didn't want to get into her feelings about them at the moment. She had enough to deal with.

"I don't get it. Your mom is a nice person. I'm sure she wants to help you if there's something wrong." After a moment of silence, he said, "Did you do something bad? Is that why you don't want to go home?"

Hallie had to restrain her anger that he would ask that. She hadn't done anything. *She* wasn't the problem. But Charlie was the only person she had to help her right now and starting a fight wouldn't help. "No, Charlie," she said with only a little agitation in her voice. "I didn't do anything wrong. But my mom won't help me. I told you, she doesn't listen. I tried talking to her already."

She took a deep breath and let it out slowly. "I need you to keep helping me." She reached out and placed a hand on his arm. "I need you to be a friend right now and just trust me." She grabbed her backpack and pulled out the ten-dollar bill that was tucked inside. "Here," she said handing it to him, "use this and buy me some food in town. That way you can just bring me one or two little things each day and your dad won't keep getting suspicious about too much missing food."

Reluctantly, Charlie accepted the money. "I'm not supposed to go to town alone."

Hallie kept her eyes locked on his, imploring him to help.

He sighed. "Dad works later tomorrow. I guess I can sneak out and get a few things for you."

Hallie grinned and popped another cracker in her mouth. "Thank you, Charlie! I knew I could count on you. And I'll try to be more careful when I sneak in and out."

Charlie nodded and got up to leave. Hallie grabbed his hand to stop him. When he looked at her, she said, "Don't buy any granola, okay? I'd rather eat dry cereal."

Rebecca L. Marsh

Chapter 7

Owen rubbed his eyes and started the coffee maker, anxious to feel the rush of caffeine to his system. When he opened the cupboard to get a mug, his eyes caught sight of the pink and blue mug Carrie Ann left there. She used to come over some mornings and have coffee with him before they both went to work. His heart sank at the sight, yet he found it difficult to tear his gaze away from the mug. Letting his fingers touch it, he thought about Carrie Ann's smile and the way she'd always made mornings more joyful. He couldn't deny that he missed her—he missed her a lot.

He ought to take the mug back to her, but the thought of doing that made his chest tighten. As long as the mug stayed in his house, it felt like she might change her mind and come back to him. He pushed the pink and blue mug to the back of the cupboard where he would know it was there, but wouldn't see it again if he didn't want to.

Why couldn't Carrie Ann be happy with the relationship they had and give him the time he needed before moving forward? Marissa said Carrie Ann loved him, but if she really did, wouldn't she wait for him and respect his need for a slower pace?

Owen grabbed a mug and closed the cupboard. He set it in place and told the Keurig what size cup to make. Then he ran a hand through his hair while he waited for the coffee maker to do its job. With a sigh, he dared to ask himself the question everyone else was asking: *why wasn't he ready to move forward with Carrie Ann?*

He certainly had strong feelings for her. *Was it love?* His heart raced at the question and he realized he didn't want to answer it. He'd loved Casey for years, and Charlie aside, all she'd ever given him was heartbreak. Owen had to admit he wasn't sure he wanted to be in love or to know if he already was.

He put cream and sugar in his coffee, then put two slices of bread in the toaster. Walking to the bottom of the stairs, he called, "Charlie, come down for breakfast."

Once he and Charlie had their breakfast, he drove the very short way to the church where Charlie went for day camp and dropped his son off. "Have a good day," he told Charlie.

With that done, Owen headed to Larry O'Conner's house where his job was to stain a fence and replace some rotting boards on the deck. He finished the job just before lunch and decided to eat his sack lunch in the park before heading to the next job.

Hopping back into his car, he sneezed a few times and realized his eyes were beginning to itch. His allergies were acting up. He reached into his glove compartment for the allergy pills he kept there. The bottle was empty. *Not again,* he thought. He was terrible about letting that happen.

He drove to the grocery store and went to their pharmacy section to find what he needed. The drug store would be faster and easier, but he didn't want to see Carrie Ann, so he avoided it. Of course, in this small town, he knew he couldn't avoid seeing her forever.

When he saw that the grocery store was out of the medicine he needed, he sighed heavily. His avoidance would have to end right now.

Owen drove the short distance to the drug store and sat staring for a moment. *Get out of the car. Putting it off won't help.* He groaned, hoped Carrie Ann wasn't the one at the counter, and forced his feet to move.

His hopes were dashed the second he walked in and saw Carrie Ann putting a new display of cough drops together near the front of the store. Keeping his head down, he tried to rush straight to the allergy meds without drawing her attention. Maybe Cory would check him out at the pharmacy counter.

"I see you, Owen. So, you can stop trying to sneak past me," Carrie Ann said without looking away from the display she was working on.

Owen sighed. "I'm not sneaking," he lied. "I'm just in a hurry to get my allergy pills and get back to work."

"You let the bottle go empty again, huh?"

The way she knew him so well tugged at his heart. "Yeah, so I'll just go get them and be out of your way." He started to walk again, but her voice stopped him.

"You're not in my way." She looked at him now and their eyes locked. "And if you decide you're ready for a relationship that isn't stuck in place forever, I'm here. I'm ready to talk." She looked down and a purple-streaked strand of hair fell forward over her cheek. Owen had to resist the urge to reach out and pull the tendril back for her.

She looked so sad, and Owen's heart seized. A part of him wanted to pull her into his arms and promise her anything she wanted, but he didn't. Something held him back, though he wasn't sure what. It was, he supposed, the same thing that made him act the way he had the night he and Carrie Ann broke up.

They had gone out dancing that night, and while she was in his arms, smiling up at him, she said, "It would be nice to get married in the fall, don't you think? We could honeymoon in Vermont or some other place where the air is cool and crisp. We'll spend all our time curled up in each other's arms next to a roaring fire."

Her eyes danced with the words, but they weren't dancing for real anymore because Owen's feet stopped, and his mouth went dry. When he didn't respond, Carrie Ann's expression sobered. "We still can't talk about getting married?"

Owen swallowed. "I don't think I'm ready yet. I like what we have now."

"It's been two years, Owen. Don't you think that's long enough? I'm ready to move forward. I'm not getting any younger." She pulled out of his embrace and stood with her eyes on his.

Owen forced a smile and tried to make light of her words. "You're hardly old. We have plenty of time."

Her lips tightened and a few seconds ticked by before she answered him. They were long, uncomfortable seconds, her eyes searching his. Her voice came back soft but with an undertone of agitation. "I want to have kids, Owen. You know that. So, if you're not prepared to move forward and don't think you're going to get there really soon, then you need to tell me now."

He looked down, unable to say his next words while looking her in the eye. "I don't know when I'll be ready for all that. Right now, I'm not. I just want to enjoy being together."

Daring to look back up, he saw her eyes glisten with a mixture of anger and sadness. "That's not enough for me."

Bringing his attention back to the present, Owen stared at Carrie Ann, trying to find some right words. Giving up, he trudged on to the allergy aisle and grabbed his pills. He carried the box to the counter and Carrie Ann wordlessly checked him out. As he reached the door to leave, she called out, "Say hi to Charlie for me. Tell him I miss him."

Hallie wiped sweat from her forehead and took a sip of her water. She tried to read her book, but the heat was so oppressive, she was having a hard time focusing. It was almost bad enough to make her want to tell Charlie's dad she was here—almost. She'd thought about telling him that morning after she woke up shaking and gasping. The nightmares had plagued her again. At home, when she had a bad dream, there was the comfort of other people in the house. And even though her mother had brushed it off when Hallie tried to tell her what she was afraid of, there was still comfort in her mother's presence after a terrible dream. Still, if she told any of the adults where she was and they didn't believe her about the danger that drove her to run away, then the nightmare might come true.

Fanning herself with one of the crossword puzzle books, Hallie decided that, no matter how hot and unpleasant it was, she had to stand firm. This might be the hardest summer of her life, but it *could* be worse.

She smiled with relief when Charlie opened the door and stepped out into the garage, carefully carrying a stack of items from the store. He walked over to her, behind the boxes, and set the stack down. Hallie looked it over: a box of Coco Puffs, Goldfish crackers, a pack of individual applesauce cups, a loaf of bread, and a jar of peanut butter.

"I'll still try to bring you a little something each day and that way this stuff will last longer," Charlie said.

"Great! This looks good. You made good choices." She kissed him on the cheek, and he smiled shyly.

He reached into his pocket and handed Hallie the little bit of change. She frowned at it. "I guess this is all I have left. I better make the food you bought last."

Before Charlie had a chance to say a word in response, Hallie's eyes snapped up to meet his and she said, "Because we are not telling your dad or anyone else that I'm here."

He nodded solemnly, looking down.

Hallie felt a stab of guilt in her chest. "I'm sorry. I know you don't like doing this for me."

He glanced up. "I like helping you. I just don't like sneaking around." His face scrunched up and he fiddled with the hem of his shirt. "It reminds me of the way it felt to be with my mom. I'm not sure why. I don't remember much about that time, but I remember some of the feelings. I didn't even know those feelings were bad until I was here for a while."

41

Hallie touched his arm. She knew a little about how Charlie's mom left him and that she had a drug problem. She was sorry to stir up bad feelings for him. "I wouldn't ask you if there was another way."

He nodded. "You want to come in and use the bathroom?"

Hallie nodded vigorously, anticipating the air conditioning. "I'd love to."

"I'm going to do my laundry tomorrow and I'll bring your stuff out to you when I can," Charlie said as they headed into the house.

"It will be nice to put on clean clothes again. Thanks for that, Charlie." She pulled at her sweaty shirt, relishing the cool air on her skin. "I guess I'll go clean up as much as I can for now."

Charlie glanced at her again, taking in the dampness of her clothes. "I've got some old T-shirts and gym shorts you could borrow if it would help."

"You really are the best friend." She beamed at him.

"I'll get them for you and leave them outside the bathroom door so you can put on something clean and dry. Leave those and I'll put them with the rest of my laundry."

They walked upstairs together, and Hallie hurried into the bathroom. It felt good to wash herself off a bit, put on clean clothes, and use the toilet. It truly is the simple things you miss.

When she returned to the kitchen where Charlie waited, he looked up from a comic book and smiled. "You want some real food to eat?"

She shrugged. "I don't want your dad to get suspicious again."

Charlie hopped up and went to the pantry, pulling out a single-serve container of Chef Boyardee ravioli. "I can heat this up for you and I'll tell him I had it for a snack if he asks. As long as we don't take too much food, I think it will be okay."

"Sure. Some real food would be nice." Hallie sat down at the table while Charlie heated up the ravioli.

"Be careful, it's hot," he warned, putting the container down in front of her and handing her a spoon.

She drew in a deep breath, enjoying the rich scent of tomato sauce, and scooped a small bite, blowing on it before putting it in her mouth. "That tastes good." She took another bite and sighed. "I miss my mother's cooking. I didn't ever think I would wish for vegetables instead of Coco Puffs, but I'm starting to."

"I think I can help you with that." Charlie went to the refrigerator and grabbed a small bag of raw carrots. He handed them to Hallie. "Dad puts these in my lunch all the time and I get tired of them. You can take them, and no one will miss them."

Hallie accepted the bag. "Raw isn't exactly what I had in mind, but I'll take it."

"Beggars can't be choosers?" Charlie said with a grin.

Hallie rolled her eyes as he mimicked her statement. "My mother's words will haunt me every day now." She looked up from her food and met Charlie's eyes. "But I'm grateful still. Thanks for being a friend when I need it."

He shrugged. "You'd do it for me."

Hallie nodded and ate more of the ravioli. After a few bites, she spoke without looking up. "Tell me more about your cousin."

"Maisy? She's nice." Charlie's face scrunched up. "I don't think she likes her baby sister though."

"How come?"

"Are you asking why Maisy doesn't like Sylvie, or why I think that?"

Hallie thought with her mouth tight. "Both, I guess."

"Well, I don't know why she doesn't like the baby, but I see the way she looks at Sylvie when she doesn't think anyone is paying attention," Charlie said, leaning back in his chair.

"What way is that?" Hallie looked quizzically at him. She wasn't sure why, but she wanted to know the answer.

Charlie furrowed his brow. "I don't know. She just looks at Sylvie like there's something about the baby that upsets her."

"Probably because her mom has to spend all her time with that baby now," Hallie said with certainty. She knew all about that problem. "At least it wasn't twins."

"Maybe, but it seems like something more to do with the baby to me. And I'm not there all the time, but it seems like Aunt Marissa and Howard are still making time for Maisy. Besides, you said you like your brothers even though they take up all your mom's time."

Hallie nodded gloomily. "I do like them. I love them. I love my mom." A tear slid down her face. "I just wish she would listen." She struggled to keep herself from breaking down and sobbing.

Charlie stared at her. "You could tell me, you know. I've kept the secret about you staying in the garage. Don't you think you can trust me?"

Hallie hesitated. A part of her did want to talk to someone, tell what she feared, and how the nightmares made it hard to sleep. But she knew she could never do it. Just thinking about telling made her throat tighten and her mouth go dry. And, even if she did feel like she could tell someone, it wouldn't be a boy. He would never understand.

"It isn't about not trusting you, Charlie. I just can't." She met his eyes with a look that pleaded for his understanding.

He let out a heavy breath and nodded, but his disappointment was clear.

Hallie finished the last bite of her ravioli. "I'm done with this. I guess I better get out of here before your dad comes home."

Charlie threw the little container away and washed her spoon before walking her back out to the garage.

When Owen arrived home that evening, the heaviness he'd felt in his heart at the drug store filled his whole body. All he wanted to do was go to his bed and lie down, but he'd have to wait for that. There was dinner to make, and after that, he had a rescheduled drum lesson. He put the fingers of his right hand to his temple just thinking about listening to a pre-teen play the drums. He hoped his head could handle the half-hour lesson.

Opening the refrigerator, Owen stared at the pork chops he planned to cook for dinner. He did not have the energy to cook. With a sigh of resignation, he closed the fridge, opened the freezer, and pulled out a frozen pizza. He tore off the plastic and placed it on a round pan before setting the oven.

While he waited for the oven to heat up, Owen tidied up the kitchen counters a little, clearing off some old mail and other junk they didn't need any longer. As he flipped through the things in his hand, making sure he didn't throw away anything important, he spotted a receipt from the grocery store. He squinted at it, trying to read the small print. As he read the list of purchases, his nose scrunched up. Coco Puffs and Goldfish crackers? He hadn't bought those things.

The oven beeped, letting him know it was time to put the pizza in. He set the receipt down on the counter, intending to ask his son about it later, and tossed the other papers in the recycle bin.

Once the pizza was in the oven, Owen went to the living room and laid down on the couch, hoping his head would feel better by the time dinner was ready.

When the oven timer dinged, Owen was startled. Apparently, he'd dozed off. He sat up slowly, noticing that his head felt better. The drum lesson might not be so bad after all.

"Charlie, dinner!" he called as he passed the staircase on his way to the kitchen. By the time the pizza was sliced, Charlie ran into the kitchen and sat down at the table.

"All right, pizza!" Charlie grinned.

"I didn't feel like cooking tonight, so you get lucky," Owen said. He put a slice of pizza on each of their plates. "Would you say the blessing?"

Charlie shrugged and recited a simple blessing, then they both dug into their food.

"How was day camp?" Owen asked.

"Today was pretty cool. We took a hike in the woods and the counselor told us which plants were edible if we ever got stranded in a forest."

Owen smiled at his son's enjoyment of the outdoors. "That's great! Maybe we can go sometime, and you can show me the edible plants."

"Sure, Dad. How was your day?"

Owen sighed. "It was okay."

"Something go wrong?" Charlie asked.

Owen forced a smile. He wasn't going to talk to Charlie about how seeing Carrie Ann had affected him. "No, just a long, hot day. I'm a little worn out." He held up his slice of pizza. "That's why I didn't want to cook."

Charlie accepted Owen's answer and spent the rest of their meal talking about Tony and Cameron, the boys he'd made friends with since starting day camp.

When they were done eating and the few dishes were washed, Owen picked up the receipt on the counter and held it up. "Did you go to the grocery store?" he asked Charlie.

"No."

Owen didn't miss how fast the word flew from his son's mouth or the way Charlie's eyes widened at the question.

"Really?" Owen raised an eyebrow. "Because I know I didn't buy these things."

After only the briefest hesitation, Charlie said, "Well, maybe Aunt Marissa or Howard left that receipt when they came to dinner."

Owen couldn't say with certainty that Charlie's suggestion was impossible, but it was extremely unlikely. Why would either of them leave a receipt here? "I doubt that."

Charlie shook his head. "I don't know, Dad."

Owen didn't like the fact that his son was almost certainly lying, but he also didn't have the time or energy to deal with it any further at the moment. He started toward the door to the garage, but Charlie jumped in front of him.

"Where are you going, Dad?"

"Ricky's lesson was rescheduled from tomorrow to today. I need to go open the door out there and let the heat out."

"Wait!" Charlie's voice pitched high, and Owen saw fear in his eyes. "I made a mess out there earlier. I'll just go clean it up first."

Skeptical, Owen said, "We can go together, and you can clean up while I get the door opened up."

Charlie refused to get out of Owen's way. "No, Dad, I don't want you to see what I was doing. It's something I'm working on for Father's Day."

Smooth, Owen thought. But what if his son was telling the truth? He didn't want to ruin it if Charlie really was working on a surprise for him. "Okay, but I'll be out there in five minutes to get ready for Ricky's lesson."

"No problem. I'll be fast." Charlie raced past Owen and out to the garage.

Still doubtful about his son's motives, Owen pressed his ear to the door, not sure what he expected to hear. When hushed voices came to his ear, his eyes widened in surprise. What was going on out there? He couldn't make out much of what was said, but when he heard a mention of the window, he hurried to the back door in the kitchen, went out, and walked to the side of the garage where the window was. He got there just in time to see a young girl slipping out.

Chapter 8

"Hold it right there, young lady." The voice stopped Hallie in her tracks. Slowly, she turned to face Charlie's dad.

"Hallie?" he said in surprise "Is that you?"

She nodded, keeping her eyes on the ground.

"What are you doing in my garage?" Owen demanded.

Hallie brought her eyes up enough to see his face but didn't meet his eyes. "Hiding."

"Hiding? From what?" He walked over, peered in the window, and said, "Charlie, get out here."

Hallie didn't answer the question and hoped he'd forget he'd asked it. Charlie opened the garage door and slunk out to stand next to her, his head hanging. Hallie felt bad for getting him into trouble.

"Hallie? What are you hiding from? Do your grandparents know you're on the island? Does your mom know where you are?" Owen asked.

Choosing to ignore the first question, Hallie said, "No, my grandparents don't know I'm here. My mom thinks I'm at a friend's house. At least, I think she still thinks that."

Glancing at Owen's face, Hallie saw his brow crinkle. "How long have you been here?"

She shrugged. "A few days."

"A few days?" Owen's voice registered shock. He turned his eyes on Charlie. "You've been hiding someone in our garage for a few days?"

Charlie nodded, keeping his eyes down.

"Oh, for heaven's sake." Owen pinched his forehead between his thumb and ring finger and paced a few steps back and forth. "This is a big mess you two have made. We'll have to let your mother know you're here, Hallie."

"No, please!" the plea burst from her lips. "I just want to stay for the summer, then I'll go home."

Owen stared at her. "I can't let you stay here even one night without telling your mom where you are," he said, then glaring at Charlie, he added, "now that I know. I certainly will not hide you for the summer." He looked at his watch. "I've got to go teach a drum lesson. Charlie, take Hallie inside and get her a snack. When I'm done with the lesson, I'll be in and we will talk about all of this. Do *not* try any more sneaky moves."

Charlie nodded sullenly and led Hallie into the house through the kitchen door. Once they were inside, away from Owen, Hallie sighed, but she knew the relief she felt would be short-lived.

Owen tried desperately to stay focused on teaching the drum lesson, but it was difficult when he knew his son had been hiding another child in their garage for a few days and now he was going to have to deal with the situation. He hadn't missed the fear that laced Hallie's voice and shined in her eyes when she'd begged him to keep hiding her for the summer. *Why for the summer?* Obviously, he couldn't do it. For his son, such an action was bad behavior, but for him, it would be criminal. Yet, that fear tugged at his heart and it wasn't hard to grasp why Charlie had helped her hide out.

When Ricky hit a cymbal with an unnecessary amount of force, Owen's mind came back to the lesson. He corrected his student and forced his head into the job of teaching for twenty more minutes.

The lesson finished, and Ricky gone, Owen walked around the garage and found Hallie's camp behind several stacks of boxes. Clever girl. He hadn't even noticed they'd been moved.

He trudged into the house and found Charlie and Hallie at the kitchen table. Hallie was polishing off a plate of cheese and crackers. Owen pulled out a chair and joined them. He wasn't sure where to start.

"Don't be mad at Charlie," Hallie said, starting for him. "He was just trying to be a good friend."

Owen studied his son. Charlie's head hung in shame, eyes on the woodgrain of the table, finger tracing the lines. "I know he was," Owen said.

Charlie glanced up, surprise on his face. "You're not mad?"

"I'm not sure what I am." Owen ran a hand through his curls. "Charlie, I know you wanted to help a friend, but you're old enough to know better than this."

"I know," Charlie said, hanging his head again.

"He does know," Hallie spoke up. "He wanted to tell you. He tried to talk me into it, but I begged him not to."

Owen turned his attention to the girl before him. He hadn't seen her in three years, and she'd grown and changed a lot since then. She was a foot taller, and her face had matured. "And why didn't you want to tell me you were out there?"

Her lips tightened as she met his eyes. "Because I knew you'd tell my mom."

Owen shook his head. "What's this about, Hallie? Why would you run away?"

"I just need to get away from home for the summer because my mom doesn't listen," Hallie said.

"You're not making sense. But if you wanted to come to the island for the summer, why didn't you ask your grandparents? I know they would love to have you stay with them."

Hallie crossed her arms over her chest. Her eyes flashed with defiance. "I don't want to see them."

"Why not, Hallie? They love and miss you."

She glared at him, fire in her eyes. "If it wasn't for them, my dad would be here and none of this would even be happening."

Owen was baffled. He'd often wondered why Hallie stopped coming for summer visits but hadn't wanted to pry. "Hallie, your dad died in the middle east. He was a brave man. Why do you blame your grandparents for that?"

"They wanted him to join the Army. If he hadn't, he wouldn't have died." Tears brimmed in the girl's eyes and emotion laced her words. "He should still be here ... with me and my mom. If he was, everything would be fine."

Owen knew Daniel had wanted to join the Army, and while his parents were proud of him and supported his choice, they hadn't pushed him into it. He thought about making that point, but the way Hallie's chin turned up and the rigidness of her posture told him it wouldn't help. Her mind was made up on that subject.

He chose to move on in a different way. "Hallie, I want to help you, but I can't let you stay here without the consent of your mother. So, we can either call her and let her know where you are, or I can call your grandparents and let them call your mom."

With a deeply entrenched frown, Hallie considered these options. "If you call my grandparents, do I have to go to their house tonight?"

"I don't know. We'll have to see what they say and what your mom says."

"Call them then," she said, looking away and staring out the window.

Owen stood up, retrieved his phone, and with a sigh, dialed Cory's number.

Hallie paced back and forth in Charlie's room while her friend sat on his bed and watched.

"Maybe it will all work out," Charlie said. "Your Granddad is the nicest person I know. He'll want to help you. I know he will."

A tear trickled down Hallie's face and dripped onto the carpet. She wasn't surprised Charlie would think that. Her granddad was known in town for his joyful attitude. Anyone entering the local drug store would hear him back in the pharmacy singing or telling jokes. But she saw him differently. "You don't know anything, Charlie."

He glared at her, and her heart sank. *What am I doing?* This boy was a good friend who went out of his way to help her against his better judgment. "I'm sorry," she said. "But I won't stay with them. I hate them."

Charlie's face clouded with sadness. "Don't say that, Hallie. I know they love you."

Hallie closed her eyes and reached deep for patience, then answered in what she hoped was a level tone. "Drop it, Charlie. I'm not going to change my mind about them."

"But you don't want to go home to your mom either. If you stay with them, you don't have to."

The little patience she'd mustered up drained away and she stopped pacing and stomped her feet. "I don't want to stay with them! Why can't you get that?"

Charlie shrank back against his headboard and dropped his head.

Not knowing what to say anymore, Hallie sagged down on the edge of the bed. She was going to lose a good friend if she kept yelling at him. But he didn't get it and she had no intention of explaining anything more to him.

They were still sitting in silence when Owen called up to them and asked them to come downstairs. Her grandparents had arrived.

Her belly full of butterflies, Hallie forced wobbly legs to carry her downstairs where her grandparents awaited her.

When she reached the bottom, she stopped, her courage failing her.

Charlie grabbed her hand and squeezed. She glanced at him and saw the encouragement in his eyes. He wanted to be there for her even after the way she'd yelled at him. She nodded at him and continued toward the kitchen.

As she and Charlie walked in, Hallie saw her granddad standing near Owen. His hair was a tiny bit grayer since she'd last seen him, but otherwise, he looked about the same. He was short and had a round belly. When she was little, Hallie loved to climb into his lap and wrap her arms around him. Part of her wanted to run to him and throw her arms around him now. But then she thought about her father. No, she would never hug her granddad again. So, she restrained any thought of running to the man before her, and instead, planted her feet and fixed him with a steely glare.

"Hallie?" Granddad began. His eyes took her in. "You're so tall now and so beautiful." He stopped a moment, continuing to study her. "But what are you doing on the island? When did you get here?"

"Why don't we sit down and talk about all that," Owen interjected.

Granddad nodded and took a seat at the table along with Owen. Charlie tugged Hallie in the direction of the table, but she didn't budge.

"Hallie," Owen said, "We're going to talk about it … or we can just skip right to calling your mom."

Letting out a loud breath, Hallie reluctantly sat at the table and faced her grandfather. He met her eyes and waited for an answer to the questions he'd already asked.

"I got here four days ago," she said.

"That doesn't answer my first question. Why did you come? And where does your mother think you are?" Granddad asked.

"I just needed a place to go for the summer." Hallie didn't like the question about her mother's beliefs about her whereabouts.

Granddad sighed at the answer that didn't say anything. "You could have come and stayed with your grandmother and me if you wanted. You know we'd be happy to have you."

"So happy she didn't come with you?" Hallie pointed out her grandmother's absence sarcastically.

"She's still sitting with Mr. Leachman and she can't just leave the old man alone. She'll be happy to see you as soon as she can."

Hallie remembered the old man her grandmother looked after during the day when his daughter and son-in-law were working. She was still strangely upset that her grandmother hadn't dropped everything to come see her and she was a little angry with herself for caring.

She chose to feign indifference. "I don't want to stay with you."

Granddad's eyes showed hurt at her words, but he deserved it.

"Hallie, why do you need a place to stay for the summer?" he asked.

"Mom decided I was old enough to stay home alone this summer while she and Dustin are at work, but I didn't want to stay there alone all day." Hallie certainly wasn't going to tell him the whole reason.

His face scrunched up. "And you felt hiding in a hot garage all summer would be better?"

She nodded.

"Surely there's more to it than that." Granddad leaned forward in his seat and rested his arms on the table. "What you're telling me doesn't make sense. Where does your mother think you are? Because I'm certain she doesn't know you're on the island."

Seeing no way around the questions now, Hallie looked away and said, "She thinks I'm at Cammie's house."

"For four days?"

Hallie shrugged, keeping her eyes averted. "Wouldn't be the first time. She's always busy with the twins and doesn't care if I'm gone a while."

Granddad sighed and then there was a heavy pause before he spoke. "I'm sure it's true that your mother is busy these days, but I *know* she loves you. I'm sure she *will* care when she finds out you're not where she thinks you are."

Hallie stayed silent. She wasn't going to volunteer anything.

"Why don't you want to be at home for the summer?" Granddad asked.

"Because my mom doesn't listen."

Granddad let out a frustrated breath. "Is there something that happened she didn't listen about?"

She spared him a glance, then dropped her eyes. "There are some kids that were bullying me, and she hardly even cared."

"I see," Granddad said, but Hallie could tell he found her claims hard to believe. It wasn't a lie, at least not exactly, but it wasn't the real reason she was on the island. She wasn't going to tell him *that* no matter how many times he asked.

There was silence for a moment except for the sound of Granddad drumming his fingers on the table. "We have to call your mom, Hallie. There's no way around that. When we talk to her, I see two options. Either you go home, or you can stay here, on the island, with your grandma and me."

"No! I won't go home. I can't. And I'm *not* staying with you." She glared at him.

"There are no other options, Hallie. What else do you expect me to do?" Granddad asked, his tone becoming agitated, something Hallie knew was unusual for him.

"Couldn't she stay here with us?" Charlie interjected. "We've got plenty of room."

Owen's face registered surprise at this suggestion as did Granddad's.

Charlie turned pleading eyes on his father. "Please, Dad?" He really was the best friend.

Owen scratched his head. "I guess we could make that work ... *if* it's okay with Hallie's mom and grandparents."

Granddad drummed his fingers again, then frowned in Owen's direction. It was obvious he felt bad about taking Owen up on the offer but didn't know what else to do. "I suppose if you're all right with it, I am. Would we be able to get her into day camp with Charlie?"

Owen shook his head. "No, it's full. I can see if she could stay with Howard during the day. He's home with the girls for the summer. And Marissa would be there on the days she isn't working."

Granddad nodded reluctantly. His eyes were sad, and Hallie could tell he was deeply hurt by her rejection. She felt a twinge of regret, but not enough to overrule her anger about her father's death.

"Okay, we can ask your mother, Hallie. If she's all right with it, then we'll work it out," Granddad said.

Owen stood in the doorway of his kitchen and wondered at how quickly things could change in life. Earlier in the day, the biggest thing on his mind was his breakup with Carrie Ann. Now he might be taking on the responsibility of another child for the summer—a child who was running from something and clearly didn't want to say what.

He'd already called his sister, informed her of what was going on, and talked to her and Howard about the possibility of Hallie staying at their house during the day while Owen was working. They had readily agreed to help. Howard remembered Hallie from summers past, and while

Marissa had never met her, she knew Cory well from the drug store and was more than happy to help.

With that sorted out, Owen was waiting while Cory called Amanda, Hallie's mom, to tell her what was going on. Cory stood near the window with his phone at his ear, and Hallie watched from the table, where she sat with the Oreos and milk Owen had given her. Charlie had taken the comic book one of his friends lent him and gone to the living room to wait.

"Hello, Amanda?" Cory said. "Yes, I'm sure it is a surprise to hear from me. I've had a little surprise myself today." He rubbed his head while he listened. "It's Hallie, she's here on the island." … "Amanda, calm down, she's fine." … "She *didn't* come to me. I wish she had, but we both know why she didn't." … Cory sighed deeply. "Let's not get into that. We need to talk about Hallie now." … "Yeah, I know I was the one who brought it up. I'm sorry. I'll drop that for now if you will." … "She was hiding in someone's garage." … "No, not a random stranger. Someone she knows from when she used to visit. His son was helping her hide out." … "Amanda, honestly, it's not like that." … "Fine, I'll put the phone on speaker, and she can tell you herself."

Cory turned from the window, touched his phone's screen to switch to speaker, and set the phone down on the table in front of Hallie. Then he sat down in the chair next to her. "You're on speaker now, Amanda. Hallie can hear you."

"Hallie?" Amanda's voice rang out from the phone.

"Yeah, mom, I'm here." Hallie twisted her fingers in her lap.

"What in the world are you doing on the island? You said you were at Cammie's house," Amanda demanded.

"I know. But I had to leave, Mom. I don't want to stay home by myself this summer."

"So, you ran away?"

"I had to! You wouldn't listen to me. I asked you not to leave me home alone for the summer." Hallie's eyes brimmed with tears, which tugged at Owen's heart while he watched.

"Hallie, we don't have enough money for day camp this year with the twins in daycare, and you're twelve years old. Lots of kids your age stay home alone in the summer time." Amanda sounded mildly defensive.

"It's always about what the twins need, and you don't care about me anymore." Hallie's voice cracked and a tear ran down her cheek.

"Hallie, that is *not* true. I love you and I care about you, but we can't afford the day camp. The boys can't stay alone, they're just babies, but you can. It isn't because I love them more."

Hallie sniffed and crossed her arms over her chest. "Well, I'm not doing it. I'm gonna stay here with Owen and Charlie for the summer."

"What? No, you're not, Hallie. I don't even know them."

"Amanda," Cory interrupted. "She seems adamant about not staying home for the summer, and she won't stay with Doreen and me. But Owen has offered to let her stay here with him and his son. And I know them. Owen's a good man. Hallie will be safe here, and I'll keep an eye on her too."

"She's twelve, Cory. I'm not letting her spend the summer with a boy," Amanda insisted.

"Charlie's just a friend, Mom. You don't have to worry about anything like that," Hallie said.

Owen stepped forward. "Amanda? This is Owen. If it'll make you feel better, I'll promise you that Hallie and Charlie won't be left alone together. Charlie goes to a day camp during the day for most of the time I'm at work. And my sister and brother-in-law have agreed to let Hallie stay at their house until I'm home, that is, if you agree to this plan. Howard, my brother-in-law, is a teacher, so he's home during the day with my two nieces."

"Hallie's my daughter. She's my responsibility and she should be home with my husband and me," Amanda said.

"No, Mom, please!" Hallie cried, wiping wet cheeks with the back of her hand. "I can't come home. Not until summer's over."

Except for Hallie's soft sniffles, the room went silent while everyone waited for Amanda's response. After a few long seconds, a heavy sigh came from the phone. "I'm not agreeing to the whole summer yet, but you can stay for now, until we can figure things out."

Owen watched as the anxiety drained from Hallie's face and was replaced by relief. "Thank you, Mom. Thank you."

Cory patted Hallie on the shoulder. "Why don't you go to the living room with Charlie now? I want to talk to your mom another minute."

Hallie nodded and hopped up. She hurried out of the kitchen and headed to the living room. Her voice rang out as she went. "I get to stay for now, Charlie!"

"Would you like me to leave too," Owen asked.

Cory shook his head. "No, you're in this as much as anyone now."

Owen took a seat at the table.

"Amanda, Hallie seems scared to death when we mention sending her home. Do you have any idea why?" Cory asked.

"There's nothing bad going on here in our house if that's what you're getting at," Amanda said defensively.

"I'm not implying anything. I'm just asking if you know a reason." Cory shifted in his seat.

"No, I don't." Amanda's tone remained curt.

"She keeps saying that she's here because you don't listen. And ... she mentioned something about bullies bothering her and how you didn't care. I'm sure that isn't true, but is there anything going on that might be causing her to say what she's saying ... and to run away?"

"Of course I cared about the bullying. But that happened at school, not at home, and I did listen. It took a while for the school to do what needed to be done, mostly because no one ever saw what was going on and the other kids insisted they didn't do anything." Amanda sniffed and emotion laced her voice. "Hallie thinks I didn't listen because I told her she still had to go to school. What other choice did I have?"

"I'm sorry. I know you did the best you could. And Hallie obviously feels left behind because of the babies needing your attention. That's not your fault," Cory was quick to add. "But think about it, Amanda, is there anything else you can think of that might be causing Hallie to feel fearful about staying home alone this summer?"

There was a pause, then Amanda said, "I honestly can't think of anything."

"Well, for now, she's fine here. Maybe, as she relaxes, we can get her to tell us why she ran away in the first place," Cory said.

Amanda sighed. "Sure, fine. But I want to hear from her every day."

"I'll have her call you in the evening," Owen said.

Amanda agreed to that, then Cory said goodbye to her and hung up. He looked at Owen. "Thank you for what you're doing."

"No problem," Owen said. "You and Doreen helped me out back when I was a new father with a traumatized kid. The least I can do is help you now." And besides that, Owen couldn't turn away from the fear in Hallie's eyes. How could he possibly say no when they didn't know what caused her fear?

"We need to try and get her to tell us why she came here. No twelve-year-old bullies are going to bother her when she's at home alone. She could lock them out. There has to be something else."

"You don't think it's her step-father, do you?" Concern etched Owen's face at the thought.

Cory's brow furrowed as he considered that. "I never met the man, so I don't know a thing about him, but if it was him, then why is it only the summer Hallie's worried about? He's always there. I think it must be something else."

Owen nodded. "Maybe spending time with Maisy and Charlie will be good for her. Maybe, in time, she'll talk to them."

"I hope so, and if she does, I hope they'll convince her to tell us too." Cory stood up and walked to the window again. He looked out for a long moment, then turned to Owen again. "I'm also hoping there might be a chance for Doreen and me to rebuild our relationship with Hallie. But she won't make it easy." He met Owen's eyes. "Maybe you could help provide some opportunities for that."

"I'm sure there will be times when I'll need someone to keep an eye on the kids. After all, I promised not to let them be alone together, and Marissa and Howard won't always be able to help," Owen said conspiratorially.

With a hint of a smile on his lips, Cory thanked Owen, then went to the living room and said goodbye to Hallie before leaving to go home.

Chapter 9

With Charlie's help, Hallie gathered her things, along with the stuff she'd borrowed, and headed into the house. She felt both elated and nervous about moving into the house. It would be wonderful to sleep in a bed rather than a concrete floor ... and air conditioning would feel amazing. But she didn't really know Owen, not anymore. She was only nine the last time she'd spent a summer on the island, playing with Charlie. It was a little strange to think she'd be moving in with them now. *Was it stranger than hiding in their garage?* Hallie shook her head at that thought. At least they weren't sending her home.

Once in the house, Owen led her to the guest room upstairs. It was across the hall from Charlie's room and had a big four-poster bed with a red and white quilt.

Hallie glanced at Owen. "I get to sleep here?"

Owen grinned. "That's right! Beat's a hard garage floor, huh?"

Hallie nodded. "Yeah."

"Well, go ahead and put your stuff down," Owen prompted. "Then you can go get yourself ready for bed. If you want to take a shower, go ahead. Do you have a toothbrush with you?"

"Yes, I have a toothbrush and some soap." Hallie dropped her backpack on the floor near the big antique dresser.

Owen studied her. "Are those Charlie's clothes you have on?"

Hallie's cheeks reddened and she dropped her gaze to the floor. "Yeah. I couldn't pack much. Charlie was going to wash mine for me, and he offered to let me borrow something because I was getting so sweaty in the garage."

"It's fine, Hallie. Don't be embarrassed. I'll get your clothes from Charlie and wash them for you tonight."

Hallie didn't like the idea of Charlie's dad doing her laundry. "I can do it," she said quickly.

Owen opened his mouth to speak, then stopped and nodded. Maybe he'd noticed the flush of her cheeks. "Okay. Go see Charlie and gather everything up, then I'll show you where the laundry room is before you head into the bathroom."

Hallie nodded, and Owen left the room. When he was gone, she gathered up everything she had to wash and headed for Charlie's room. She guessed she would have to wash clothes often, but at least now she could.

After getting her laundry started, Hallie went into the bathroom. She took a shower and brushed her teeth. Then, before climbing into bed, she went back to the laundry room and put her clothes in the dryer. They would be wrinkly in the morning, but at least they'd be clean.

On her way back to the guest room, Owen called goodnight to her. She smiled, feeling grateful for all he was doing for her. No wonder Charlie was such a good friend. He'd had a great example. And now that she was here, she felt sure she could convince her mother to let her stay for the rest of the summer.

With that thought in her mind, Hallie slipped into the big bed, snuggled under the covers, and sighed as the cool indoor air blew on her. In seconds, she was fast asleep.

Hallie stared out the window as she rode in the passenger seat of Owen's truck, watching as they passed all the island houses. Owen had the radio turned off, leaving the inside of the vehicle quiet except for the sound of the road under the tires. The silence felt awkward, but Hallie wasn't sure she was ready to have a conversation with Owen. She felt self-conscious being alone with him, but Charlie had been picked up by a friend who took him to his day camp. Soon they'd arrive at the home of Owen's sister and Mr. Paxton, where she'd be spending her days while she stayed on the island. That would probably be awkward too, at least at first.

"Here we are," Owen said as they pulled into the driveway of a modest single-story house.

Hallie took it in, letting her eyes roll over this new environment. She liked the blue color of the siding and the big front porch with rocking chairs and a swing. The island was full of pretty houses.

Hopping out of the truck, Hallie followed Owen to the front door, staying a couple of steps behind him. He pressed the doorbell and, as they waited, Hallie's stomach filled with butterflies. *Whatever spending summer here is like, it's better than going home.*

Moments later, a girl with light brown hair and glasses opened the door.

"Good morning, Maisy," Owen said. He turned, and with a hand on Hallie's shoulder, maneuvered her closer to the door. "This is Hallie," he said to the girl. Then he looked at Hallie, gestured to the other girl, and said, "Hallie, this is my niece, Maisy."

Maisy smiled shyly. "It's nice to meet you."

The corners of her mouth turning up just a bit, Hallie said, "Nice to meet you too."

"Come on in," Maisy said, opening the door wider. "Howard is in the kitchen with Sylvie."

They walked inside and down the hall to the kitchen where Mr. Paxton sat in a chair at the table feeding a tiny baby. His head was down showing its bald top, his eyes on the infant who kicked her feet while she sucked down milk noisily.

He looked up and grinned at Hallie. "There's a face I've missed seeing. And boy have you grown!"

Hallie smiled and tried not to look at the floor. "Hi, Mr. Paxton."

"It's good to see you, Hallie. Come meet our little Sylvie."

Hallie stepped forward for a closer look at the baby. She was very pale-skinned with blue eyes and sprigs of red hair. "She's cute."

"I hear you have a couple little ones at home now too," Mr. Paxton said.

"Yes, I have two baby brothers. They're seven months old now."

"Then I bet you're a pro at helping out with babies, and I can sure use all the help I can get. With you and Maisy to help, I should be in good shape." He leaned forward and spoke in a softer voice as if the words were meant only for Hallie. "But don't worry, I won't ask you to help too much. Maisy is excited to have another girl around that she can do fun stuff with. Sylvie won't be doing much this summer except eating and sleeping."

"And pooping," Hallie blurted out.

Owen and Mr. Paxton laughed. "You're right about that," Mr. Paxton said, his eyes dancing with amusement.

"Well," Owen said. "I've got to get going. I'm scheduled to fix the Johnsons' dishwasher this morning. I'll be back around four o'clock to pick you up, Hallie."

Hallie nodded.

"Okay then, have a good day." Owen turned and left.

"Are you hungry, Hallie? I'm going to make some breakfast for Maisy and me as soon as little bit gets done with her bottle," Mr. Paxton said.

"I ate some cereal already." Hallie's stomach rumbled loudly as if in protest.

With a smile, Mr. Paxton said, "Sounds like your stomach wants something more. Would you like an egg or a waffle?"

She shrugged. Both sounded good, but she didn't want to ask for too much. "An egg, I guess."

The baby smacked her lips as the last bit of milk drained from the bottle. "And she's done." He put Sylvie on his shoulder and began to pat her back. "With the appetite this girl has, I'll be making eggs for her before I know it."

Once the baby burped, Mr. Paxton set her down in a baby seat, strapped her in, and went to work making eggs and waffles.

Hallie turned when she felt a tap on her shoulder. Maisy's blue eyes met her brown ones.

"Want to see my room before breakfast is ready?" Maisy asked.

"Sure," Hallie said. She followed the younger girl down the hall until they came to the third door.

Maisy pushed the door open and revealed a room filled with pink frills and Hello Kitty décor. "I know it's a little babyish," Maisy said. "But soon, when Sylvie is a little older, we're going to paint it purple and get some new decorations. I'm really over the Hello Kitty stuff now."

Hallie glanced around the room, taking in the white four-poster bed and matching dresser. "I love purple," she said, "and it will look great with your bed and everything."

Maisy beamed. "Purple is my favorite color now. I picked out a really pretty bedspread." She ran to her dresser and picked up a picture. "See, this is the one I'm going to get."

Hallie took a look. It was lovely with swirling shades of purple. "That's really nice."

"Do you like cats?" Maisy asked, changing the subject.

Hallie nodded.

"I got a kitten for my birthday last year. His name is Chester. He's a big cat now and he's probably hiding under my bed if you want to meet him."

"Will he come out?"

Maisy shook her head. "Probably not yet. But once he gets used to you being here, he will. If you want to see him now, you'll have to look under the bed."

Hallie got down on her knees and Maisy did as well. Poking their heads under the bed skirt, Maisy said, "See, there he is."

"Hi Chester," Hallie cooed to the orange and white cat that was crouched against the wall at the head of the bed. In response, the cat scooted closer to the wall and turned his head away.

"See, he's shy. But he'll get used to you soon," Maisy said as they both stood back up.

For an awkward moment, the two girls stared at each other. Hallie wished she could come up with a subject to talk about, but nothing came to mind. Finally, Maisy broke the silence. "Do you like to draw?"

"Sometimes. I'm not that good at it though."

"I love to draw. I won a contest at school this year." Maisy beamed. "Want to see the picture I drew?"

"Sure." Hallie shrugged.

Maisy grabbed Hallie's hand and led her into the hallway, pointing at a framed drawing on the wall. "Mom and Howard were so proud."

Hallie studied the rendering of a pond surrounded by green grass and trees. "It's pretty. You're a lot better than me."

"What do you like to do? Video games?"

Hallie scrunched up her face. "Sometimes, I guess. But not much. I like music and hanging out with my friends." Maisy was barely eleven. Hallie wasn't sure if she'd understand or if she still wanted someone to play dolls with.

"Do you like the beach?"

"Yeah. I'm a good swimmer."

"I'm getting pretty good at swimming too, but I still like staying on the sand most of the time. We'll go to the beach some days while you're here."

Hallie frowned. "I don't have a bathing suit with me."

Before Maisy could answer, Mr. Paxton called out to them. "Food is on, girls. Come and get it!"

The beach topic forgotten, Maisy headed for the kitchen and Hallie followed. They sat down at the table and Mr. Paxton placed a plate in front of Hallie with a waffle and a helping of scrambled eggs. She smiled, breathing in the sweet scent of the waffle. "Thank you, Mr. Paxton."

"You can call me Howard," he said, sitting down with a plate of his own. "You might as well. Maisy does. Besides, we're here to have some summer fun. No need to be so formal."

"Okay," Hallie said, picking up her fork and preparing to dig into the food on her plate.

Marissa stared at the end cap in front of her. Carrie Ann wanted her to set up a display of seasonal summer items and she was having a hard time figuring out what to do with it. Maybe she should put the sunscreen at the top and beach toys in the middle, with a selection of beach towels on the bottom. About to start lining sunscreen bottles up on the shelf, Marissa stopped, noticing the utter quiet in the store. There was no humming or singing or laughter coming from the pharmacy. Usually, Cory's exuberant personality rang through the store one way or another.

Curious, Marissa left the sunscreen where it was and headed to the back corner where the pharmacy was. As she approached, she saw Cory sorting some pills into a bottle. The expression on his face was sullen.

Marissa frowned in concern. She'd never seen Cory like this. He always had a smile on his face.

Reaching the pharmacy counter, Marissa said, "Cory, are you all right?"

He glanced up. "Of course. Why wouldn't I be?"

Marissa placed her hands on the counter and studied him. "You're not singing or humming. You're not smiling."

"No one smiles all the time." He twisted a lid on the pill container and set it aside.

"If you were anyone else, I'd agree."

He glanced at her. "You've seen me unhappy before."

"Only a few times in more than two years of knowing you. And all of those times were on the occasions when you and Doreen came to the grief support group." Marissa had moved to the island with her daughter two and a half years ago on the heels of losing Kevin and Kyla. When Marissa recovered from the shock of their drowning, she'd swallowed a handful of pills and almost died. When she moved to the island, looking for a fresh start, her psychiatrist insisted she join the grief support group he hosted. Cory and Doreen attended the group a few times, looking for support in the loss of their son. "I've never seen you at work without a smile."

Cory sighed. "I guess I've just got a lot on my mind."

Marissa tilted her head in consideration. "I know your granddaughter is here under strange circumstances and I know your relationship with her isn't what you'd like it to be, but I thought you would be feeling more hopeful." Marissa shrugged. "She's here, so there's a chance to work on whatever is broken between you."

With a nod, Cory said, "I am hopeful about that, but …"

"You're disappointed she didn't want to stay with you," Marissa finished for him.

"Yes, and I'm concerned about why she ran away in the first place. There has to be something going on that's pretty big to make her do that. Kids her age might threaten to run away, and they might even pack a bag and head to a friend's house. But Hallie lied about going to a friend's house, then hopped on a ferry and came to an island where she has relatives she doesn't want to see." He met her eyes.

"Something is up, and it isn't good. But she won't tell us what it is."

"Yeah, I see your point. Maybe she'll open up in time, tell someone why she did it." Marissa stopped for a moment, not sure if she should ask the question that was on her mind. She went ahead tentatively. "Cory, it's fine if you don't want to answer, but I was wondering, what did happen between you and Hallie?"

Cory closed his eyes and rubbed the space between them. "What happened was Daniel's death."

Marissa's forehead wrinkled and she waited for more.

"Hallie's mother, Amanda, always hated Daniel's decision to join the Army and she blamed Doreen and me for it. She chose to believe he joined because we pushed him into it." He met her eyes. "We didn't. Daniel started talking about joining the Army when he was nine. We supported him is all.

"Hallie didn't pay much attention to her mother's feelings about us before her father's death. She used to come to the island for a month every summer. That's how she got to know Charlie."

Cory's face darkened. "But after we lost Daniel, Hallie latched onto her mother's anger toward us. She was angry and needed a target for all that emotion. Doreen and I became that target." His eyes grew moist as he said, "We lost Daniel and, in a way, we lost Hallie at the same time. This is the first time she's come back to the island since."

Marissa reached for Cory's hand and squeezed it. "I'm sorry. I hope you get some answers about why Hallie ran away. And I hope you can repair your relationship with her."

Rebecca L. Marsh

Chapter 10

Her third evening after leaving the garage, Hallie found herself wearing Charlie's gym shorts and t-shirt again while preparing to wash her own clothes. It was Thursday, and she planned to politely ask Owen if he'd take her to get a few things over the weekend. She was sure her mother would be willing to send a little money to pay for it. She didn't need much, a couple more pairs of shorts, a few t-shirts, and a pack of underwear would do ... and maybe a bathing suit.

In the two days she'd spent with Howard and Maisy, they hadn't yet gone to the beach, but when they did, Hallie wanted to be able to get in the water. She loved the ocean. And she was beginning to think Maisy would be a fun friend to swim and play with at the beach. They were doing well together so far. The two of them spent a lot of time on the front porch, Maisy with a sketch pad, and Hallie with a book to read. When they weren't doing that, they played with Chester, who wasn't hiding any longer, and talked about their friends and the music they liked.

Just as Hallie gathered all her clothes to take to the washer, the doorbell rang.

"I'll get it," she heard Charlie call.

Hallie headed downstairs to the laundry room, but Charlie stopped her halfway down. "Hallie, your grandma is here."

Hallie sucked in a deep breath. "I don't want to see her."

"She says she brought something for you." Charlie looked at the carpet. "My grandmother isn't always easy to get along with, but I'd never refuse to see her or talk to her. I'm so glad to have a grandmother. I wish I had a grandfather like you do. But I know what it's like not to have any grandparents at all. Before I came here, I only had my mom—and she wasn't a very good mom."

"Charlie, I keep telling you, you don't understand."

He looked up to meet her eyes. His glistened with emotion. "I know I don't."

Hallie stood still for a moment after Charlie pushed past her and went to his room. She didn't want to admit it, but a part of her missed her grandparents. When she was little, she loved spending time with them here on the island. But she didn't know how to forgive them for what happened to her dad. She didn't want to.

Reluctantly, Hallie continued down the stairs. She moved slowly one step at a time, and as she went, she was keenly aware of each beat of her heart. Emotions roiled through her, causing her dinner to go sour in her stomach.

She hated her grandparents. They were the reason her father was dead. He only joined the Army because they wanted him to, and he didn't want to disappoint them. If not for them, he'd be alive today.

But Hallie didn't always hate her grandparents. Once she'd loved them. Her mother's anger at them was always there. She could remember the way Mom blamed them even when Daddy was alive. Hallie hadn't paid much attention back then. Daddy seemed happy when he was home, and her grandparents were good to her. They doted on her, and she always loved coming to the island to spend a month with them in the summer.

When her father died, however, Hallie was filled with hurt and rage, and her mother's words told her where to direct it. It was her grandparent's fault her father didn't come home. It was their fault he would never swing her around in the air again, read to her again, or smile at her again.

As time passed, Hallie didn't think about that anger as much. But there were moments when her father's loss hit her just like it was happening all over again. In those moments, the anger flared up inside her fresh and hot. Being back on the island brought that anger back too, but it also brought something else—something that was fighting a war with the anger. Hallie wasn't sure what to call that emotion. It was a longing of some kind. All she knew was that, as she neared the end of the stairs, it grew stronger, and she had to fight to tamp it down and remember she was angry.

She'd felt it the other night too when Granddad came to see her, but it was stronger now. Hallie didn't know if that was because her feelings for Grandma were stronger, or because of what Charlie said to her about living without any grandparents in your life, something she knew well from the past three years. Or maybe it was because the longing was growing stronger each time she had to face one of her grandparents. All she knew at the moment was that she was fighting like crazy to push away the memory of feeling safe in her grandmother's arms and of grandma's smile that was so much like Daddy's. She had to fight to hold onto the anger because letting go of it felt like betraying her father.

Reaching the last step and shuffling into the hallway, Hallie made a point to avoid eye contact with her grandmother.

"Hallie! Honey, it's so good to see you!" Grandma rushed toward her, arms open. When Hallie stepped back, Grandma let her arms drop. "I've missed you."

"Charlie said you had something for me," Hallie said in a tight voice.

In response, Grandma picked up a bag and held it out. "I thought you might need a few things."

Reluctantly, Hallie reached out and took the bag. She peered inside and saw an assortment of new clothes. She fought back the excitement she felt in being given a bag of exactly what she needed and made sure her face held no emotion when she glanced back up. "Thank you," she said, maintaining a frosty edge in her voice.

"I called your mother to make sure I got the right sizes. You've grown so much since I saw you last."

Hallie nodded.

"I'm sorry I haven't been over to see you sooner, Hallie. I wanted to come, but I couldn't make it that first night and after that ... well, your Granddad thought you needed a little time."

Hallie remained silent and kept her face impassive. Part of her, though, wanted so much to feel Grandma's arms around her. *No! She's the reason Daddy is gone.*

"Hallie, we want to know you again. Please give us a chance," Grandma pleaded.

Emotions twisted inside Hallie's chest—anger, hurt, pain, and growing ever stronger, longing. Feeling her resolve beginning to break and tears welling in her eyes, Hallie shouted, "My daddy's dead because of you!" Then she turned and ran back up the stairs. Slamming the door behind her, she rushed into her room and threw herself on the bed as sobs erupted from deep inside her.

After a quiet first weekend with Owen and Charlie, Hallie found herself eating breakfast with Maisy Monday morning at Howard and Marissa's house. She'd learned quickly to hold off on breakfast until she arrived there. Howard, it seemed, enjoyed cooking breakfast and the food he made was delicious. This time, however, Marissa sat at the table with them, feeding baby Sylvie. She had the day off from the pharmacy and would be spending it with them.

"Let's go to the beach today," Howard said with a grin when they were finished eating.

"Yay!" Maisy said excitedly. She turned to Hallie. "Did you bring a bathing suit?"

With a grin, Hallie nodded. Though she didn't want to admit it, she loved all the clothes her grandmother gave her and looked forward to wearing the purple and green tankini bathing suit.

"Perfect!" Howard said. "It'll be Sylvie's first trip to the beach."

"And that means we need to bring the shade tent for her," Marissa said.

"I'll make sure it goes in the car," Howard said. He looked at Maisy and Hallie. "You girls go put your suits on and get ready. Don't forget to put on sunscreen."

"I know *I* won't forget," Marissa said, pushing red curls back from her pale face. "The sun hates me. And that reminds me, make sure you bring the umbrella."

"Got it." Howard headed outside to start packing what they needed.

Maisy grabbed Hallie's hand. "Come on, let's get ready."

Hallie pulled her swimsuit out of her backpack and went into the bathroom to change while Maisy changed in her room. The suit fit surprisingly well considering she hadn't been able to try it on, and the colors looked nice on her.

Once ready, Hallie walked out into the hall and found Maisy waiting for her. "Wow, I love your suit! And mine is purple too," Maisy said pointing to her bright, purple and pink suit.

"Yeah, I like yours."

Maisy leaned in closer and quietly said, "I like yours better. I didn't want one with pink in it, but my mom worries about me swimming and she wanted a color that stood out."

"Why does she worry about you swimming?"

Maisy's face darkened. "That's how my dad and sister died. Last summer was the first time Mom would even go back to a beach or let me go. She hates it when I'm in the water. It scares her. Fortunately, I like the sand better than the water anyway."

"Oh." That information sinking in, Hallie wondered what it would be like to revisit the place where someone you loved had died or even to have been there when it happened. Maisy had been there, too, when her father and sister died. Hallie couldn't imagine what it would have been like to be there when her dad died. She swallowed hard looking Maisy in the eye. "Isn't it hard for you to go to the beach?"

Maisy shrugged. "It's a different beach. And ... I don't know ... the place isn't really what bothers me. I still like the beach."

There was something strange in the way Maisy said that the place didn't bother her. Somehow, her tone and body language told Hallie there was something that *was* bothering her—bringing the memories back. She chose not to ask about it, but as she was unsure of what else to say, silence filled the space until Marissa stepped into the hallway from her room. Sylvie was in her arms wearing the smallest bathing suit Hallie had ever seen.

"Are you girls ready?" Marissa asked.

"We're ready." Maisy threw a beach towel over her shoulder.

"Sylvie looks so cute in her suit," Hallie said, stepping closer to Marissa and the baby in her arms who wore a bathing suit covered in colorful butterflies.

As if on cue, Sylvie squirmed and made some noises.

"She seems to appreciate the compliment," Marissa said as they all headed for the door.

Jumping out of the car when they arrived at the beach, Maisy grabbed Hallie's hand. "Come on, let's get the bag with the sand toys. I want to build the biggest sand castle ever with a moat."

"Can we swim first?" Hallie asked. "It's already hot."

Maisy shrugged. "Sure, I guess. Mom, can we swim now?" She turned toward her mother who was carefully taking the baby from the car.

Marissa glanced at Maisy. "Wait until we get all the stuff out and set up on the beach. I don't want you in the water until Howard and I can keep a good eye on you."

Looking at Hallie, Maisy raised an eyebrow. "Might as well start with the sand. It'll take them a while to set things up. They've never used the baby tent before."

"How long can it take?" Hallie wrapped her towel around her neck and followed Maisy to the back of the car to get the sand toys.

Maisy smirked and whispered, "Hopefully not as long as it took them to put the crib together."

With a sigh, Hallie said, "Let's build that castle."

The sand castle was about half done when Howard and Marissa finished setting everything up. "All right, you girls can swim now," Marissa said.

Hallie could hear the reluctance in her voice. "We'll be careful," she said. "Come on, Maisy, let's go."

"Shouldn't we finish this first?"

"It'll still be here when we get back. Please, I'm hot."

Maisy stood up and brushed sand from her knees. "Okay."

"This will be fun. Come on!" Hallie took Maisy's hand and pulled her into a sprint toward the water. By the time their toes got wet, they were both giggling.

"That's cold!" Maisy said, gasping as the water hit her thighs.

"It's easier if you just get in fast." Hallie continued forward, but Maisy pulled her to a stop.

"I don't like to get in fast. Let me get used to it on my legs first."

"Okay." They stopped and stood where they were with the waves crashing against their legs. Hallie squinted toward the beach where the adults and baby were. "Your sister is so cute. I've never seen such a tiny bathing suit."

Maisy shrugged. "I guess."

Scrunching her face up, Hallie asked, "Don't you like your little sister?"

"She's okay." Maisy seemed to be aiming for a dismissive tone, but there was something stronger in her body language. Maybe Charlie was right and Maisy didn't like the baby.

"I have two baby brothers," Hallie said.

Maisy looked at her but didn't say anything.

"They're seven months old now. My mom had them after she married my step-dad. Now, my mom doesn't have much time for me. Still, I like my brothers. They're cute and more fun now that they can sit up."

"My mom still spends time with me." Maisy's words came as a simple statement of fact and carried little emotion. She wasn't giving anything away, Hallie realized. If there was a reason she didn't like her sister, she wasn't going to share it today.

As she slipped out of the shower and into clean clothes, Marissa tried to still her trembling hands. She took several deep calming breaths, but the trembling didn't stop.

"Is it my turn with the shower?" Howard asked, stepping into their bathroom.

Before Marissa could answer, the look on her face told him she was still struggling.

"Hey," he said, taking her hands in his, "you did great today."

She nodded. Going to the beach was still difficult for her. It was impossible to be there and not remember the worst day of her life—the day she lost her first husband, Kevin, and their oldest child, Kyla. When she looked at the sandy beach, the memory of them both lying lifeless on another beach invaded her mind. When she looked at the water and its crashing waves, she couldn't help thinking of their last moments—when they'd been struggling for their lives. And there was no escaping the sound of the waves.

Allowing Maisy to step foot in the ocean was immensely difficult, but Marissa knew she couldn't keep her daughter from doing this normal thing forever, especially not when they lived on an island. Fortunately, Maisy wasn't a daredevil like her father and big sister had been. Still, Marissa hated seeing her in the ocean. She'd managed this time by letting Howard watch Maisy and Hallie while she focused on the baby.

"It's still hard. I worry. I think I'll always worry." Marissa looked into Howard's compassionate, blue eyes.

He kissed her forehead. "I know. It isn't easy to step out into your worst fear."

"I'll be okay now, I think."

Howard let go of her hands and pulled her in for a hug. "Listen, Sylvie is snoozing and Maisy and Hallie are settled with a movie to watch. Why don't you take a few more minutes in our room while I shower? Then I'll make us some dinner."

She shook her head. "No, it's my turn to cook. I'll be all right, really."

He picked up one of her hands and held it out where they could both see how it continued to tremble. "I'm not taking no for an answer. Give yourself a break."

Deciding he was right, she nodded her agreement and headed into their bedroom to rest.

Rebecca L. Marsh

 **Chapter 11**

Hallie reluctantly slid out of Owen's truck in front of her grandparents' house. She closed the door and stared at the lovely yellow house in front of her. A row of petunias, pink and white, lined the sidewalk up to the house. Her gaze traveling to the wide porch, she saw the wicker chairs with floral cushions that she remembered from previous visits. It all looked the same, and she could remember sitting in those chairs with Granddad shucking corn, or with Grandma reading to her.

Glancing back at the truck, Hallie gave Owen one last pleading look.

"You'll be fine," he reassured her. "It's only a few hours and they love you."

Gathering all her resolve to combat the longing that accompanied the onslaught of memories, Hallie dragged her feet up the steps. Charlie was already on the porch and had knocked on the door.

As Hallie reached the porch, the door swung open and granddad's smiling face met her.

"Hi, Mr. Hobbs," Charlie said.

"Hello, Charlie. It's good to see you." Granddad's gaze went to Hallie. "Hello, Hallie. Come on in. Grandma just took a batch of cookies out of the oven."

The scent of the warm cookies drifted out and Hallie breathed it in. She wanted one, but she didn't want Granddad to know. "We already had dessert."

Charlie threw her a scowl. "Speak for yourself. I'll take a cookie!" He rushed through the door and headed toward the kitchen. "Hi, Mrs. Hobbs. Those smell great!"

Hallie didn't budge from the porch.

"You can stay on the porch if you want," Granddad said. "But the bugs get pretty bad after the sun goes down." He met her eyes. "And besides that, we'd like a chance to spend a little time with you."

"I guess it doesn't matter that I don't want to," she scoffed.

With a sigh, Granddad stepped out onto the porch and shut the door. He sat down in one of the chairs and motioned for her to sit in the one next to it. She walked to the railing and leaned against it instead.

"You used to like coming to see us. Remember what that was like, the fun we used to have?" Granddad said.

"That was *before* my father died." She crossed her arms over her chest and fought to keep the memories he spoke of from her mind.

"And because he died, you believe what your mother says about it being our fault?"

"My mother doesn't listen lately, but she wouldn't lie to me." Tears of hurt and anger brimmed in Hallie's eyes. She swiped at them before they could fall.

Granddad pursed his lips in thought, then said, "I don't think she's lying to you. I think she just wants someone to blame other than your dad. I think she wants that so badly that she's convinced herself it's the truth."

"It is the truth," Hallie spat the words at him.

"No, Hallie. Grandma and I did not push your dad to join the Army. He wanted to." His voice stayed calm and even and his eyes searched hers. She supposed he was looking for an indication that his words may have changed her mind. They hadn't.

She met his gaze with a hard stare. "I don't believe you."

His eyes dropped and he nodded. "Okay. Come in when you're ready. But don't leave the yard." He got up slowly, gave her one last glance, and headed into the house.

Once she was sure Granddad was out of earshot, Hallie let go of the deep, shuddering sob she was holding inside. When she decided to come to the island for the summer, she hadn't thought about what it could lead to. She never considered how painful it might become. If there was one topic she wanted to avoid, it was her father and his death. And when she did think about it, having someone to blame allowed anger to override grief—anger was easier than grief. However, that anger was harder to hold onto each time she saw or spoke to one of her grandparents.

Hallie did remember how much she once enjoyed spending time with them, and it made her long to welcome them back into her life. But if she did that, she would have to let go of the anger—or worse, believe joining the Army was what her father had wanted and shift the anger to him.

Squeezing her eyes shut, Hallie took a deep breath and pushed the thoughts of her father and the confusion her grandparents were causing out of her mind. She wiped a few lingering tears from her face; then opening her eyes, she walked to one of the chairs, sat down, and opened the book she brought with her.

After dropping Charlie and a very unhappy Hallie off at Cory and Doreen's house, Owen headed to the community center to meet with his swing dance group. Tonight would be his first meeting with the group since his breakup with Carrie Ann. That meant he was going to need to be paired up with a new dance partner. He figured Louise Hatton might be interested, since her husband only joined the group to make her happy and had twisted his ankle at the last meeting.

He sighed, looking at the building in front of him. He'd enjoyed dancing with Carrie Ann. Though he loved all the members of the group, most of them were sixty or older and it was fun to dance with someone closer to his own age.

Carrie Ann never had to stop because her knees couldn't take it anymore or because she was winded when he was just getting warmed up.

Resigned to going back to having an older partner, Owen hopped out of his truck and headed inside. He smiled as he moved to join the group in the center of the room where they were socializing. Then his smile fell and he gaped as his eyes reached the back of the group. Carrie Ann stood before him, laughing as she talked to some of the other ladies.

Carrie Ann's gaze traveled to meet his. After staring at one another for a few seconds, she disengaged from the women she'd been talking to and stepped over to stand in front of Owen.

"Did you really think I'd stop coming just because we broke up?" she asked.

"I … well," Owen stammered, searching for an answer to her question that was clearly a challenge. "You only started coming because of me."

She raised an eyebrow. "That's true. The first few times, I came to spend time with you. After that, I didn't need to come for that reason. You and I were dating and doing lots of other things together besides dancing. At that point, I continued to come because I enjoyed it. I still enjoy it. I'm not going to quit just because you and I broke up."

Owen nodded, taking one step back from her in order to reclaim some personal space. "Fair enough. I guess we can find another couple to switch partners with."

Carrie Ann cocked her head to one side. "It's just dancing, Owen. Surely we're both grown up enough to spend a couple of hours dancing together every other week." She put her hands on her hips. "Besides, it makes the most sense for us to stay paired up. Everyone else is twenty-five years or more our senior. If we switch, we'll both have to slow down a bit so no one breaks a hip."

"Or an ankle." The comment slipped out before Owen even thought about it as the memory of Larry Hatton's recent incident came back to his mind.

Carrie Ann nodded. "Or an ankle. I'm glad you see my point."

Owen sucked in a deep breath and let it out slowly. Two hours with Carrie Ann in his arms would weaken his resolve. But he didn't have a good argument, not without touching the emotions he wanted to push away. "Fine. But we're here to dance, not talk."

She shrugged. "Fine. I don't have anything to say."

When the music started, Owen took Carrie Ann into his arms and tried with every fiber of his being to ignore the feelings pulsing through him.

Hallie stayed on the porch for over an hour, but once the sun went down, the bugs began buzzing around her. For ten minutes, she swatted them away, but when she felt them biting her, she knew she needed to go inside. If she stayed on the porch, she would be covered in bites by the time Owen came back.

She closed her book, sucked in another steadying breath, and walked to the door. Turning the knob and opening the door as quietly as possible, Hallie hoped she could sneak inside without anyone noticing. As soon as she stepped inside, however, her grandma walked into the foyer. They stared at each other.

"I don't want to talk," Hallie said. "I only came in to get away from the bugs."

With tight lips, Grandma studied Hallie's face. "If you want to be alone, you can go in the front sitting room. Charlie and Granddad are in the living room watching TV and I'm just going to grab my knitting bag before I join them."

Hallie nodded and started into the sitting room to her right.

"And there are still cookies in the kitchen if you decide you want one," Grandma said before walking away.

Determined to be as sullen and uncooperative as possible, Hallie sat down in the chair closest to the foyer and opened her book. She tried to keep her attention on the story she was reading, but the smell of fresh cookies drifted in the air, distracting her. The kitchen was just through the next door. She could probably sneak in there and grab a cookie without anyone knowing she'd moved.

Setting her book aside, she stood and tiptoed to the kitchen door. She peeked in and confirmed that no one was around. The cookies were lined up on a paper towel. Hallie crept over to it and picked up a soft, gooey, chocolate chip cookie. The aroma filled her nostrils and made her stomach grumble. Then, as she bit into her sugary treat, the sound of laughter rang out from the living room.

Hallie didn't know why, but she found herself quietly walking to the other side of the kitchen that joined up with the living room. No one saw her. They were all looking at the TV in the other direction. As she watched Charlie laughing with her grandparents, her chest began to ache with the desire to join them.

No! She forced herself to remember why she couldn't do that. With a deep, steadying breath, she turned and headed back into the sitting room. Once there, she finished eating her cookie. When it was gone, she looked at the chair where she'd been reading, but she didn't want to read anymore.

Hallie walked to the lovely black piano and ran a hand across it. Granddad used to play for her and teach her simple songs. She sat on the bench and touched the keys with her fingers, pretending to play one of the songs. *I still remember the right keys.*

Getting up, she walked around the room and looked at the pictures and objects on the shelves. She stopped at a picture of her in Daddy's lap. Tears welled in her eyes as she studied the photo. They were so happy—*she* was so happy.

Tearing her eyes from the picture, Hallie's gaze landed on a row of DVDs. The spines were labeled with names and events. She ran her finger along the row until it landed on one that said: DANIEL AND HALLIE. Hallie pulled it out from the row. She desperately wanted to watch it, but she didn't want her grandparents to know of her interest. *I could sneak it out and take it with me tonight.* But there were no TVs at Owen's house and there was no way to watch in privacy at Howard and Marissa's house. If she wanted to watch it, she'd have to do it here.

With a sigh, she put the DVD back on the shelf, walked back to the chair by the foyer, and picked up her book.

Rebecca L. Marsh

Chapter 12

The following morning, Hallie sat at Owen's kitchen table scowling at the toast she was buttering. She had spent most of the night awake, thinking about the DVD at her grandparents' house. If her mother had any videos of Daddy, Hallie wasn't aware of them. Now that she knew there was one at her grandparents' house, she longed to see it. Still, pictures just weren't the same. Watching a video of Daddy would be the closest thing to having him with her again. She needed that, but how could she have it without giving in and letting her grandparents know she wanted something from them?

"Hallie, pass the butter please," Charlie said in a chipper tone.

With an irritated grunt, she shoved the container at him.

"Geez, you're a grump today," Charlie said.

She turned tired, angry eyes on him, and his brows flew up in response.

After gingerly reaching across the table and grabbing the butter container, Charlie finished his breakfast without another word.

When it was time to leave the house, Hallie was grateful Owen had to drive Charlie to camp also because it allowed her to climb into the backseat and silently stew while Owen talked to Charlie.

Arriving at Howard and Marissa's house, Hallie hopped out of the truck and started for the door.

"Have a good day, Hallie," Owen called after her. "See you this afternoon."

Realizing she was being rude to him for something that wasn't his fault, she forced herself to turn around and wave. Then, as Howard had told her she no longer needed to knock before entering, Hallie went into the house and walked back to the kitchen to let them know she was there.

Howard offered to make her an egg biscuit, but she declined as politely as she could and went into the living room to be alone for as long as possible. She sat down on the couch and let her head fall back against the headrest. With a sigh, she closed her eyes.

The next thing Hallie knew, Maisy was shaking her shoulder. "What?" she moaned.

"I thought you were going to help me build a fort in the backyard today," Maisy said.

"Can't you let me sleep a little while first? I didn't sleep well last night."

"Howard's taking us to the park this afternoon. If we're going to work on the fort today, it has to be this morning. You promised you'd help me." Maisy looked at her with pleading eyes.

Hallie blew out a long breath. She didn't want her roiling emotions to lash out at Maisy. That wouldn't be fair.

"Fine," she said, "let's go build a fort."

Maisy responded with a wide grin and a hand held out to help Hallie up. Hallie accepted it and they headed out to the backyard where a small stack of old boards waited for them along with a box of nails and two hammers.

Skipping out ahead, Maisy pointed to a spot between two trees. "Let's build it here. The trees will help us get it started."

Hallie nodded and moved to pick up one of the boards. She stood it up against one of the trees. "Like this?"

Maisy nodded, hurrying over with a hammer and nail. "Perfect! We'll nail it to the tree and then go from there."

For a few moments, the two girls worked in silence, hammering nails into the board and tree. Then Maisy broke the silence. "Did you have a bad dream or something?"

Hallie darted a glance at her. "No. Why?"

"You said you didn't sleep well. Usually, when I don't sleep well it's because of a nightmare."

Hallie could relate to that. She sometimes had terrible dreams in which her mind conjured up images of what her father's death may have been like. Although, lately, when she had nightmares they were about someone else—the someone who'd driven her to run away.

"It wasn't a dream. I just couldn't sleep." Hallie picked up another board and lined it up with the corner of the one they'd nailed to the tree. Maisy hurried over with a nail and began to connect the two boards.

When that one was firmly in place, Hallie said, "You hold the next board and I'll do the nails."

Maisy trotted to the pile of boards and grabbed one. She put it in place and Hallie began to hammer in the nails.

"Were you thinking about your dad? Is that why you couldn't sleep?" Maisy asked.

Hallie squeezed her eyes shut with the pain of the question.

"Ouch!" Maisy screamed. "You hit my finger."

Realizing she'd swung the hammer with her eyes shut, Hallie stammered out a response. "I didn't mean to."

Tears streamed down Maisy's face as she cradled the injured hand against her chest. "It hurts." She glared at Hallie. "You did that on purpose!"

"No, I didn't," Hallie said defensively.

"I saw you swing with your eyes shut."

Hallie paused, that truth stabbing at her. "That doesn't mean it was on purpose." Her voice wasn't so defensive this time. Instead, it was pleading. "I shouldn't have done that, but … it was only because you asked about my dad. I didn't mean to hurt you."

Rather than answer, Maisy took several long breaths while continuing to cradle her hand.

"I'm really sorry," Hallie said. "How bad is it? I can go get Howard."

Maisy eased the injured hand away from her chest and glanced down at it. "I'm not sure how bad it is. It hurts."

"Can I look?"

Maisy held the hand out with her other one protectively cupping it, and Hallie studied the damage. "It's swelling. We should show it to Howard. I'll go get him."

Maisy shook her head. "Let's just go inside and let him look."

Together, they headed into the house. Maisy was still sniffling and protecting her hand as they looked around for Howard.

"Maisy's hand is hurt," Hallie blurted out when they found Howard in the baby's room, rocking her. "I hit it with the hammer by accident."

Maisy shot her an agitated glance but didn't dispute the story.

"Let me put Sylvie down and I'll have a look." Howard gently laid the baby in her basinet and turned to Maisy. "Let's see it."

Maisy held her hand out to him and he took it in his with the same care he gave the baby. "There's swelling. We need to put ice on it, but first, I need to try to determine if the bone is broken." He met Maisy's eyes. "I'll be as gentle as I can, but I need to see if it hurts when I move it."

Maisy bit her lower lip and nodded.

Howard carefully and slowly bent the finger at each joint, looking for a sudden reaction from Maisy. When her level of pain remained constant no matter how the finger was moved, Howard said, "I don't think it's broken. We'll get an ice pack on it and you'll need to be careful with it for a while. No more building today."

Maisy's eyes darted up from her finger to Howard's face. "But if it isn't broken ..."

"I don't think it is. But it's still hurt and swollen. The fort will have to wait. Let's go get some ice." Howard guided Maisy out of the baby's room and toward the kitchen while Hallie trailed behind. He took ice from the freezer and put it in a plastic bag, then wrapped it in a towel. "Go sit in the living room and we'll get this on your finger."

Maisy complied and sat on the couch. Howard put a pillow on her lap, and after asking her to rest her injured hand there, put the ice pack on top. "Sit here with the ice for a bit and I'll be back to check on you."

When he left the room, Hallie walked over and sat next to Maisy. "Want to see what's on TV?"

"Sure and you can sleep. I guess you get what you wanted," Maisy huffed.

"I didn't want to hurt you. I told you that. It's just when you brought up my dad … it upset me."

Maisy cast a hard look at Hallie. "You act like you're the only one who knows what it's like to lose your dad. I lost mine too, you know … and more than that."

Hallie sighed, knowing Maisy was right. If anyone could understand, it was her. "Yeah, I know. It's just being here … and having to see my grandparents. And last night …"

Maisy's expression softened. "Last night what?"

Hallie hesitated, considering whether or not she wanted to tell Maisy about the video. "Last night when I was forced to go to my grandparents' house, I found a DVD and the label says it's a video of me and my dad. I want to watch it. I want to see my dad's face. But I don't want Grandma and Granddad to know I want something from them."

Maisy furrowed her brow. "Why not? Why don't you like them?"

"Because they're the reason my dad joined the Army and that's why he's dead."

"So, if you hate them, then why did you come to the island? I still don't get why you ran away in the first place."

Anger rose in Hallie's chest at Maisy's question, but she didn't want to snap and put a wedge between them again. "I don't want to talk about that. I have my reasons, okay?"

Maisy shrugged. "Fine. Turn the TV on."

"Be careful with that finger," Howard said to Maisy when they arrived at the park.

"I will," Maisy responded.

Howard pointed to a bench under an oak tree. "Sylvie and I will be over there. You two have a good time."

When he'd moved away, Hallie turned to Maisy and asked, "What do you want to do?"

Maisy glanced toward the playground, then looked at Hallie. "We could take a walk around the pond."

Hallie agreed and they headed toward the small, man-made pond in the center of the park. As they neared the water, Maisy pulled her toward the bridge that spread across from one side to the other. This was the spot where Granddad used to take her fishing when she was younger. She remembered the way he'd patiently taught her how to cast her line and how he always baited her hook for her because she didn't like to touch the worms. His smile filled her mind as she thought about the first fish she ever caught. He was so proud of her. No matter how hard she tried not to care, somehow that still meant something to her.

Stepping onto the bridge, Hallie pushed the memories away and kept pace with Maisy.

"I love this place," Maisy said. "It's so pretty."

"Yeah, it's nice." Hallie forced a smile.

They stopped and stood at the center of the bridge, looking out at the water. The only sounds were from the birds. Then Maisy said, "Maybe you should give your grandparents another chance."

"Why should I do that," Hallie scoffed. "Because they're so nice?" She was sick of hearing that.

"Because they miss your dad too," Maisy said without taking her eyes from the pond.

"So what if they do?" Agitation swelled inside Hallie's chest.

"Even if you're right and they did push him to join the Army, they didn't want him to die. He's their son."

"I know that."

"So, maybe if you gave them the chance, they could help you, and you could help them." Maisy turned and regarded Hallie. "You should tell them you want to watch the video."

Still looking at the water, Hallie answered with a sigh.

"Let's walk back to the playground," Maisy suggested.

Nodding, Hallie gratefully started walking again.

When they reached the playground, Maisy glanced around. "No one is on the swings. I'm going to go over there."

"Sure, I like the swings."

"No," Maisy said putting a hand out to stop Hallie from following. "I want to be alone for a little while."

"Why?"

Maisy eyed her. "You don't want to talk about why you ran away. I don't want to talk about why I want to swing alone."

Hallie's forehead crinkled. "Fine. Go be alone. I'll find something else to do."

She watched for a moment as Maisy headed toward the swings wondering why it was so important that she go alone. Then, kicking at the dirt, she walked to the bench where Howard sat.

He smiled at her. "Having fun?"

She shrugged.

"Where's Maisy?" Howard asked.

"On the swings. She wanted to be alone for some reason." Hallie sat down on the bench next to Howard.

"Maisy only goes to the swings when she wants to feel close to her sister."

Hallie furrowed her brow. "Her sister is right here."

"Not Sylvie, her other sister, Kyla. The swings were Kyla's thing. Maisy wants to be alone because she's thinking about her."

"Oh." So that was it. Maisy was remembering her dead sister.

The peaceful sounds of the park were broken when Sylvie began to cry.

"Can I pick her up?" Hallie asked when Howard reached for the infant carrier.

"Do you know how to hold her?" he asked.

Hallie nodded. "I helped with my little brothers when they were this age. I know I have to support her neck."

Howard smiled at her. "Go ahead then."

Hallie reached into the baby seat and placed one hand under the baby's head and one under her rear, then lifted her from the seat. She put Sylvie on her shoulder and bounced gently until the crying stopped.

"You've got the knack," Howard said with a grin.

"The bounce always worked with Tyler and Tyson. They still like it." As she said the words, her heart ached from how she missed the boys. Her lips turned down, she said, "I hope they don't forget me while I'm here."

"Don't worry. I'm sure they'll remember their big sis as soon as you pick them up and bounce them."

Hallie smiled and sat back down on the bench with the now content baby, enjoying the warm bundle against her chest. Then she glanced at Howard and saw his face had darkened. She followed his gaze and saw he was looking toward the swings where Maisy sat on one swing and was turned to face another one. She appeared to be talking to the empty swing. Hallie thought about asking Howard if he knew what Maisy was doing, but the concern that laced his features silenced her.

Chapter 13

Marissa took a quick look in the mirror. She liked the black jeans she'd put on and the ruffled top. However, she wasn't happy about the extra plumpness around her middle that remained from her pregnancy. She had already been a little overweight before the baby, and it was harder losing the baby weight this time than it had been ten years ago.

With a sigh, she decided it was time to add a few sit-ups to her daily routine. But for now, there was nothing she could do about it.

Stepping into her bathroom, she did the best she could to tame her unruly red curls. Then she headed into the living room where Howard was packing up the diaper bag.

"I'm ready when you are," she said.

Howard turned and smiled at her. "Are you sure? It'll be our first time leaving Sylvie with someone else."

"I know. It's hard to leave her with anyone but you. But she'll be in good hands with Uncle Owen. And I think we need a date night." She moved closer to him and kissed his cheek.

"I think so too. Sylvie is ready to go."

"I'll go get Maisy and we can head out."

Once they were all in Marissa's minivan, they drove the short distance to Owen's house and dropped the girls off. That done, they headed to the island's Italian restaurant.

"So, who goes first?" Marissa asked after they'd ordered their meals.

Howard looked up and smiled. "I think it's your turn."

"Okay." She let her eyes travel over the other tables near them trying to decide which one to pick. When she and Howard first began to see each other, they'd started a people-watching game in which they took turns picking a nearby table and guessing about the occupants.

Marissa indicated a table to her left where a large family sat. There were four children, all under the age of seven. The older two fought over the last bread stick, the youngest, crying, struggled to free herself from a highchair, and the other was busy painting his face with spaghetti sauce. The father was attempting to settle the war over bread, and the mother was offering an array of toys and pacifiers to the little one, hoping to quiet her down. Neither noticed the tomato sauce face art.

"She's a stay-at-home mom. Money is tight, so they don't do babysitters. But today is her birthday, so her husband insisted on taking the family out to eat. And right now, they both regret that choice," Marissa said.

Howard raised an eyebrow at her. "I don't know those kids—the older ones, I mean—and since there's only one elementary school on the island, I'm pretty sure they're here on vacation."

Marissa scowled at him. "Or they may have just moved here."

"Could be," he said with a hint of skepticism. "But they're probably vacationers."

"Possibly," Marissa agreed as the waiter arrived with their meals—chicken parmesan for Howard and fettuccini alfredo for Marissa. They began to eat, then after a few bites, Marissa said, "Your turn."

Howard let his eyes roam the dining room. "Over there," he tipped his head to his left and forward a bit to indicate a table where a young couple sat. They were dressed up more than most of the other people in the restaurant, the young man in a shirt and tie, the young woman in a short, black dress. The woman looked unhappy and the man appeared sullen.

"They were set up on a blind date, but she's upset because he doesn't look like his picture. And him ... well, the poor guy doesn't know how to bounce back from her instant disappointment."

A small smile spread across Marissa's face as she shook her head. "Sorry, but you've got it wrong. Those two are married already."

Howard scowled at her. "How do you know? I've never seen them before."

"You mean besides the rings they're wearing? They've been into the pharmacy a few times." Marissa picked up her bread stick and took a bite.

"Are they new in town?"

Marissa pursed her lips in thought. "I think they've been here for about five months. But they don't have kids yet, so you wouldn't see them at the school."

"I see the rings now. I must be slipping." He met her eyes with a shrug. "Well, if they're married, then it looks like it's date night." Howard lifted his glass and took a sip of his sweet tea. "Same as us."

Marissa grinned. "Except we put less effort into our clothing." She leaned closer to him and whispered, "And I'd have to say we're having a better time."

Howard returned her smile. "Let's keep the good times rolling with dessert and a stroll around town."

"The cheesecake?" Marissa asked.

"Definitely."

Once they finished their dessert and boxed up their leftovers, Marissa and Howard left the restaurant for a walk along Main Street. Marissa remembered the first time they had attempted an evening walk after a dinner date, back when Marissa was still grieving the loss of Kevin and Kyla and wasn't ready to think of Howard as anything but a friend. That walk had ended quickly when the sounds of the nearby ocean brought back the memory of Marissa's worst day—the day she lost half of her family.

While that sound did sometimes still make her think of her lost husband and daughter, enough time had passed and the pain was no longer raw. She could put the thoughts aside now and focus on enjoying her time with Howard. He, however, seemed unusually quiet since leaving the restaurant.

"Is something wrong?" Marissa asked as they walked arm in arm.

He glanced at her, then returned his eyes to the sidewalk ahead of them. "I was thinking about Maisy."

"Did something happen today?" Marissa asked with mild concern.

"No, not really. We went to the park. She and Hallie walked to the pond and then Maisy asked for some alone time on the swing."

"That's not unusual."

"No, but when I looked to see how she was doing, she was sitting on one swing and had turned to face another one that was empty. And … it looked like she was talking to the empty swing." He looked at Marissa again. "I haven't seen her do *that* before."

Marissa sighed. "I saw her do something similar the night we had dinner at Owen's house. She went to Betty's yard and when I looked out the window, she was standing up facing the swing and it looked like she was talking."

They walked in silence for a moment. "When she's with you, does she ever pay attention to Sylvie?"

"No," Marissa said, her voice somber. "I have to admit that worries me."

"Do you think she feels like she's lost something? Like we aren't paying enough attention to her?"

"I think we've done everything we can to make sure she doesn't feel that way."

"I know, but maybe she still does."

Marissa took a deep breath, thoughts of what she and Maisy went through three years earlier when they'd lost Kevin and Kyla ran through her mind. Marissa's attempt to avoid the grieving process had put a giant wedge between herself and Maisy. There was no way she was going to let their issues, whatever they were, take them down a road like that one again.

"Do you think we should be worried about it?" Howard asked.

"I think maybe we should ask her about it."

Howard put an arm around her shoulders. "Maybe we should wait on that. It doesn't seem that serious yet. Confronting her might cause problems instead of solving them."

Marissa stopped and turned to him. "If there's an issue with her, I don't want to let it fester." She searched his face as her fears ramped up. "I've learned my lesson about avoiding problems."

His eyes full of compassion, Howard put his hands on her shoulders. "This isn't the same, honey. And we won't avoid it. I just want to give her a little space first to see if she works ... whatever this is out on her own."

Marissa sighed. "All right, but if we keep seeing what we have been, we'll have to talk to her and maybe bring it up with her psychologist." She pulled his hands from her shoulders into her own hands and smiled at him, pushing away her worries. "But maybe right now we should put that aside and try to enjoy our time together. We don't get a lot of that these days."

A grin spread across Howard's face and he leaned down to lay a kiss on Marissa's forehead. "You're absolutely right. Let's enjoy tonight and I'll pray over Maisy."

At his words, a surge of emotion brought tears to Marissa's eyes. She dipped her head and dabbed her eyes with the back of her hand.

"You okay?" Howard's brow furrowed in concern.

Marissa nodded, turning her face up to his. "Sometimes you say something that reminds me how lucky I am to have found you."

"Not to nitpick, but I'd have to say *I* found you. It took some work to convince you to see me as more than a friend."

She nodded as they began to walk again. "True enough. I'll start praying about Maisy too. I'm glad you brought that up."

He wiped a stray tear from her cheek. "Never hurts to consult the One who knows everything we don't."

"I wish I'd done more of that a few years ago. Maybe I wouldn't have gone so long trying to avoid the grieving process. Maybe I wouldn't have ended up literally talking my daughter off of a cliff." Marissa's mind flashed back to the day she'd found herself searching the town for Maisy, then discovered her standing at the edge of Tara's Pointe, a cliff that was named for the daughter of the town's founder who fell to her death there.

"There's no point playing the maybe game. Yesterday is gone. Today is enough to worry about." He pulled her in for a hug. "Besides, we said we were going to enjoy tonight."

"I think I said that actually. I guess I need to listen to myself." She took his arm again. "It's a beautiful night. And I think Owen can handle the girls for a short while longer."

Owen knocked lightly on Hallie's door. "Mind if I come in?"

"Go ahead," she called back.

He eased the door open and glanced inside. Hallie sat on her bed with her knees against her chest and her chin resting on them.

"Is everything okay?" he asked.

She shifted and raised her head. "Yeah, I'm fine."

The way she was sitting and the pensive look in her eyes told a different story.

Owen stepped forward and rested a hand on one of the footboard posts. "I saw your grandma today. She's disappointed about the way you tried to stay away from them the evening you and Charlie went to their house."

"It's her fault," Hallie said with agitation. "If she and Granddad hadn't pushed my father into the Army, he'd be alive now. And if he was, I wouldn't have needed to run away."

Owen's face crinkled with worry. "What does that mean, Hallie? Does it have something to do with your step-father?"

She looked away. "Not exactly."

Owen took a few more steps toward her, his jaw clenching at the thought that Hallie might have been mistreated. "Has he hurt you?"

A flicker of surprise registered in her eyes as she turned back toward him. "No. Dustin's not like that."

Relief washed over Owen and he felt his muscles relax. *Thank God.* "Charlie tells me that you miss your little brothers."

"Yeah, I do." She looked down at the quilt on her bed and ran a finger along one of the color blocks. "I hope they still know who I am when I get back."

"I bet they will." Owen wasn't sure it was a good idea, but he voiced the thought in his head anyway. "I know you miss your dad. Everyone who knew him does. But if things had gone differently, if he hadn't joined the Army, then your brothers wouldn't be here."

Hallie's head jerked up and she glared at Owen with her brows drawn together.

"That doesn't mean anyone is glad he's gone. But those little boys couldn't exist without your step-father."

"So I should be glad my dad is gone," she spat the words out like vinegar.

Owen sucked in a deep breath as a stab of regret hit him. Maybe this was the wrong tactic. Hallie still hadn't let go of her anger. She might not be ready to understand what he meant.

"No, of course not. What I mean is, you love both your dad and your brothers—brothers you couldn't have if your dad was never in the Army, if your mother had never married your step-dad. So, wouldn't it be better if you could remember your dad and how you love him, but also see the good in what you've gained? Not because it's good that your dad is gone, but because God took that bad thing and gave you something good out of it."

Hallie inhaled sharply and let the breath out with force.

Owen crept closer and sat down in the chair beside the bed. "How much has Charlie told you about his mom?"

Her expression changed to one of annoyance with the subject change. "A little. His mom left him here with you."

Owen nodded. "And that was really hard for him, losing his mom and finding himself with a dad he didn't know." Owen didn't mention that it was quite an adjustment for him as well. "At first, he cried for his mom every night, and I wasn't much comfort because we didn't even know each other. But over time, we got to know each other and now our relationship is strong. Even so, Charlie is still sad that his mother isn't a part of his life, but if she hadn't left him, he and I would never have become father and son."

Hallie's brows drew together in confusion. "But you'd still be his dad if his mom hadn't left."

Owen shook his head. "Actually, no. When his mom dropped him off here, she thought I might be his father, but didn't know for sure. A couple years ago, we had a DNA test done. As it turns out, I'm not Charlie's biological father. And even if I were, I doubt his mother would have ever told me he existed had she not been looking for a safe place to leave him."

"You mean you're not his dad?"

"I'm not his biological father, but I am the one his mother chose to list as father on his birth certificate. And since the other man his mother was involved with when she got pregnant with him is dead, there's no need to take any legal action. Also, I love Charlie and want to raise him. So, I may not be his biological father, but I am his dad."

"But you're saying that if his mother hadn't left him, he wouldn't have you and you wouldn't have him."

"Yes. And I'm saying that, because we're both glad to have each other, it doesn't mean he doesn't miss having a mother in his life. But there was a good thing that couldn't have happened without the bad thing."

Hallie shrugged dismissively. "So, I love my brothers. That doesn't mean I should forgive my grandparents."

Owen sighed. "What do you gain by continuing to be angry with them? They're your best link to your dad. And you're their best link."

When she answered him with a scowl, Owen stood up and said, "Charlie, Maisy, and I are going to play a game. We'd love it if you joined us." He stopped just before leaving and turned back. "Oh, and I need to tell you, next weekend Charlie and I will be going to the mainland for his and my nephew's birthdays. Marissa and Howard are going as well. So, you'll be staying with your grandparents while we're gone."

Hallie put her legs down and straightened her back. "What? No! I'll come to the mainland with you."

Owen met her eyes. "Your mother barely agreed to let you stay here. She's not going to let me take you on a trip. So, it's your grandparents' house or home to your mom."

When Hallie came downstairs and joined them for a game of Uno, Owen was surprised. With a smile, he said, "You decided to join us."

She shrugged, not meeting his eyes. "I'm tired of sitting in my room."

Owen grabbed the deck of cards and began to shuffle them. "Whatever the reason, we're glad to have you. Take a seat."

She sat down between Charlie and Maisy. Her face still showed irritation, but Owen chose to ignore that. He dealt the cards. "All right, Maisy, you're first," he said as he flipped a card over from the deck.

Two hands into the game, Hallie began to look more relaxed. She even smiled as she threw down a draw two card for Charlie. When Sylvie began to wail, Owen tossed his cards down. "Sorry, guys, I'm gonna have to leave the game."

"Yes! That means I'm winning," Charlie said with a grin and a fist in the air.

"I suppose it does. You can thank your little cousin." Owen stood up and pushed in his chair.

Stepping into the living room, he went to the infant seat and reached in to pick the baby up. He put her on his shoulder and bounced gently until the cries abated. "So, what is it, Sylvie? Do you need a bottle or a diaper change?" He carried her to the couch where a blanket was already laid across the seat and put her down to check her diaper. "Looks like we'll start with some dry pants and then a bottle."

Owen was just finishing up with the diaper change when he heard the doorbell. "Now who could that be?" He picked up Sylvie and strode to the front door. When he swung it open, Carrie Ann's face met him.

His eyes meeting hers, Owen's chest tightened. He stared at her.

"Hi, Owen," she said.

"W-what are you doing here?" he stammered.

She raised her eyebrows. "Nice greeting."

"Sorry, but ..."

"Don't worry, Owen, I only came for my mug."

"Your mug?"

She pushed a lock of hair behind her ear impatiently. "Yes, Owen, my mug—the one I left over here when we were dating."

His brain clouded by her presence, Owen kept staring. She looked beautiful and her vanilla-scented body spray wafted toward him. He licked his lips as he stared at hers and remembered what it felt like to kiss her. Everything in him wanted to pull her toward him and kiss her now.

She rolled her eyes. "Can I come in and get it if you aren't going to?"

Shaking his mind from the fog, he narrowed his eyes at her. "You drove over here just to get a mug?"

"It's on my way home from work and I happen to like that mug."

Owen raised one eyebrow. "You never work this late."

She crossed her arms over her chest. "I had some things to do in town before heading home, not that it's any of your business." Sighing when he didn't move from the doorway, Carrie Ann said, "Can I have the mug now?"

"Not tonight, Carrie Ann. I've got a house full of kids." He raised the arm that held Sylvie as an indication.

Her face scrunched up. "Are the kids holding my mug hostage?"

"No."

"Did they break it?" She leaned on the doorjamb.

"No. It's just not the best time."

"Owen," she said, leaning closer to him, "is there some reason you don't want to give me back my mug?"

He shifted his weight. "No, of course not."

"Then it seems like I should be able to come in for just a few minutes and get my mug. What can it hurt?"

Owen swallowed. For reasons he couldn't explain, the thought of her taking back the last thing of hers that remained in his house hurt a lot. He wasn't going to tell her that though. Instead, he stepped back and allowed her inside.

Sweeping past him, Carrie Ann headed straight for the kitchen.

Before Owen could catch up, he heard his son's voice ring out, "Carrie Ann!"

When he reached the kitchen, Charlie had his arms wrapped around Carrie Ann.

"Are you and Dad working things out?" Charlie asked, his eyes hopeful.

Carrie Ann glanced at Owen for a second, then turned her attention back to Charlie. "I'm just here to get my coffee mug." Her voice was laced with sadness.

Charlie wilted. "Oh." He glared at Owen before sliding back into his seat at the table, arms crossed over his chest. Owen felt a stab to his heart. He didn't just miss having her around for himself, but for what she gave to his son. If only she wasn't giving him an ultimatum.

Glancing at the other kids, Carrie Ann said, "Hi Maisy. And Hallie, it's been so long! You've really grown up."

Maisy smiled and waved.

"Hi, Carrie Ann," Hallie said.

"It's good to have you on the island again. I know your grandparents have missed you," Carrie Ann said.

When Hallie looked down uncomfortably, Carrie Ann moved toward the cupboard over the coffee maker. "I guess I'll just get that mug now." She pushed a few mugs around, then glared at Owen. "Where is it?"

He shrugged, pretending not to know.

Carrie Ann shifted her weight to one side and put a hand on her hip. "Where did you put it, Owen? I left it right here."

"He moved it to the back," Charlie called out, his voice still laced with resentment.

Staring at Owen, Carrie Ann's eyebrows went up. He did everything he could to keep from showing the irritation he felt with his son at that moment.

She turned back to the cupboard and began pulling mugs out until she reached the one she was searching for. "All the way to the back, Owen? Really?"

"It must have gotten pushed back when others were used and washed," he lied and attempted a nonchalant posture when she turned toward him.

"Yeah, I'm sure that's what happened." She rolled her eyes. They both knew he was the only one who would be using any of the mugs, and the ones he used generally stayed right in the front. The only time they got shifted was just before Christmas when he moved the holiday mugs to the front.

Carrie Ann put all the mugs back in the cupboard except the one she'd come for, and just as she turned back to Owen, the baby squirmed and began to fuss.

"She needs to be fed," Owen said.

Holding the mug up, Carrie Ann said, "I've got what I came for. I'll get out of your way so you can take care of her."

She headed toward the front door and Owen followed. Each step closer to watching her leave made his heart heavier. When she took hold of the doorknob, he reached out and grabbed her hand.

"I don't want you to go," his voice was a near whisper.

Carrie Ann turned and met his eyes. A silent moment passed between them before she responded. "I'd like to stay. You know what it takes to make that happen."

"I just want to put things back the way they were." Owen felt his eyes grow moist with his pleading words.

Her lips tightened for a moment. Then she spoke softly. "Owen, I can't tell you how much I want to say yes. But what would that achieve? I love you. I want to be with you. But I won't stay in a relationship that stands still indefinitely." Tears rolled down her cheeks as emotion filled her voice. "I deserve more."

"More than me?"

She shook her head. "Don't do that, Owen. You know that's not what I mean. When you're ready to move forward, call me." She opened the door and walked out without looking back again.

Chapter 14

Hallie tossed and turned in her bed, winding herself up in the sheets as nightmare images played through her mind. She was in her mother's house—alone—and someone was at the door. She cringed in the corner, her heart galloping, as she watched the knob jiggle.

"You think a locked door is going to stand in my way," a man's voice called out. "Don't you know I've got the key?"

As the key slid into the lock, Hallie jumped up and ran to her room, slamming the door shut behind her. Her eyes darted around in search of a hiding place. The only place that seemed reasonable was the bed. Flattening her body on the floor, she began to crawl underneath. Just as her fingers touched the wall on the other side of the bed, she heard the door open and a hand latched onto her ankle.

"Got you now, little girl. We gonna have some fun."

Hallie screamed and her eyes flew open. She panted for a moment until her heartbeat slowed. She was in her room at Owen's house. She was okay.

Untangling herself from the sheets, she stretched and dragged herself out of bed. After a shower, she shoved clothes into her backpack in preparation for the weekend she would spend at her grandparents' house. She didn't want to go, but after a week to think about it, she decided it didn't have to be that bad. She'd simply stay in her room most of the time. As she saw it there were two benefits to the situation. First, her grandmother was an amazing cook. So, she'd eat well. Second, it opened up an opportunity to possibly watch the video. She might even be able to watch it without them knowing. Besides that, she wouldn't be home.

And after her nightmare, the need to be anywhere but there was as clear as ever.

She went into the hall bathroom and began packing her toiletries. When she'd done that, she pulled her hair into two elastic bands, then took a glance in the mirror, scowling at the image staring back at her. Maybe she'd use some of the time alone over the weekend to attempt braiding her hair. It wouldn't be as good as what her mother could do, but anything would be better than the ponytails.

When her bag was packed, she headed downstairs and dropped it off by the front door before settling into a chair in the living room to read while she waited for Owen and Charlie.

Hallie made it through two pages before Charlie came bounding into the room and joined her on the couch. She looked up and smiled at him. "I hope you have a good time celebrating your birthday with your family." They'd already had a small celebration for him three days earlier on his actual birthday.

Charlie nodded but didn't smile. His expression was pensive. "Don't you want to see your family?" She asked, closing her book and sitting up straighter.

"Of course I do." He hesitated. "But I want to talk to you about something."

"Okay, what?" She couldn't think of any reason for him to be upset with her, but he was acting like he might be.

He twisted his fingers together in his lap as he avoided making eye contact. "Hallie, it really hurt your grandparents' feelings that night we went over there and you stayed away from them."

Hallie was about to protest, but before she could get a word out, Charlie spoke again. "I know you're mad at them 'cause of what happened to your dad. I don't really get that, but—" He shrugged. "Well, I guess I don't have to get it. But Hallie, I don't like the way you're hurting them." He looked at her with moist eyes. "They've always been so nice to me.

When I first came here, your granddad always made me laugh and I didn't laugh much then."

Charlie stopped talking, but Hallie didn't know how to respond when her friend was sitting in front of her with tears in his eyes.

After a long moment of silence between them, Charlie said, "Could you try to be a little nicer to them this weekend?"

She let out an exasperated sigh. "I'll try."

He smiled now. "Thanks, and bring me back one of those cookies if you can."

"Okay," she said as he stood up and started to leave. "And Charlie?"

He turned and met her eyes.

"I'm glad they helped you back then."

Marissa jumped when Howard walked up behind her and wrapped his arms around her waist.

"I'm sorry I startled you," he said. "I just couldn't help myself when I saw such a beautiful sight."

Turning her head to glance at him for a moment, Marissa said, "That's okay. I guess the ferry still makes me a little jumpy." She wrapped one arm tighter around her infant daughter and with her other hand, she grasped the railing in front of her. The ocean waves splashed against the large boat as it slowly chugged toward the mainland. Seagulls flew behind it, squawking. Two-and-a-half years ago, when she and Maisy first moved to the island, Marissa hadn't been able to come above deck on the ferry. She'd needed to stay in the car and grit her teeth the whole ride. She'd come a long way, but it was still a battle.

Howard kissed the top of her head. "You're doing great."

The two of them sat down on the bench that ran along the outside wall of the boat's bridge. Howard held Marissa's hand as they watched a group of pelicans dive for fish.

"We saw dolphins!" Maisy said excitedly as she ran up to them.

"That's awesome," Howard said.

Maisy nodded. "They were swimming next to the boat and this lady started throwing crackers at them. Then one of the ferry workers told her to stop." She sat down next to Marissa. "Charlie and Uncle Owen went to the other side of the boat to see if there are any dolphins over there, but I wanted to sit down for a minute."

"Perfect," Howard said. "You can keep your mom company while I run to the restroom."

A moment after Howard walked away, Sylvie began to fuss. Marissa checked her diaper, but she was dry as a bone. Deciding the baby must be hungry, she turned to Maisy. "I need you to hold your sister for just a minute while I get a bottle ready for her."

Maisy's expression went instantly from lighthearted to tense. "I'll get the bottle for you," she volunteered.

"It's not that simple, sweetie. I need to mix the formula."

"I can do that." Maisy hopped up and reached for the diaper bag that sat at Marissa's feet.

"You don't know how and it will be much easier for me to do it while you hold Sylvie."

Maisy stared at her, jaw clenched, then sat back down on the bench. "Okay," she mumbled.

As Marissa gently placed the baby in Maisy's arms, it didn't escape her attention that her older daughter was not only uncomfortable holding the baby, but she was also trying very hard not to look at her sister.

Marissa mixed the bottle up quickly as the infant continued to fuss. When it was ready, she turned to Maisy and held the bottle out to her. "Why don't you feed her?"

Maisy shook her head, a strange desperation in her eyes.

"She needs to get to know you too. You're her big sister," Marissa tried.

"I don't want to." Maisy's forehead crinkled in a pained expression.

"Okay. Let me take her." Marissa's heart dropped at Maisy's response. She took Sylvie back into her arms and began to feed her, expecting Maisy to hop up and go back to the railing with her cousin. Instead, she stayed on the bench, sitting rigidly, and turned away from Marissa.

"Maisy," Marissa spoke in a lowered voice, "what's wrong?"

"Nothing." Maisy crossed her arms over her chest as she continued to look in the opposite direction.

Unsure how to push forward, Marissa tried the least intrusive tactic she could think of. "Something must be. You were happy a moment ago and now you're not."

"I'm fine."

"Except you don't want to hold your sister." Marissa knew she was charging forward into territory that might create problems between Maisy and herself, but after the way Maisy had just behaved, she needed to know what was going on.

"I said I'm fine," Maisy growled her response.

"Sweetie, if something is going on, we should talk about it."

As Sylvie noisily sucked the milk from her bottle, Maisy turned for a moment, gave Marissa a fiery gaze, then yelled, "I don't want to talk about it!" She stood up and stomped away toward the railing just as Howard returned.

"What in the world happened while I was in the restroom?" Howard asked, scratching the bald top of his head.

Marissa sighed. "I tried to talk to her about why she doesn't want to hold Sylvie."

Howard frowned. "I thought we were going to wait and give it some time."

"Yeah, I know. But I don't think we can wait. I think we need to address it."

Letting out a heavy breath, Howard dropped down next to her. He didn't say anything, but his posture was stiff.

"So, you're mad at me too?" Marissa asked as the baby finished her milk. She tossed a burp cloth over her shoulder before moving Sylvie and beginning to pat her back.

"I'm not mad," Howard said, but his tone was tight.

"You *are* mad."

He turned and met her eyes. "I just don't think today was the right time to address the issue. We're going to your mom's house to celebrate two birthdays. This weekend is supposed to be fun." He turned his eyes forward again and looked out to the ocean. "Do you think opening this door with Maisy is a good idea right before we see your mom?"

Marissa sighed. He had a point.

When Owen and Charlie dropped her off at her grandparents' house, Hallie glanced back at them for a moment before slinging her backpack over her shoulder and ambling up the front steps. Her stomach churned as the door loomed in front of her. But there was nothing she could do about it. This weekend with her grandparents was going to happen. Letting out a breath, she rang the doorbell and waited.

The door opened and Grandma's face looked out at her with a broad smile. "Hallie, come on in." Grandma opened the door wide for her and waved at Owen as he drove away. "Let's get you settled upstairs."

"I know the way," Hallie said in a clipped tone. Her grandmother's smile fell away, and Hallie felt a stab of regret as she thought about the promise she'd made to Charlie. Changing her tone, Hallie said, "It's the same room I stayed in before, right?"

"Yes."

"Okay. I'll go up and put my stuff in there." Hallie started toward the stairs. She was halfway up when her grandmother's voice stopped her.

"Your granddad and I would like to have lunch with you."

Hallie turned and met her grandmother's hopeful eyes. "Call me when it's time."

She continued up the stairs and found her way to the second door on the right side of the hall. It was already opened and a neat and tidy bedroom awaited her. The double bed was covered in a feminine, flowery bedspread and lots of matching pillows. The walls were a pale blue, matching some of the flowers. A chest of drawers stood against one wall. It was made of a dark wood that matched the headboard on the bed as well as the little nightstand. On another wall stood a tall bookshelf that was filled with things from her father's childhood as well as pictures of him. This room, Hallie knew, used to be her father's room. When she was born, her grandparents changed the bedspread to make the room more girly for when she came to stay with them.

Hallie dropped her backpack next to the bed and walked around the room. She glanced at the mementos of her father's youth that he'd chosen to leave behind—a trophy from little league baseball, a hat with the name of his high school, and on one of the shelves all his school yearbooks were arranged along with some other books he'd left. She ran a finger along the spines of the yearbooks. Maybe she would look through some of them while she was here.

When one of the framed pictures caught her eye, Hallie picked it up and studied it. Her father's face looked back at her. He was wearing his Army uniform and the expression on his face was serious, but behind the seriousness, Hallie also saw something else. There was a gleam in his eyes. Though she hated to think it could be true, she had to admit, he looked proud.

She put the photo down, brushing away that gleam she saw. He was probably just proud of making it through his training. It didn't mean he wanted to be there.

Hallie pulled out an old photo album that was wedged in next to the yearbooks and took it to the bed to look through it. Propped against the pillows, she began to flip through the pages. Picture after picture showed her the years of her father's childhood. He'd been active in several sports and he had lots of friends.

Hallie was on the last page, tracing the angles of her father's handsome face when her grandmother's voice beckoned her to come downstairs for lunch. With one last look at her daddy's face, she set the album aside and scooted off the bed.

When she reached the kitchen, Hallie found her grandparents seated at the table waiting for her.

"Come take a seat," Granddad said with a smile. Once she was settled, he continued, "We know being here wasn't what you wanted, but we want you to know that we're so happy to have you with us this weekend."

Hallie peeked up at him and gave him a tight smile. Since the comments she had in mind were snarky, she resisted voicing them, and instead, turned to the plate in front of her.

"I hope you still like peanut butter and jelly sandwiches," Grandma said.

Glancing at her, Hallie gave a curt nod. Though she didn't want to admit it, they were still her favorite. And Grandma had even cut the crust off for her and sliced it into little triangles. Next to the sandwich, cut-up strawberries and blackberries filled her plate. Her mouth watered in anticipation.

"Well," Grandma said, "go ahead and eat. After lunch, Granddad has to go in to work for a little while and my knitting group is coming over. I thought maybe we could go to the pond later when all that's over and you and Granddad can fish."

With one of the sandwich triangles halfway to her mouth, Hallie stiffened. "I'd rather stay here and read." She thought about the video and added, "Or maybe watch TV a little."

As Hallie bit into her sandwich, secretly relishing the taste, her grandparents' disappointment was visible. Granddad's mouth drew into a frown and Grandma's posture drooped. Their desire to spend time with her was obvious. The strange part was the way all of that made Hallie feel. Instead of feeling pleased with herself, she felt a sinking sensation in her gut.

With no desire to contemplate the emotions that were hitting her, she shoved the rest of the small sandwich into her mouth and tried to focus only on her food.

"Hallie, how are you and Maisy getting along?" Grandma asked, her tone artificially cheery.

"Fine." Hallie popped a strawberry into her mouth.

"What have the two of you been doing so far this summer?" Grandma tried an open-ended question before taking a bite of her sandwich.

Hallie shrugged. "Different stuff."

Grandma sighed, and they ate silently for a few minutes.

"I hear you went to the beach and that you girls are building a fort," Granddad said.

Hallie nodded, but with the mention of the activities she and Maisy were doing together, responses bubbled up inside of her, and this time, they weren't snarky. She clamped her lips closed and held them back. She would try to be nicer to them as she told Charlie, but she wasn't ready to let them in the way they wanted. For her father, she was determined to remain angry with them.

With her silence, her grandparents gave up and they finished lunch without another word. Granddad left for work, then Grandma's group came and they all went into the family room.

Hallie took the opportunity to wander around the house a bit. She spent some time on the porch swing and she looked through another photo album she found. Then she found herself drawn back to the living room. She sat at the piano and tried to remember some more of the songs she used to know. When she was tired of that, she found herself back at the shelf staring at the DVD she desperately wanted to watch.

"You're welcome to watch them," Grandma said, surprising Hallie and making her jump.

Hallie spun around and faced her grandmother who had just stepped into the room from the foyer.

"Sorry, I didn't mean to startle you," Grandma said.

"I thought you were in the other room with your group."

"They all just left. Didn't you hear us in the foyer?"

"No." *Was I really that caught up looking at this DVD?* Hallie thought. She moved closer to the chair that was in front of her and gripped the back of it with both hands.

"It's just you and me here now." Grandma nodded toward the shelf. "Is there a video you'd like to see?"

Hallie squirmed. She didn't want anyone around when she watched the video. She'd been hoping she could slip it off the shelf and take it to her room, then look for an opportunity to watch when no one was around. But that chance might not come. She pointed to the one she wanted to watch. "I want to watch it alone."

Grandma nodded. "I understand. Would you like me to get it started for you?"

"No, I can do it." Hallie bristled at her grandmother's claim of understanding but tried to keep her tone even. *You don't understand anything.*

"You go ahead and take it to the family room. I've got some gardening to take care of before Granddad gets home."

At the mention of gardening, a memory played through Hallie's mind of when she was younger and loved to help Grandma in the garden. She remembered the feel of the dirt in her hands and her grandmother's encouraging smiles. She sucked in a sharp breath with the emotions that rolled through her, feelings that she didn't welcome.

Turning to the shelf, she snatched the DVD and headed into the family room without another word.

Rebecca L. Marsh

 **Chapter 15**

Sitting in the back of his sister's minivan, Owen was puzzled by the behavior he saw around him. Charlie was fine, chattering about their weekend and the ferry ride. Everyone else was silent. Howard looked a bit irritated; Marissa chewed her nails and sneaked peeks at Maisy who sat with her arms crossed over her chest and an expression Owen was struggling to identify. He didn't know if she was sad or angry, but she certainly wasn't happy.

"I wonder what Grandma got me for my birthday," Charlie said, bouncing in his seat.

Owen glanced at his son, glad the mood in the car wasn't affecting him. "I don't know. I guess you'll find out soon." He held back from sharing that he hoped the gift would be something that fit in a minivan that was full of people and luggage already.

"I'm going to teach Alex what I learned in day camp about edible plants and how to tie knots," Charlie said.

"The knot-tying is good, but Alex is only turning seven. I wouldn't want him to accidentally eat the wrong plant. So, maybe you should leave that out," Owen told him.

"Oh." Charlie scratched his head. "I didn't think of that. I guess you're right."

"I'm sure you'll have lots of fun with your cousin and get some fantastic gifts." Owen smiled at his son. Then he looked around the van again. Everyone remained the same. Charlie pulled out a comic book to look at and the car went silent again. What was going on?

When they arrived at his mother's house, Owen was relieved—a feeling he didn't usually associate with visits home. But it would have to be better than the car ride had been. He slid the side door open and got out of the van ahead of Charlie and Maisy. Howard opened the other side door and lifted the infant seat out. By the time they were all out of the van, Owen's mother was out of her house and waiting for them on the front porch. Charlie ran toward her, but Maisy beat him there and threw her arms around her grandmother like she was grabbing a lifeline. Mary Lynn returned the embrace and motioned for Charlie to join in. He quickly accepted.

Watching as he trudged through the yard, Owen couldn't help but smile at the affection. He just wished his niece's behavior didn't feel so reminiscent of the way she'd been three years ago.

When the adults made it to the porch with the baby, Mary Lynn tore herself away from her older grandchildren. "There's my newest baby," she said, grinning at Sylvie.

"Want to hold her, Grandma?" Howard asked.

"I most certainly do," Mary Lynn said.

Owen didn't miss the sour expression that overtook Maisy's face. His heart dropped. It wasn't the first sign he'd seen of an issue with the way Maisy felt about her baby sister, but it was concerning. And it might be getting worse.

"Oh, look at this little one," Mary Lynn said as the baby was placed in her arms. She ran a hand over the red fuzz atop the infant's head, and as she did, Maisy's expression became even tighter.

Owen pushed a hand through his head of blond curls and frowned at his niece. What was going on with her?

As his mother cradled Sylvie in the crook of one arm, she held the other out. "Just because I'm holding a baby doesn't mean I don't want hugs from my children."

Marissa's worried expression dropped momentarily and she walked into their mother's embrace. When she moved back, Owen hugged his mother.

"It's hot out here. Let's get inside and get all of you settled," Mary Lynn said.

They all followed her inside, grateful for the air conditioning.

"Do you have room for all of us here, Mom?" Owen asked.

"I could squeeze all of you in, but Carter has space for you and Charlie. It will probably be more comfortable that way."

Owen nodded, relief washing over him. He always found staying in his mother's house a little stifling, but at the moment he was even more concerned about his sister and niece and where their behavior was headed. It might be better if he and Charlie were elsewhere. "That's just fine. We'll be happy to stay with Carter and Isabelle. Charlie's looking forward to spending some time with Alex."

Mary Lynn smiled at Charlie. "I'm glad to hear that. Boys your age don't always like to make time for younger kids."

Charlie shrugged. "He's my cousin. I've got time for him."

Owen patted his son on the back. He was such a good kid.

They all moved into the living room, and Mary Lynn turned her attention to Owen again. "How is Carrie Ann doing?"

"They broke up," Charlie blurted out with a dramatic eye roll.

Mary Lynn raised a brow. "I see."

"All because Dad doesn't want to get married," Charlie added. Owen fought the urge to drop his head into his hands.

"Really?" Mary Lynn gave Owen an appraising look, the kind he used to get growing up when he somehow didn't measure up. "She seemed like a good fit with you, Owen."

He looked down, wishing the conversation would change. He was certain his mother would not understand. "I'd rather not discuss it."

"Okay," she said amiably, but her expression continued to judge him.

"My friend Hallie is living with us for the summer, Grandma. Did Dad tell you about that?" Charlie asked.

Mary Lynn's head snapped back to Owen sharply. "You have a girl living with you for the summer? Do you think that's wise?"

Owen sighed. "It's not like that, Mom. Hallie and Charlie are only friends. She's staying in my guest room, and honestly, she's spending more time with Howard and Maisy than she is with us."

"She ran away," Charlie said and Mary Lynn's eyebrows went up again. "She was hiding in our garage."

"She ran away? Shouldn't you send her home then?" Mary Lynn asked.

"I will at the end of summer," Owen said. "Her mother knows where she is."

"And she's okay with it?" Mary Lynn adjusted the baby in her arms and bounced her a couple of times.

"She is allowing it after Hallie begged to stay on the island for the summer," Owen said.

"Why for the summer?"

Owen shrugged helplessly. If only he knew. "That's what we'd all like to know. She won't say, but she was desperate not to be sent home until the end of summer. We're hoping she'll open up and tell one of us eventually."

"And where is she this weekend? You didn't leave her at your house alone, did you?"

Owen sighed. Did his mother think he was that incompetent? "No, she's still on the island at her grandparent's house."

"If her grandparents live on the island, why doesn't she just stay with them?"

"'Cause she's mad at them," Charlie said.

"She wasn't excited about staying with them for the weekend, but I told her the only other option was to go home," Owen said.

"Sounds like this is a complicated situation," Mary Lynn said.

"You could say that," Owen agreed.

"Well," Mary Lynn said, "I've got a pot roast in the oven for dinner. Carter and Isabelle should be here any minute to eat with us." She grinned at Charlie. "And tomorrow we'll have the big birthday celebration for you and Alex."

Hallie lay in bed, staring at the ceiling. She could not sleep. Her mind kept circling back to the video she'd watched and her father's face. The image of her younger self, sitting on his knee and looking adoringly up at his handsome face filled Hallie's thoughts. She wanted to see more of the videos from the shelf downstairs—needed to. They were all she could think about.

She glanced at the clock on the bedside table and saw it was past midnight. She rolled over and closed her eyes, trying to find sleep.

When it still eluded her twenty minutes later, she threw the covers back and slid out of bed. Tiptoeing past her grandparent's room, she made her way down the stairs and into the living room. She went to the shelf and squinted at the DVDs in the moonlight. Pulling one from the shelf, she padded into the family room and put the disk in the player. Dropping to the floor in front of the TV, she stared at the screen and watched intently as her father's face filled it.

In this video, Daddy was just a little boy. He smiled at the camera and slammed two toy trucks together on the floor, making a crashing sound as he did.

Then Granddad's voice came through. "Daniel, are you going to drive a big truck when you grow up?"

Daddy looked up and smiled. He was missing a front tooth. He shook his head. "No way. I want to be a G.I. Joe."

He put his attention back on the trucks and slammed them together again.

"G.I. Joe is just a toy, and your name is Daniel," Granddad said.

Daddy looked up again and shrugged. "I'll be G.I. Daniel then. I'm gonna be in the Army."

"Really? Why do you want to do that?"

Daddy's little boy face turned serious. "I want to get the bad guys. I want to be like Uncle Dennis."

Hallie watched the rest of the DVD without hearing a word that was said. She stared at the screen unable to believe what she just heard. Her grandparents were telling the truth. Daddy *did* want to join the Army. It hadn't been their idea. They hadn't forced it on him.

When the video came to an end, Hallie put the disk back in its box, turned off the TV, and put the video away on the shelf. Practically in a trance, she trudged up the stairs and into her room, slipping into bed.

For most of the night, she continued to stare at the ceiling. Tangled emotions rolled through her. She didn't know which was worse: to be angry at her grandparents or what she felt now. She was both sad and angry with her father for choosing the Army instead of choosing to stay home and safe with her and her mother. And she was angry with her mother for convincing her it was her grandparents' fault and stealing away years she could have had with them. They were her only link to her father now. And her mother took that from her with lies. At the same time, she wasn't sure how to let go of the feelings she'd had for her grandparents for the last few years and forge ahead.

After hours of contemplation, Hallie finally fell into a fitful sleep.

Chapter 16

When Hallie awoke, light streamed in through the window, making her squint. She rubbed her sleep-crusted eyes and glanced at the bedside clock. It was almost nine-thirty. Feeling the effects of a restless night, Hallie groaned and rolled over. She squeezed her eyes shut and tried to fall asleep again, but her tangled thoughts ran loose in her mind.

She threw the covers off and stretched before crawling out of bed. Stumbling out of her room, she made her way downstairs and to the kitchen. When she reached the doorway and saw her grandparents sitting at the table in their church clothes, she stopped and gaped at them. She didn't know what to say to them or how to act. She had been angry with them for so long, and now she didn't know what she was feeling. Whatever the emotion was, it was strong, and without understanding why, her eyes filled with tears and her chest began to heave.

When her sobs grew louder, her grandparents realized she was there and turned, looking at her with confused expressions. Grandma got up from her seat and closed the gap between Hallie and herself. "Hallie, what's wrong?"

"I ... I ...," was all Hallie could get out before allowing herself to fall into her grandmother's arms.

Grandma pulled her in and held on to her. The embrace felt to Hallie like a drink of water when your throat is parched. She reached around Grandma's middle and held on tight.

"Sweetheart, whatever is wrong?" Grandma asked again.

Hallie loosened her hold and looked up. When she did, she noticed that Granddad stood next to Grandma now and his concern-filled eyes were locked on her.

She took a few deep, steadying breaths and stepped back. "I know the truth now. I know you were telling me the truth." She sobbed again. "I know my mother lied to me."

Her grandparents looked at her intently but didn't speak.

"I couldn't sleep last night, so I came down here and watched another video. It was an old one. Daddy was just a little boy and he said ..." Hallie's forehead wrinkled as she tried to control her emotions. "He said he wanted to join the Army."

Grandma and Granddad nodded. They weren't smiling or saying *we told you so*.

Hallie turned and went to the table, grabbing the back of a chair and holding on to it. She couldn't keep looking at their faces. If she did, she'd burst into tears again. "I don't know how to feel now. I was wrong and I was really mean to you. And my mother ... she lied to me."

Granddad came up behind her and put his hands on her shoulders, giving them a gentle squeeze. "I told you before, Hallie, that you shouldn't think of it as a lie. Your mother never wanted him to join the Army and she wanted—maybe needed—someone to blame. And I think over time, she began to believe it herself."

"It is a lie!" Hallie wrenched away and turned teary eyes on her grandfather. "If she wanted to blame someone, she should have blamed him. He wanted to do it and he stuck with it and chose to risk his life even when he knew mom and I were counting on him. And she kept lying after he died and that lie made me angry with you. She stole the time I could have had with you."

"Hallie," Grandma stepped around the table to face her, but Hallie didn't look her in the face. "Are you mad at your mom or your dad?"

"I'm mad at both of them! And I'm not sure how to stop being mad at you." She shook her head. "And I feel other things. I don't know what they are."

"Whatever time we lost with you, we can make up for it now," Granddad said. "It won't do any good to be angry about what can't be changed."

"Hallie," Grandma said, "I'm glad you know the truth and that, I hope, you're ready to give us another chance, but you need to forgive your mom. Your father is gone, and while we love you so, so much, you need your mom. And she needs you."

Hallie turned and walked to the sliding glass door on the back side of the breakfast nook. She stared out at the backyard. "I don't know if I can. She lied to me. How do I trust her?"

"Has she lied to you about anything else?" Grandma asked.

Hallie thought about it. She couldn't think of any other lies. "I don't think so. Mostly she just doesn't listen to me."

Grandma didn't address Hallie's last statement, and instead, focused on the first. "This lie came from a place of hurt. Daniel always wanted to join the Army. You saw that in the video you watched, but your mother could never see that as anything other than him choosing something else over her. That isn't what it was. He loved her and he loved you. He also loved his country and had his own dreams. It wasn't a matter of choosing one thing over the other. Still, the fact that he joined when she didn't want him to made her feel like she was put in second place. So, she told herself it was our fault. If she could believe we pushed him to join, then she could believe that he didn't really want to. And that allowed her to feel like she was more important to him than the Army."

"But it never needed to be a contest," Granddad added. "Just because a person chooses a career that is dangerous or takes them away from their family for periods of time doesn't mean they love it more than their family."

Slowly, Hallie turned from the glass door and looked at her grandparents. "I've missed you both. But how do I get rid of all the bad feelings inside me?"

Granddad smiled just a little. "You've been angry with us for a long time, but you know the truth now. The bad feelings will fade with time. How about we just work on getting to know each other again with no pressure?"

Hallie nodded as some of the tension in her belly relaxed. "How do we start?"

Granddad looked at his watch and Grandma grinned. "We start with you eating some breakfast and getting dressed for church. This afternoon, we can spend some time together."

"Doing what?" Hallie asked.

"Why don't you think of some ideas of things you'd like to do? After church, we'll get some lunch and decide which of your ideas to go with," Granddad said.

Hallie looked from his face to Grandma's. Their smiles and easy manner helped her relax. "That sounds good."

Owen awoke when he felt someone poking him in the ribs. With a groan, he cracked his eyes open and saw the face of his nephew who was leaning over him.

"Hi Alex," Owen said.

"Today is the birthday party." Alex bounced on the bed.

Owen smiled at his nephew's enthusiasm. Charlie was looking forward to the party too, but his excitement was less exuberant. Watching Alex, Owen realized he missed the days when Charlie was younger.

He sat up in bed and grabbed Alex around the waist, pulling the boy close to his face. "We're going to have so much fun!"

"Yay! Let's wake everyone else up."

Owen glanced at the window. There was only a hint of light coming through the curtains. He looked at the clock. It was only six o'clock. "I think we should wait a little longer, buddy." He ruffled Alex's hair. "But since we're both up, let's go see what we can make for breakfast. I'm sure your mom and dad won't mind if I make use of their kitchen."

"I want pancakes."

"Well, I guess we'll just have to see what we can find. But you know what you have to do first?"

Alex looked at him quizzically. "What?"

"Help your old uncle out of bed. You can do that, right?"

Alex giggled and grabbed Owen's hand. He began to pull, and Owen made a show of trying to get up. "That's it, keep pulling." When his feet hit the floor, he sighed dramatically. "You did it, bud. Now let's go see what we can rustle up."

He followed Alex down the hallway to the kitchen and started looking through the cupboards. Spotting a box of pancake mix, he said, "Pancakes it is."

Alex jumped up and down. "Yay!"

"Want to help me mix this up?"

"Okay."

"Let's find a big bowl and a measuring cup," Owen said.

Alex pointed to another cupboard. Owen opened it and found the large bowl. Alex didn't know where the measuring cup was, so Owen looked around. When he found one, he measured out the pancake mix and then water into the large bowl. Looking through a few drawers, he found a whisk and handed it to Alex. "Stir it together with this."

Alex nodded and took the whisk. He began to stir, sloshing the ingredients. Owen took hold of his hand. "Easy buddy. Slow and gentle, okay? We want it to stay in the bowl."

While Alex stirred, Owen pulled a skillet out and started it heating on the stove. "Should we make some eggs to go with it?"

Alex nodded, and Owen laughed at the smear of pancake mix across his cheek. "Okay. Let's get the pancakes made, and we can keep them warm while we make the eggs. Maybe by the time we get the pancakes done, the rest of the house will be awake."

Pointing at the coffee maker on the counter, Alex said, "When Daddy makes coffee, Mommy always gets up."

"You know what, you're right. We need coffee. *I* need coffee." Owen found a can of coffee and a filter and got the coffee maker started. The aroma alone made him feel more alert.

He got to work making the pancakes with Alex helping, and just as the last of the batter hit the pan, Carter trudged into the kitchen wearing a bathrobe and rubbing his eyes.

"Daddy," Alex said, jumping down from the stool he had been standing on. "It's party day!"

Carter smiled. "It sure is and it looks like you two are up early for it."

"I was too excited to sleep anymore," Alex said hopping back up on the stool.

"His excitement spilled over into my room," Owen said as he flipped the pancake.

Carter chuckled. "Sorry about that, brother."

"No need to be. I'm enjoying his youthful enthusiasm. Charlie's a tween now. Few things get him out of bed early anymore. And those things will dwindle more as time goes on."

"Well, you're welcome to visit and enjoy the enthusiasm here anytime you want," Carter said. He stepped forward and kissed the top of his son's head. "Special occasions aren't even required to get this guy out of bed early."

Owen smiled at him. "I'll keep that in mind."

By the time Owen finished making the eggs, Isabelle and Charlie were up. They sat down and ate breakfast together, and Owen marveled at how enjoyable it was. He and Carter had often disagreed over the years, and though they loved each other, their time spent together wasn't always easy. Sipping his coffee and glancing around the table, he thought about the way Maisy behaved the day before and wondered if their family was about to hit a bump again.

By the time they arrived at Mary Lynn's house for the party, Alex wasn't the only one who was excited. Charlie jumped out of the car just as quickly as his younger cousin, and his face was alight with a grin. Owen's heart surged with joy as he watched his son run toward the house.

He turned to his brother. "Looks like Alex's excitement is infectious."

"It usually is," Carter said.

The three adults headed to the house and found Mary Lynn in the living room. Owen glanced around and marveled at all the decorations.

"Mom, you've outdone yourself. I've never seen such a festive display," Owen said.

Mary Lynn, looking perfect in a blue silk blouse and ivory slacks, turned to look at him. "Only the best for my grandsons. This is a double birthday party, so double the decorations."

"Thanks, Grandma, this is great!" Charlie said before hugging Mary Lynn.

Alex jumped up and down in the center of the room. "When do we start?"

Mary Lynn laughed. "Well, I planned on serving lunch first, then the cake, then the presents. But now I wonder if we can wait that long. I see a little boy who might burst."

"I am bursting!" Alex cried.

"Besides that, we had pancakes and eggs this morning," Charlie said. "I'm still full."

"I see." Mary Lynn tapped her chin. "I guess we'll just have to rearrange the order of events. Maybe," she drew the word out as she met Alex's eyes, "we should do the gifts first."

Alex whooped and clapped his hands.

With a chuckle, Mary Lynn turned to where Owen stood with Carter and Isabelle. "How much syrup was on those pancakes?"

"Not as much as you'd think," Isabelle replied.

Mary Lynn returned her attention to the boys. "We can get started just as soon as everyone is in here. Why don't you boys go find your aunt, uncle, and cousins?"

The boys left the room, Alex at a sprint and Charlie trying to keep up without running. Their voices could be heard as they rounded up the rest of the family, then the two of them came running back into the living room. Moments later, Howard and Marissa walked in with the baby. Maisy was the last to arrive, and when she entered the room, she skulked to a chair in the back corner and sat down without saying a word.

Owen frowned wondering what was going on with her. Before he had much time to consider it, his attention was pulled away by his mother's voice.

"Time for the gifts," she called in a sing-song voice. "Who goes first?"

"Me! Me!" Alex begged.

Charlie laughed. "Alex should be first, Grandma. He's the youngest."

Mary Lynn smiled adoringly at Charlie, "So he is. All right, Alex, I think I have a present with your name on it over here." She picked up a box wrapped in bright green paper and handed it to Alex.

"Yay!" he said before tearing the paper from the box. "Wow, a chemistry set. Look, Mom, it's full of fun experiments to do at home."

"Great," Isabelle said with a tight smile. "I can't wait."

"I think that should be a father and son activity," Carter said. Isabelle turned to him and smiled with relief.

"Charlie, this one is for you," Mary Lynn said, handing him a festively wrapped gift.

He accepted the box and began to unwrap it. Though he didn't tear into it with as much zeal as his younger cousin, the look on his face showed his joy. When the wrapping paper was off, Charlie pulled the flaps of a plain cardboard box open and his face lit up. He flipped through the contents, then looked up at his grandmother. "Comic books!"

"There's something else in there. Did you see?" Mary Lynn asked.

Charlie flipped through again and pulled a book out. He studied it.

"You seem to be having such a good time learning about the outdoors this year at your day camp, I thought you might like something to help you learn even more," Mary Lynn said.

"Thanks, Grandma. This is great!" He turned to Owen. "Look, Dad, it's a field guide that tells all about plants and animals."

"That's nice, Charlie. I bet you'll learn a lot," Owen said, grateful his mother had chosen a gift they could all be happy with.

They continued with the gifts until all were opened and the floor was filled with wrapping paper.

Marissa smiled as she watched her nephews finish opening their gifts. The boys were pleased with their presents, and everyone was enjoying watching them. Or at least Marissa thought everyone was enjoying the moment until she glanced at Maisy in the corner of the room. She sat with an impassive look on her face. *Is she still upset about our conversation on the ferry?* Marissa thought her daughter would be over that by now.

With a sigh, she tried to focus on the birthday fun. Moving Sylvie to one arm, she began to help pick up the wrapping paper that littered the room.

"Lunch or cake next?" Mary Lynn asked when the paper was all picked up.

"Cake!" Alex bounced.

"I think it would be better to start with lunch," Carter said. Isabelle nodded her agreement.

Mary Lynn raised an eyebrow as she watched Alex bounce around, still asking for the cake. "I think your parents might be right, young man. If we give you cake right now, you might bounce all the way to the moon. Let's go get some sandwiches."

Alex wilted and let out a heavy breath. "Okay," he said reluctantly. "Can I have ham?"

"Of course you can," Mary Lynn told him.

They all made their way into the kitchen, had lunch, and then Mary Lynn brought a large cake out with a set of candles on each end.

"All right, boys," Mary Lynn said, "time to sing and blow out the candles."

As they sang Happy Birthday to the boys, Marissa watched Maisy hang back behind the rest of the group. She wasn't singing and she still looked unhappy.

"Make a wish, guys!" Carter said when the singing was done.

Both boys closed their eyes for a moment, then Charlie counted to three, and they blew their candles out together.

Mary Lynn strode forward and pulled all the candles out of the cake. Alex licked the frosting off them while Carter cut the cake into squares and began filling plates.

When they were all finished with the cake, Mary Lynn picked up her camera and snapped a few pictures of the boys, laughing at the frosting on Alex's nose. "Let me get a picture of all my kids and grandkids," she said. "All of you squeeze in together."

They all moved in close, putting the shorter people in the front, and Mary Lynn snapped a couple of shots.

"Oh, these are nice," Mary Lynn said, looking at her camera screen. "Now I want to get one with just my grands. Come on, Charlie, Alex, and Maisy. Sit in these chairs." She moved three kitchen chairs close together and the kids sat down. Then Mary Lynn approached Marissa. "Let me have Sylvie. She needs to be in the shot too."

"Do you want me to get her infant seat?" Marissa asked.

"No need," Mary Lynn said as she took the baby. She walked over to the kids. "Maisy, hold your sister please."

Maisy's face drained of color. "I don't want to. Charlie can hold her."

"She's your sister. And I wanted to have you girls in the middle and the birthday boys on either side."

Maisy shook her head furiously. "No, I don't want to."

Mary Lynn hesitated, furrowing her brow. "Okay. Charlie, you move to the middle and let Maisy have your seat."

Charlie complied without complaint and Mary Lynn placed the baby in his arms. She asked the kids to smile and snapped a couple of pictures. Watching, Marissa saw how tight and unnatural Maisy's smile was.

After the pictures were taken, the kids dispersed and Mary Lynn approached Marissa, holding the baby in one arm. "Is there something going on with Maisy? She's been sullen since you got here yesterday."

"I'm not sure what is going on with her. She doesn't ever want to hold Sylvie. We're a little concerned that she isn't happy being a big sister," Marissa said.

Mary Lynn glanced down at the infant that now slept in her arms. "She was excited about it when you were pregnant."

"I know. I'm not sure what changed." Marissa glanced down, away from her mother's gaze. "But I insisted she hold Sylvie for a short time on the ferry so I could get a bottle ready. She's been agitated ever since."

"I see. Have you asked her why she doesn't want to hold the baby?"

Marissa sighed. Her mother meant well, but she always pushed. "Yes, I pressed her on that during the ferry ride. She wouldn't answer and got mad at me for asking." Marissa met her mother's eyes. "I shouldn't have pushed it then. I think I ruined this visit for her. I just wish I knew what was going on."

Mary Lynn nodded. "I think you need to find out." She went silent for a beat. "Maybe I should talk to her."

"Oh, Mom, I think it would be better to back off for now. She's already unhappy. Let's not make this visit any more strained." Marissa silently prayed her mother would listen and not push Maisy.

Mary Lynn's lips tightened, then she said, "Waiting isn't going to make it go away, Marissa."

Shame flowed through Marissa as it always did when her mother brought her back to the past and painful memories filled her mind. Three years earlier, she had caused her daughter a great deal of pain as she tried to avoid the grieving process. Her desperate need to remove any reminders of the husband and child she'd lost made it impossible for Maisy to grieve the way she needed to and heal.

Taking a deep breath, Marissa forced herself to look her mother in the eye again. "I know, Mom. Howard and I will deal with it, just not right now."

Mary Lynn kept eye contact a moment, then nodded. "Okay. Now what is this I hear about your brother and Carrie Ann?"

Relief washed through Marissa with the change of subject. "The simple answer is, Carrie Ann wanted to move their relationship forward, and Owen wanted to keep things as they were."

Mary Lynn raised one eyebrow. "So who broke up with whom over this?"

"Carrie Ann broke up with Owen. But she didn't want to. She wants to get married."

"I see." Mary Lynn sat down at the kitchen table and Marissa followed suit.

Marissa watched as her mother silently considered the information. "I guess he just isn't ready," she said without much conviction. Marissa didn't want her mother's love of meddling to find a target with Owen, but in truth, she couldn't understand her brother's reluctance to move forward with Carrie Ann either. Over the past couple of years, she'd seen Owen happier than ever before. Why he would let that slip away from him was a mystery to her. In fact, she was surprised that he hadn't done the asking himself a long time ago.

Mary Lynn stroked her chin in thought, then looked up. "They've dated a good while. What more could he need to be ready?"

Marissa shrugged and her mother sat in quiet thought.

Mary Lynn looked up at Marissa and smiled. "I think I'm just going to go lay this little Angel down in her bed." Her chair scraped the floor as she pushed back from the table and stood.

"Watch out, Owen. She's coming your way," Marissa whispered to herself as she watched her mother walk away.

Chapter 17

Hallie's stomach growled in anticipation as a waiter set a plate full of chicken tenders and fries in front of her. She licked her lips and picked up a fry. By the time she doused her fry in ketchup, the waiter had put her grandparent's meals on the table and walked away.

"Thanks for lunch," Hallie said before stuffing the crispy potato into her mouth.

Smiling at her, Granddad said, "You're welcome. Now, tell us your ideas for things to do."

Hallie took a sip of her soda. "I know we just went to the pond yesterday, but I think I'd like to go fishing again." She looked at her lap feeling ashamed again of the way she'd been treating them. "I always used to like it when you took me fishing, Granddad. But yesterday ..." She picked at a piece of chicken, keeping her gaze down.

"Yesterday is gone," Granddad said. "Today is a new day, and I never get tired of fishing."

Hallie lifted her eyes to meet his, grateful for his loving response. Her lips curved up in a smile.

"If you want a change of scenery, we could go to the pier," Grandma said.

Hallie hadn't been to the pier in a long time, but she recalled a fishing trip there when she was six. "You think I'd catch a baby shark again?"

"You never know." Granddad's eyes twinkled as he took a large bite of his club sandwich.

They ate in silence for a while, then Hallie said, "Later, after we're done fishing, could I watch another video of my dad?"

"Sweetheart," Grandma said, "you can watch as many of those old home movies as you want."

Hallie took another bite of her chicken, chewed, and swallowed. Then, meeting her grandmother's warm, deep brown eyes, she asked, "Would you watch with me this time?"

A smile lit Grandma's face. "I would be happy to." She scooped up a forkful of coleslaw and ate it. "You know, I pull those videos out once in a while anyway. I like to see my son's face and think of him."

Hallie's lips tightened as the emotions that went with loss flowed through her. When she felt like she could speak without crying, she said, "That's why I like watching them too. I miss seeing him and pictures aren't as good."

Grandma reached out and covered one of Hallie's hands with her own. Hallie looked at it, feeling the warmth of the touch. "We'll remember him together," Grandma said.

Finished with their lunch, Hallie and her grandparents went home to change clothes and gather the fishing gear before heading to the pier.

Hopping out of the car, Hallie closed her eyes for a moment as she sucked in the salty beach air. Opening them, she gazed out to the ocean that seemed endless and watched seagulls and pelicans swoop through the air. Now that her anger was subsiding, she was beginning to remember how much she loved the island and all the happy times with her grandparents.

"Let's stop in at the bait shop," Granddad said. "I haven't done any pier fishing in a while. We need to get the right bait."

"Do I have to touch it?" Hallie asked.

Granddad grinned at her. "Are you really fishing if you don't?"

Hallie wrinkled her nose. "I don't like touching worms."

"What about shrimp?" he asked. "I can get some of those."

"Are they alive when we put them on the hook?"

"Live ones work better because the fish like their food fresh. That's why the bait shop only sells them live."

"Oh," Hallie said, a little deflated. "Will they bleed?"

Shaking his head with a chuckle, Granddad said, "Don't you worry, I'll bait your hook."

Grinning, Hallie remembered having similar conversations with him in years past. He always gave in and agreed to bait the hook for her.

After buying the bait, they walked out onto the pier. The ocean breeze swept across their faces and carried a fishy smell.

"Let's go all the way to the end," Hallie said, her voice trailing into the wind.

"Of course. Deeper water means a better catch." Granddad marched toward the end of the pier carrying the fishing rods and bait. Hallie followed with the tackle box and Grandma trailed behind them.

When they reached the end of the pier, Granddad set the poles down, leaning them against the railing, and put the container of bait down on a tall bench. "Remember when I used to have to lift you up to get you on this bench, Hallie girl?"

"I remember." The memory flowed through her and brought warmth to her soul. "I think I can get there on my own now." She set the tackle box down in the middle of the bench and then lifted herself onto one end.

"There you have it," Granddad said. "You don't need my help anymore."

"Yes, I do. Just not for this," Hallie said.

Grandma walked to the railing at the pier's end and breathed deeply. "It's a lovely day and the air is perfect."

"You gonna fish with us, dear?" Granddad asked Grandma.

She turned and smiled. "For a while. But only if you bait my hook," she teased.

He laughed. "I guess I gotta take care of my girls, don't I?" He went to work getting the rods ready and baited all the hooks. "Here we go," he said, handing out rods. "Hallie, go ahead and cast your line first."

Hallie did as he said, sending her line out as far as she could. Her hook plopped into the water disappointingly close to the pier. She huffed and slumped her shoulders.

Granddad patted her back. "That's okay. We're up high, so you just need to work on throwing out more. It went further than you think, but some of the distance you gave it was at a downward angle and it's a long way down. You need to let gravity do that part for you. Here, watch the way I toss mine." Taking time to show and explain the difference in his motions, he cast his line. It sailed out several feet further than hers.

Taking hold of her reel, Hallie said, "Let me try again. I'll do it just like you."

"Leave it where it is for now. There're fish up close to the pier too. No sense starting over just yet."

"Sometimes you even get a better catch up close to the pier," Grandma said as she cast her line. "Fishermen drop bait on occasion and it attracts fish."

All of their hooks in the water, they sat quietly on the bench and waited. Hallie glanced at their shadows on the grey boards of the pier. Warmth rose up in her chest as she watched her own shadow between those of her grandparents. Then the puffball ponytails at the sides of her head caught her attention.

"Grandma?" Hallie said, hesitantly. It still felt strange to ask them for anything. "When we get back to your house, could you braid my hair?"

Grandma smiled warmly. "Sure I can. If you like, I can do that while we watch one of the videos."

"That sounds good. Thanks! I hate these ponytails."
Grandma shifted in her seat and Hallie heard her sniffle. "I'm happy to do it for you."

Rebecca L. Marsh

Chapter 18

Owen slouched in his seat and leaned his head against the headrest in the back of Marissa's van. Everyone in the car was quiet. Charlie sat reading the field guide his grandmother gave him. Maisy stared out the window while, next to her, Sylvie slept. In the front seat, Howard and Marissa sat silently as Howard drove them toward Owen's house. Owen wasn't sure if the silence was because it was late in the afternoon and they'd been traveling or if they were all contemplating their own thoughts and feelings.

As for him, it was contemplation. He and his mother had always struggled to relate to one another. That was nothing new. Normally, he let unpleasant conversations with her roll off his back. But this time he found that difficult. Her probing about his breakup with Carrie Ann hit a nerve. He'd hardly been able to respond to her questions because thinking of Carrie Ann, and being faced with questions about his avoidance of commitment, made his stomach hurt. *What does that mean?*

Owen closed his eyes and tried to relax. They'd be home in a few minutes and it would be time to pick Hallie up from Cory and Doreen's house. Then he'd need to think about getting some dinner together for them. Or maybe he'd just take the kids out for dinner.

When they reached his driveway, Owen raised his head. He squinted and strained to see better when he realized someone was sitting on his porch steps. Seeing it was Carrie Ann, he sighed. *I don't have the energy for this today.*

The van stopped in front of the house. "Here we are," Howard said. "Let me help you get your bags out."

"No need," Owen replied. He was hoping to send Carrie Ann on her way without any fuss. "Charlie and I can handle it."

"Okay. I guess we'll see you in the morning when you drop Hallie off," Howard said.

Marissa turned in her seat to look into the back of the van. "Bye, Charlie," she said. Once Charlie returned her salutation, her eyes fell on Owen. There was a hint of sympathy in them. Owen didn't know if that was because Carrie Ann was waiting on him or if she was still feeling sympathetic about his being targeted by their mother. "Bye, Owen."

"See ya soon, sis." He smiled at her to let her know he was all right. Then he and Charlie climbed out of the van.

"Charlie," Owen said, "Get our bags out of the back while I go see why Carrie Ann is here."

Charlie let out a heavy sigh but obeyed without complaint.

Owen trudged to the porch where Carrie Ann sat. Her head was down as if she was studying something on the ground. "It's been a long day, Carrie Ann. So, if you've left something else here, can you get it tomorrow?"

Her head lifted and Owen's heart dropped. Carrie Ann's face was puffy and blotched with red. Tears streaked down her face. Owen sucked in a sharp breath. Her obvious pain hit like a sucker punch. He dropped down to sit on the step next to her, and without thinking about it, took her hands in his. "What's wrong? What's going on?"

Carrie Ann sniffled. "It's Freddy Alvarez." She broke into sobs, unable to say more.

His brow furrowed, Owen thought about the fun-loving elderly man from their dance group. He asked, "What about Freddy? Talk to me, Carrie Ann."

"He's ... He's dead, Owen." She got the words out before breaking down again. Owen wrapped an arm around her and pulled her close, letting her cry on his shoulder.

Marissa's minivan pulled away and Charlie approached the porch with their bags. "What's going on, Dad? Why is Carrie Ann crying?" Though he didn't say it, Charlie's body language asked, *what did you do this time?* His arms were crossed over his chest and his eyes bore into Owen accusingly.

"Freddy Alvarez died," Owen said, ignoring his son's silent accusation.

"Oh," Charlie said, "Do I know him?"

"Not really. He was in our swing dance group," Owen answered while Carrie Ann continued to sob.

Charlie nodded. "What happened to him?"

"I don't know. That's as much as she's managed to tell me." He rubbed Carrie Ann's back soothingly.

"Charlie, could you please take our bags into the house? And after that, would you call Cory and ask him if he or Doreen could bring Hallie back over here."

Charlie's body sagged a little with the request, but he picked up their bags and headed into the house.

Owen returned his attention to Carrie Ann. Her sobs had quieted a little. "What happened to Freddy?"

She sat up and reached for the purse that sat on the other side of her. After fishing out a tissue, she wiped her eyes and blew her nose. Then she spoke softly. "It was a stroke. Antonia let everyone know this morning. And I ... I didn't know where to go except here."

Something in that statement struck Owen. If their breakup stayed firm, eventually she wouldn't come to him for comfort anymore. She'd find someone else. Thinking of that made Owen's stomach clench. "How long have you been here?" he asked gently.

She met his eyes for a second, then let them drop. "I don't know. What time is it?"

Owen glanced at his watch. "It's almost five. You haven't been sitting here all day, have you? Who's at the store?"

She sniffed. "Tim's at the store," she said without answering his other question.

"Freddy was a good man," Owen said, not knowing what else to say that might be helpful.

"The best," Carrie Ann agreed. "He was like a father to me. He's been there for me more than anyone since ..." She let her words trail off, but Owen knew the rest. Freddy had been there for her since their breakup.

Owen sucked in a breath, the pain of their lost relationship mingling with the feelings of loss. Right then, more than ever, he questioned his own choices. Watching Carrie Ann suffer tore at his heart and all he wanted to do was give her the love she needed. *So, why can't I? What's stopping me from giving her what she wants and moving our relationship forward?*

"Any idea when the funeral will be?" Owen asked.

Carrie Ann shook her head. She met Owen's eyes and they stared at each other wordlessly.

The door opening behind them made them turn their heads toward it where Charlie stepped outside. "Dad, Cory says Hallie can stay there tonight and they'll take her to Aunt Marissa's house tomorrow morning," Charlie said.

A little surprised, Owen said, "That will be helpful. I guess the weekend went okay."

"Cory sounded happy, but he usually does," Charlie said. "Are we going to have dinner soon?"

"I was thinking we could go out for dinner tonight," Owen said. Then, without thinking about it, he turned to Carrie Ann. "Why don't you come with us? My treat."

Owen watched as emotions passed over her face— surprise, uncertainty. Then she nodded. "I guess I could eat."

At her answer, it occurred to Owen that she may not have eaten in a long while if she'd been on his porch as long as he suspected.

"Come on, then," he said, "Let's keep it simple and go to the diner."

Hallie ran a hand over her braided hair, smiling. Grandma had put her hair into two nice, tight braids on either side of her head. She liked it so much better than the puffy ponytails. On Wednesday, she was going back to her grandparents' house while Owen went to his swing dance group. Grandma said she'd do the braids again if Hallie washed her hair before she came over. Grandma also said she would teach Hallie how to do the braids herself so she could still have them when she went home at the end of summer. She wouldn't have to worry about Mom not having the time for it.

Hallie turned her eyes from her book to look at Maisy, who sat next to her in their mostly completed fort. Maisy had a pad on her lap, but she wasn't drawing. The page remained blank. Instead, she was staring straight ahead at the wall of the fort.

"What's wrong?" Hallie asked.

Maisy cast an irritated glance her way. "Nothing."

"So, you just happen to like staring at walls?" Hallie said jokingly.

"Maybe I do," Maisy huffed without turning her eyes from the blank wall.

"You're grumpy today." Intending to show friendship, Hallie reached out and touched Maisy's arm. "Maybe you'll feel better if you tell me why."

Maisy pulled her arm away and scooted to the side, moving further away from Hallie. She clamped her lips shut.

Hallie studied her newfound friend. "Did something bad happen while you were at your grandma's house?"

"No." Maisy's answer came in a clipped tone.

"Did you get in trouble or something?"

"No," Maisy growled this time.

Hallie tapped her chin and considered Maisy's behavior and what she knew about her friend so far. "This has something to do with Sylvie, doesn't it?"

Maisy turned to face her, eyes flashing with anger and also hurt. She scowled rather than answering the question.

Hallie closed her book and set it to the side. "Why do you hate her?"

Maisy's forehead scrunched, her anger deepening. "I *don't* hate her."

Hallie shook her head in confusion. "Then what do you call it? You don't want to hold her or be too close to her. And now you're mad because what—" Hallie said with a shrug, "you had to spend time over the weekend in a car with her?"

"I'm not mad because I had to be in a car with her," Maisy spat the words. "You don't understand and you never will." She glared at Hallie, breathing heavily. "You want to know so much, but you won't even tell me why you're here. You haven't told anyone why you ran away or why you can't go home till the end of summer. How about you tell me that, and then I'll tell you something."

Hallie stared at Maisy, their eyes locked. Emotions swirled through Hallie as she thought about home and why she couldn't be there right now. She thought about the nightmares that kept coming night after night. Then she thought about the answers to Maisy's questions. From there, her mind roamed to a place and time she tried to never think about—a day during the spring when her parents had left her alone while they took the boys for a check-up. It was a teacher work day, so Hallie didn't have school. Something had happened that day—or it had almost happened. Luckily, her parents got home just in time to keep it from happening.

But when she had tried to tell her mother about it, Mom didn't believe her. *I'm sure you're imagining things, Hallie,* her mother had told her. The words still stung.

Hallie was certain Maisy wouldn't understand. She might not believe either, and having another person fail to believe her was more than Hallie could bear. And even if Maisy did believe her, she didn't want her—or anyone—to know. She took a deep breath, deciding to tell Maisy just a bit of the truth. "My mom was going to leave me home alone all day during the summer. She and Dustin can't afford day camp for me with both the boys in daycare. And ... I don't want to stay home alone all day."

Maisy looked at her skeptically. "Why?"

"I wouldn't feel safe. There are some weird people in our neighborhood." This was as close to the truth as Hallie was willing to go. "So, now you know," she said with finality, hoping it would be enough to stop the questions.

Maisy studied her. "That's it? Couldn't you just lock the doors?"

Hallie narrowed her eyes. "That's easy for you to say. You live on an island."

Maisy shrugged. "Islands can have weird people too."

"I don't know of anyone on this island that even compares. You really don't know what you're talking about." Hallie turned her eyes away, frowning.

"Maybe I don't. But you don't know anything about my problems either."

Hallie glanced at her friend again. "Try me."

Maisy crossed her arms over her chest like she was hugging herself. "If you laugh at me, I won't be your friend anymore."

"I won't laugh, I promise," Hallie said with sincerity.

"I don't hate Sylvie. It's just that it hurts me to be close to her." Maisy stopped and her eyes welled with tears. "My sister, Kyla, died three years ago. And she had red hair and blue eyes. Sylvie sort of looks like her. When I'm near her, it reminds me of Kyla."

Maisy went silent and Hallie waited a few seconds to see if she would say more. When she didn't, Hallie asked, "So, that's it? Sylvie reminds you of Kyla?"

"I didn't want another sister. I was hoping for a brother." Maisy said the words as if they explained something, but Hallie didn't understand.

"Why is it so bad to have another sister? Didn't you like Kyla?"

Maisy sniffed. "I didn't always like Kyla. She picked on me a lot. But I loved her."

"Okay. Then why is it bad to have another sister? Sylvie is just a baby. You don't even know what she'll be like yet."

Maisy turned to look at Hallie, her eyes flashing. "*Kyla* was my sister!"

Hallie drew back at the sharp tone and furrowed her brow.

In an instant, Maisy's anger dissolved and she wilted against the wall behind her. "I feel like having Sylvie as a sister, being close to her, is wrong. Like I'm forgetting about Kyla—like she isn't important anymore."

"Because Sylvie looks like her?"

Maisy shook her head as a tear streaked down her cheek. "I don't know. It's just how I feel."

Hallie scooted close to Maisy and put an arm around her tentatively. "Feelings don't always make sense. I get that. But I don't think loving Sylvie means you're forgetting Kyla."

Silence passed between them for a moment, then Hallie had another thought, "Would Kyla want you to be mean to Sylvie or ignore her?"

Hallie watched Maisy's face as she considered the question. Then Maisy looked her in the eye and said, "Kyla did pick on me. She wasn't always nice to me, but I know she loved me. Once, when we were outside playing, a boy started to make fun of me for having glasses. Kyla stood up for me. I'm sure she'd love Sylvie, too, if she were here."

"Then you should try to be a good big sister to Sylvie for her." Hallie tried a gentle smile and Maisy nodded.

"I'll try." Maisy took hold of Hallie's hand. "Thanks, Hallie."

"That's what friends are for," Hallie said, her eyes drifting away from Maisy's. She could feel the relief Maisy got from letting all her thoughts and feelings out. And Hallie wondered if she should trust Maisy—with the whole story of why she came to the island.

Rebecca L. Marsh

Chapter 19

Marissa left the stock room at the drug store carrying a box of first aid supplies that needed to be shelved. As she walked by the pharmacy counter, Cory's humming reached her ears and she stopped. Setting the box down, she meandered over to the counter and glanced in to see Millie, Cory's assistant, scowling at her jovial boss.

Marissa smiled, which was just enough to chase Millie away. The poor girl seemed to prefer discontent over joy.

"How's it going, Cory?" Marissa asked.

Cory turned and met her eyes with a grin. "Couldn't be better. Hallie's going to stay with us again this weekend. She's coming back to us."

"That's great, Cory. I'm sure you and Doreen are over the moon." Marissa smiled back at him. She could feel his joy. That was Cory's special gift. He found joy even when life wasn't the greatest for him, and when he was happy, everyone around him felt it with him.

"We are. In some ways, it's like getting a little bit of Daniel back." He studied her. "You seem to be feeling better than usual today too."

Marissa nodded. "Maisy's been in a good mood the last few days. So, I'm not worrying about her like I was."

"That's good to hear." Cory's face sobered. "Have you talked to Carrie Ann this morning?"

"Not really. I mean, I said good morning to her. That's about it. Why?"

"She's not herself this morning." Cory gave little information, but it spoke volumes. He wasn't the type to worry much. If Carrie Ann's demeanor was concerning to him, it meant something.

"Well, she took Freddy's death pretty hard. And the memorial service was just yesterday. Maybe that's all it is."

"I hope so. But you're her friend. Maybe you could try talking to her."

"I will. Just as soon as I get this box unloaded." Marissa picked the box up and headed to the first aid aisle.

When she was finished shelving the items in the box, she wandered up to the front of the store and found her boss at the check-out counter staring into space. "Carrie Ann, are you okay?"

Carrie Ann looked up, and Marissa could see that her eyes were moist.

"Are you still upset about Freddy?" Marissa asked, reaching out to put her hand on top of Carrie Ann's.

"Yeah, I am." Carrie Ann paused and her face clouded with emotion.

"It's more than that, though, isn't it?" Marissa asked.

Carrie Ann pulled her hand free and chewed on her thumbnail. "It's Owen."

"What about him?" Sudden concern laced Marissa's voice.

Carrie Ann met Marissa's eyes and a tear streaked down her cheek. "I don't think I can do this."

Mild frustration bubbled up in Marissa with the answer that didn't tell her a thing. *What is she talking about?* She kept her voice even. "Do what?"

"I may have to leave the island altogether. That might be the only way I can do it." Carrie Ann spoke as if she were talking to herself.

Marissa took her friend by the shoulders and gave them a little shake. "Carrie Ann, what are you talking about?"

Carrie Ann met her eyes. "I'm talking about letting go of Owen. I'm not sure I can do it unless I get away from him—far away."

Marissa sighed, letting go of her friend's shoulders. "Oh. You wouldn't leave the island, though, would you?"

Marissa certainly hoped not. And the thought made her irritated with her brother. She knew he loved Carrie Ann, so what was his issue with commitment?

"I don't want to, but it might be the only way." She shook her head. "I was doing all right. But when Freddy died, I didn't know what to do except run to Owen." Her brow scrunched. "And he was great. He gave me a shoulder to cry on. He was there for me."

"And that convinced you that you needed to get away from him?" Marissa asked the question, but she believed she understood even without the answer.

Carrie Ann nodded slowly. "It convinced me that I'm still totally, completely in love with him. It convinced me that as long as he's around me, I won't be able to move on." She met Marissa's eyes. "I'll always want him."

"I think he feels the same way even if he won't admit it," Marissa said.

"But he won't marry me. And I can't stay stuck. I want a family and a full life. I don't just want to be his girlfriend forever."

"No. I don't blame you."

Carrie Ann's pain was evident and it made Marissa's heart sink. She couldn't understand what her brother's problem was, but if Carrie Ann showed any sign of being serious about leaving the island, she was going to talk to him about this again and see if she could find out why he was so set against marriage.

Wednesday Owen had a hard time staying on schedule. He had a deck to repair, a bathroom faucet and vanity to install, and he'd promised Hal Thompson he'd be by to stain his backyard fence. But thoughts of Carrie Ann kept getting in his way and he'd catch himself staring into space, imagining her head on his shoulder. He hated to see her sad, but at the same time, he loved the feel of her body close to his. And, if he was honest with himself, he also liked the feeling that she needed him.

His stray thoughts were wreaking havoc with his concentration, and as a result, he was making mistakes. While working on the deck, he bent a ridiculous number of nails and also hit his thumb with the hammer once. The pain that caused added to his slow down.

Then, when he started work on the faucet install, he forgot to turn the water valve off first. So, he soaked himself and a portion of the Trumans' bathroom. That meant he had to clean up his mess and change into the extra set of clothes he kept in his truck before he could get started again. He'd have to hurry if he was going to finish the fence job and get home in time to feed the kids and make it to swing dance.

Should I even go tonight? The thought of dancing with Carrie Ann had him feeling both exhilarated and anxious at once. He would get to be near her and touch her. Then he'd have to let go of her again. Either that or agree to marry her.

Part of him ached to do exactly that. But he wouldn't.

He'd thought once—a long time ago—that he wanted to get married. But it hadn't worked out. In fact, it had ended with his heart crushed into a million pieces and he wasn't going to let that happen again. The only problem was, it seemed like that's exactly what was happening anyway. So now what?

Now, Owen, you stain this fence and get your head in the game, he chastised himself. He had to stop thinking about Carrie Ann … and yet, he couldn't.

When five o'clock rolled around, Owen scowled at the fence that was only two-thirds of the way done. He apologized to Hal and promised to be there first thing in the morning to finish the work. That meant tomorrow he'd have to fight to catch up. He sighed. There was nothing he could do to change it now. It was time to pick the kids up and feed them.

He tossed his tools into the back of his truck and pulled himself into the driver's seat. Reaching his destination, he trudged to the porch and knocked.

When his sister opened the door, he smiled at her, but she didn't smile back.

"Something wrong?" Owen asked.

"Yeah, I think something is wrong with you," she retorted.

Owen raised his eyebrows at his sister's remark. "What'd I do to upset you?"

Letting out a heavy breath, she closed her eyes a moment and relaxed her tense shoulders. "Nothing. I'm sorry," she said.

"Clearly there's something you're upset about."

"There is, but I'm overreacting." She turned as Hallie and Maisy approached from behind her.

"I'm ready to go," Hallie said, her voice upbeat.

Owen eyed Marissa, waiting for her to explain her outburst.

"You need to take Hallie home and I'm sure Charlie is waiting there for you. We'll talk later," Marissa said.

Owen stood in the doorway. He didn't like leaving without knowing what he'd done to upset Marissa.

"Later," she said again. "We both have kids to feed."

Nodding, he left her porch and slid into the truck with Hallie in tow.

The short ride home was filled with happy chatter from Hallie. She was so pleased with her braided hair, she and Maisy had finished their fort and were getting to be good friends, and best of all, she was looking forward to seeing her grandparents again.

Owen smiled and nodded as she talked, but didn't engage otherwise. Hallie didn't seem to need him to say anything, and his mind was in other places. Besides the renewed intensity of his feelings for Carrie Ann, he was also wondering what he'd done to tick his sister off.

As soon as the truck reached a full stop in front of Owen's house, Hallie was out the door and hurrying inside. Owen knew she wanted to take a shower before dinner so Doreen could braid her hair again tonight. Owen eased out of the truck and followed at a slower pace.

Once inside, he found Charlie on the couch with his field guide. "Hi, Charlie. I'm going to go fix dinner now," he said.

"Hey, Dad, did you know you can eat a cactus?" Charlie asked.

"I may have heard that before." Owen started to walk away.

"Want me to bring in some clover?" Charlie called after him. "That's edible too."

"I think I'll stick with the green beans I was already planning on." Owen couldn't help but laugh at his son.

Owen's distractedness continued as he cooked, leading to one burned pork chop and one burned finger. He ran his finger under some cold water, and with a sigh, put the burned meat on his plate before calling the kids to the table.

As the children sat down, Charlie wrinkled his nose and pointed to Owen's plate. "Dad, what did you do to your pork chop?"

"Nothing. It's just a little well done. More flavor that way," Owen said, pretending he'd done it on purpose.

"You're really gonna eat that?" Hallie asked, making a face.

"Yes, I am. Now let's say a blessing and eat before the food gets cold."

After Charlie said the blessing, Owen forced a smile as he cut the meat and popped a bite into his mouth. It was dry, tough, and tasted like charcoal, but he ate it anyway. After a few bites, his mind was so distracted again with thoughts of Carrie Ann, he didn't even notice the taste.

"Dad?" Charlie said.

Owen blinked and met his son's eyes. "What?"

"Are you okay?" Charlie's face was etched with concern.

"Yeah, why?"

Charlie nodded toward Owen's plate. "You're trying to cut the bone."

Looking down, Owen saw that his son was right. He set his fork and knife down. "I guess I'm done then."

Charlie and Hallie stared at him.

"Nothing to worry about guys. I'm just a little distracted," Owen insisted. "But I think the two of you should do the dishes tonight. I wouldn't want my wandering mind to lead to a broken dish."

"And what about after that? Wrecking the truck would be worse than a broken plate," Charlie said.

Owen raised his brows. "I assure you, I'll be fine by the time we leave. I just need a few minutes."

He left the kitchen and went into his room to change out of his work clothes. Glancing inside his closet, he found himself searching for the shirt Carrie Ann always liked best. *What is wrong with me?* Despite knowing it was a bad idea, he grabbed the shirt she preferred and put it on. He couldn't help himself. And deep down, he wanted her to feel what he was feeling—the longing that had distracted him all day and led to more than one injury. Of course, he didn't want her injured.

After buttoning up the shirt, he pulled on a pair of khakis and his shoes. Then he combed his hair and headed back out to see if the kids were finished with the dishes.

Half an hour later, Owen pulled up in front of the community center and headed inside. As he neared the group gathered there, he noticed their solemn expressions. Everyone was still struggling with Freddy's death. For a moment, Owen felt ashamed of himself for spending the whole day wrapped up in his thoughts about Carrie Ann when he should be thinking about Antonia and the rest of the group. They were all hurting and he was lusting over the woman he'd lost.

In the center of the group, Antonia sat sniffling with a tissue in her hand. Several of the other group members, including Carrie Ann, tried their best to offer comfort. Owen fell in line with them and offered the grieving woman a hug.

"Let's forget about dancing tonight," said Alice, one of Antonia's closest friends.

The group nodded and agreed, but Antonia spoke up and said, "No. Freddy wouldn't like that. He'd want us to dance. He loved this group and he loved to dance."

"Then tonight we'll dance in his honor," Alice said. "Let's just get paired up." She stopped and glanced around the group with an almost stricken look, and Owen knew she'd just realized that Antonia no longer had a partner.

With an inward sigh, Owen said, "I'll be Antonia's partner tonight. Is that okay with you, Carrie Ann?"

"Of course," Carrie Ann said.

"Just take the first dance, young man," Harvey said. "I'll partner with Antonia after that. Mildred likes a break anyway, don't you darlin'?"

Mildred nodded.

Then Joe and Willie spoke up and said they'd take a turn too.

Owen smiled. This seemed like the perfect way to honor Freddy. In fact, he was so moved by the outpouring of support for Antonia, he stopped thinking about Carrie Ann … at least, until his turn with Antonia was over.

Once Carrie Ann was in his arms, his desire to keep her there began to overwhelm him again. The way she smelled—like ripe strawberries—and her smile as they danced made him lightheaded. At that moment, his desire for her was so great, he had to force himself not to blurt out a marriage proposal.

Then, as soon as that thought entered his mind, a painful memory flowed through his mind and he clamped his mouth shut. *No, the answer is still no.*

Rebecca L. Marsh

Chapter 20

Hallie shoved clothes into her backpack in preparation for a weekend with her grandparents. She made sure to pack her swimsuit since Granddad said they would go to the beach. She was looking forward to spending some more time with them without Charlie around. Besides going to the beach, they were going to watch some more videos of her dad. She also wanted to look through the books he'd left on the shelf of his old room. She wondered if she would like some of the same books he'd once read.

Though she knew she could stay at her grandparents' house for the rest of the summer instead of staying with Owen and Charlie, Hallie wasn't ready for that yet. Having a relationship with them again was still new and Hallie didn't trust it that well yet. Staying at Owen's house felt safe, and feeling safe was very important. It was the whole reason she'd run away for the summer in the first place.

Even though she hadn't come to the island in three years, when she'd decided to run away, it hadn't taken long for her to decide to go to Owen's house. She could have gone to her best friend's house—she'd done that before for short stays—but she didn't think it would be a good idea to go there for the whole summer. Her mother could have easily shown up and made her go home. Or Cammie's mother might have gotten tired of having her around and sent her home. She felt it was important to go somewhere that wasn't too close to home.

With that conviction, Owen's house sprang to mind. Hallie remembered how shy and broken Charlie was when they were little, and she also remembered Owen's gentle manner. He had always been a comforting presence.

Hallie evaluated what she had packed, and satisfied, she closed her backpack and carried it downstairs. She left it by the front door and walked into the kitchen where she found Charlie with his nose buried in the new book his grandmother gave him.

"Hey, Charlie," she said.

He glanced up at her. "I'm learning how to make a spear out of a stick."

Hallie nodded. "Why do you want to learn that?"

"Cause it's cool. And because it's a survival skill. If I got stuck out in the woods, I could use it to hunt."

"You live on an island. If you got lost in the woods, someone would find you before you'd need a spear."

Charlie sighed. "It's not like I'll never leave the island. Dad and I are talking about planning a camping trip on the mainland." He cocked his head to the side. "I'm gonna know all kinds of helpful stuff."

Hallie shrugged and Charlie went back to his book.

A few minutes later, the doorbell chimed. Hallie hopped up and hurried to the door. Swinging it open, she smiled. "Granddad! I'm all set to go." She grabbed her backpack and swung it to her shoulder.

"That's great. Let's let Owen know you're leaving first, though." Granddad grinned at her.

"Yeah, sure." She stepped back and let her grandfather through the door. Then she hurried toward Owen's room and knocked. When he responded, she called to him that she was leaving with her grandfather.

"Have a great weekend, Hallie," he called back. "I'll see you Sunday evening."

"See you then," she sang out before grabbing Granddad's hand and pulling him out the door.

He laughed as she dragged him toward his car. "It's great to see you so excited about spending time with us."

"Can Grandma make cookies?" Hallie's mouth watered at the thought.

Granddad held the door open for her to get into the car and leaned close to her conspiratorially. He whispered in her ear. "She already has."

Hallie grinned. "And can we watch one of the videos tonight? I want to watch one from when I was little."

"I think that can be arranged," Granddad said after sliding into the driver's seat.

He started the car and pulled out of Owen's driveway. Hallie bounced in her seat and chatted happily with him the whole ride.

Hallie went to bed filled with contentment. Grandma made tuna noodle casserole—Hallie's favorite—for dinner and, afterward, she ate two large chocolate chip cookies. But it wasn't just her belly that was satisfied.

After dinner, they watched one of the videos of her dad. Joy filled her heart as she watched him play with her when she was a toddler. He'd loved her. And she was beginning to understand that her mother's logic was wrong. Just because Daddy chose to join the Army, it didn't mean he put that ahead of his family. Seeing him interact with them in the videos made it clear that he loved them.

As Hallie thought about it, she wondered if maybe her mother needed to watch the DVDs. Maybe if she did, she would realize she was wrong, and if she saw the one of Daddy as a little boy, the one Hallie had watched, she would understand that Grandma and Granddad didn't push Daddy into the Army. Maybe she would forgive them too. Hallie hoped so because she wanted them to love each other again.

Before getting into bed, Hallie looked through the books on the shelf. At first, she pulled out *The Hobbit* and read the first page. Wrinkling her nose, she put the book back on the shelf. Then she picked up *The Call of the Wild* and decided that she liked that one much better. She took it to bed with her and fell asleep reading it.

When she awoke the next morning, she hurried downstairs to find a plate of pancakes waiting on her. They were cut into heart shapes and covered in strawberry slices and whipped cream.

"Yum! Thanks, Grandma!" Hallie said before gobbling up everything on her plate.

When the breakfast dishes were cleaned up, Grandma told Hallie to put on her swimsuit and they headed to the beach for the day.

The three of them spent the whole day enjoying the sun, sand, and warm ocean water. They walked a long way and collected shells, they jumped in the waves, and when the sun began to sink, they packed up their things and headed home to clean up and change before going out to the local seafood restaurant for dinner.

Chapter 21

Saturday evening, Marissa and Howard, along with their girls, went to Owen's house for dinner and game night. They arrived to the smell of chicken pot pie baking. When it was finished, they all filled their bellies while Charlie and Maisy chattered on about how their summer was going. Charlie had shared his field guide with his day camp group, and that led to a few fun activities being added to the previous week. Maisy was excited to talk about the fort she and Hallie finally finished building.

Marissa smiled while she listened to her daughter. She was thrilled to see Maisy in a good mood. And, even better, Marissa had caught sight of her, more than once in the past week, giving some attention to Sylvie. She was only paying attention to the baby when no one was looking, but it was still a step in the right direction. Marissa didn't know what had changed, but she was glad to see it.

"Hallie ran away because there are weird people in her neighborhood," Maisy said.

The change of subject grabbed Marissa's attention. Owen and Howard took notice as well, their eyes growing more alert.

"What weird people?" Owen asked, his brow furrowed.

Marissa wished she'd been paying more attention to what Maisy was saying before this revelation. Since her mind had been wandering, she wasn't sure if she missed something relevant.

Maisy shrugged. "I don't know. She just said she didn't want to stay home alone during the day because there are weird people around. She doesn't think the island's weird people are as bad as the ones that live near her."

"Maisy," Howard spoke in a slow, gentle tone. "Did Hallie say why she's afraid of these weird people?"

The look on Maisy's face changed as she noticed the concerned interest of all the adults. She shrank back in her seat and her eyes went from sudden wideness to worried and welling with tears. "Hallie might get mad at me about telling you guys what she said. She's my friend and I don't want her to hate me."

Silence filled the room for a few long seconds. Then Owen put a hand on Maisy's shoulder and said, "Don't worry, sweetheart. We won't tell her what you said."

Maisy shook her head. "But if you ask her about the weird people, she'll know I told you."

"I won't use that word. In fact, I won't talk to her about it at all. Okay?" Owen said.

Maisy nodded slowly, her face uncertain. "Promise?"

"Cross my heart," Owen said, making a crossing motion over his chest with a finger. When Maisy's expression relaxed, Owen smiled. "Now, dinner's done, why don't you kids go play with Max? Betty has been asking me to send you over."

Charlie perked up. "We don't have to help with the dishes?"

"Not tonight. The adults will handle it," Owen answered.

"Marissa and I will take care of it," Howard said. "Only fair since you did the cooking." He nodded toward Owen.

"I appreciate that." Owen grinned. "I'll be happy to spend some time with little Sylvie."

"Perfect. She needs some bonding time with her uncle." Howard stood up and began to collect the dishes. "Okay kids, scoot. Max is waiting for you."

Charlie and Maisy happily jumped up from their seats and headed for the back door. As soon as they were gone, Marissa looked at Owen and asked, "If you're not going to ask Hallie about the weird people she's afraid of, what are you going to do with that information?"

"I'm going to call Cory and Doreen and let them come up with a way to bring it up without letting her know Maisy said anything. I don't want to hurt their friendship. It's been good for both of them," Owen said, standing up and scooping baby Sylvie up from her infant seat.

"That's a good plan," Howard said. "Cory and Doreen will figure something out."

When Owen left the room with the baby, Marissa slid out of her chair and went to the sink to help Howard with the dishes. She ran water into the sink and squeezed dish soap into it. Then she began washing the dishes while Howard dried them.

"Maisy's doing better lately," Howard commented.

"I was just thinking about that. It's so good to see," Marissa agreed. "Last night, before I put Sylvie to bed, I saw Maisy talking to her."

"Really? How did she respond when she saw you watching?"

"She didn't see me. I didn't want to mess it up, so I hung back." Marissa scrubbed another plate and handed it to him.

"Smart plan. We probably shouldn't push her." Howard returned a plate to the cabinet and took the next one from Marissa.

Continuing to wash the dishes, Marissa glanced out the octagonal window over the sink. Gazing into Betty's yard, she saw Charlie tossing a ball for Max who ran after it. Then she caught sight of Maisy standing in front of the swing. Her lips were moving as if she was talking to someone when no one was there.

"Howard," Marissa said, going still. She tipped her head to the window. "She's doing it again—talking to the swing."

He squeezed in next to his wife and peered out the window. "Hum. I think maybe we do need to talk to her about that."

Marissa nodded. "Yeah, it worries me."

Howard kissed her cheek. "We'll figure it out. But let's wait till tomorrow to bring it up. I want tonight to be fun for all of us."

"Me too. We'll bring it up after church tomorrow."

Once they finished the dishes, they called the kids in for a game of Monopoly and a plate full of brownies.

Hallie went to bed Saturday night with a smile on her face. Her day with Grandma and Granddad was so much fun. And she looked forward to going out to a movie with them after church the next day. She was so glad she'd decided to come to the island for the summer. While she hadn't come thinking her relationship with her grandparents would change, she couldn't be happier now that it had.

Sinking into her bed, she easily fell asleep. She slept peacefully for a few hours, but then her nightmares returned.

In her dream, she stood at the living room window at home. As she looked out, a dark figure approached. The figure drew closer and closer, and with each step he took, Hallie's heart filled with dread. She stepped back from the window and ducked behind a chair, hoping she hadn't been seen. Her heart pounded and the sound of rushing blood filled her ears. When the figure reached the other side of the window, his face twisted with a demented smile. He could see her! Then Hallie heard him say, *here I come, time for some fun,* in a sing-song voice.

She shot up in bed as a scream ripped from her throat.

Less than a minute later, when Hallie's heart was still racing, Grandma rushed into the room. "Hallie, sweetheart, are you okay?" Grandma sat next to Hallie on the side of the bed and pulled her into a hug.

"I ... I had a bad dream." Hallie sniffed, trying to calm herself down.

Grandma kissed her forehead. "What did you dream about, baby? It'll help if you tell me about it."

Hallie shook her head. The last thing she wanted was to share her fears with Grandma and have her brush them away like Mom had. If her mother didn't believe her, why should anyone else?

"Hallie, it's okay. You can tell me."

Hallie peered up into her grandmother's dark, comforting eyes and the knot in her stomach loosened. "I dreamed about a bad man."

Grandma's forehead crinkled and concern filled her eyes. "What bad man? What did he do?"

"He didn't do anything, but he wants to." Hallie whimpered at the thought.

"Sweetheart," Grandma spoke softly, worry lacing her voice. "What does he want to do to you?"

Hallie curled her legs up close to her body and turned her eyes away. "He wants to touch me."

Grandma stilled and drew in a sharp breath. "*Who* wants to touch you, Hallie?" Grandma was trying to keep her tone even, but Hallie could hear how upset she was. Still, she didn't want to say more. If she did, and Grandma didn't believe her, it would ruin everything. *Maybe she's only upset because she thinks I'm lying.*

"No, you won't believe me." Hallie pulled away from her grandmother's embrace and rolled over to face the wall.

"Sweetheart," Grandma's voice was a whisper as she stroked Hallie's hair. "I'm listening. Please, trust me. I want to help."

Hallie rolled enough to peek at Grandma's face over her shoulder. There was sincerity in the dark eyes that met hers. "Leon." Hallie's lips trembled as she allowed the truth to slip out. "He wants to touch me, and I don't want him to."

A silent moment passed before Grandma answered. Hallie held her breath, praying she hadn't made a huge mistake by telling.

"Who is Leon?" Grandma asked in a shaky voice.

Hallie faced her and studied her face. She didn't see doubt or disbelief. "He's Dustin's cousin. He takes care of our yard."

"He's the reason you ran away?"

Hallie nodded.

Grandma swallowed, then asked, "Has he ever touched you before?"

"No," Hallie whispered. "But he was about to once. Mom and Dustin came home and he stopped and acted like he wasn't doing anything. I told Mom what he was trying to do. She didn't believe me." Tears flooded her eyes with the memory. "She said I shouldn't tell lies about people, but it isn't a lie."

"Baby, It's okay." Grandma pulled Hallie close and held her. "I believe you. And you're safe here."

Hallie heard the tenderness in her grandmother's voice. And the love that flowed between them broke free a dam that Hallie hadn't realized was there. She began to sob, letting all her fear and anguish out.

"That's it, baby. You'll feel better when you let it all out," Grandma cooed.

When the tears dried up, Hallie looked up into her grandmother's face. "You believe me, but Mom doesn't."

Grandma sighed. "I suspect she can't bring herself to believe you because it's too hard. No one wants to think someone in their family is capable of hurting their child. Granddad and I will have a talk with her. You won't go home until we are certain she understands that you are not lying or making things up. And you won't go home until she assures us that Leon," Grandma spat the name out as if it carried a bad taste, "will never come near you again. That's a promise."

Hallie's lips tightened. "Do we have to tell Granddad?" The idea of her grandfather knowing what that man wanted to do to her caused shame to wash through her. *Will he look at me differently?* She felt dirty every time she thought about the way Leon wanted to touch her and she found it hard to believe that other people didn't see her that way as well. If Granddad looked at her differently, it would break her heart.

"I think we do. But don't you worry, he will believe you."

Hallie looked at the bedspread and twisted her fingers. "I still don't want him to know."

Grandma lifted Hallie's chin and met her eyes. "It isn't your fault Leon tried to hurt you that way. You didn't do anything wrong."

"I know, but ..." Hallie pulled her legs up to her chest and wrapped her arms around them. "When I think about what he wanted to do, I feel ... dirty." She tentatively glanced up at Grandma's face.

Grandma's eyes flashed with anger. "He's the one that's dirty. Not you."

Hallie latched onto those words. She desperately needed to believe them.

The next day, Hallie found it hard to think about anything other than her conversation with Grandma. In church, she found herself constantly evaluating her grandfather's face for signs that he knew about Leon. She hardly even heard the hymns they were singing. He didn't seem upset, but when his face went serious during the sermon, she wondered if it was the preacher's words that caused the expression on his face or if it was because he knew. *Would he really understand?*

Her stomach twisted in knots. *Please understand, Granddad,* she thought as she studied his face. *Please keep me safe.*

After church, they went out to lunch. Hallie ordered Chicken nuggets and forced herself to eat half of them. The knots in her stomach made it difficult. When she didn't think she could get any more down, she took tiny nibbles to make it look like she was eating.

"Not hungry today?" Granddad asked.

Hallie shrugged and glanced at her grandmother. A knowing look filled Grandma's face. Granddad didn't know yet, Hallie was almost sure of that now. She swallowed hard wishing once more that he didn't need to know.

At the movie theater, she tried to watch the animated characters on the screen, but she couldn't focus. She didn't even open the box of candy Granddad bought for her.

Once they were home, Granddad asked Hallie if she wanted to watch another one of the home videos. She shook her head and told him she was tired and wanted to take a nap. It wasn't a lie, she really was tired. She'd never gotten back to sleep after her nightmare.

She curled up on the bed in her room and exhaustion took over. She fell asleep right away. When she woke up, it was almost dinner time. Scooting off the bed, she wandered out into the hallway and stopped when she heard her grandparents' voices coming from their room. *Grandma's not making dinner yet?* Curious, Hallie tiptoed closer to their door and strained to hear them.

"It'll never work, Cory," Grandma said.

"We have to make her listen, you said it yourself," Granddad insisted.

"Yes, but I didn't mean *we* literally. If she wouldn't believe it from Hallie, she isn't going to believe it coming from us. You know that. She still sees us as an enemy."

"Then what do you suggest we do? Who is going to talk to her if not us?" Granddad huffed.

"I'm thinking Owen might be the best person to make the call. He's outside of all the issues between Amanda and us. I think she might listen to him."

Grandma wants to tell Owen too? No, no, no!

Without a second thought, Hallie burst into her grandparents' room. "You can't do that!" she cried. Heat rose through her body causing sweat to bead on her forehead. "You can't tell Owen what I told you!"

For a long moment, her grandparents stared at her with stunned faces. Then Grandma reached out for her, pulling her closer. "Come sit down, sweetie."

Hallie resisted and shook her head. "No. You can't tell him. I don't want anyone else to know." Tears began to well in her eyes.

When Hallie refused to sit on the edge of the bed, Grandma took both her hands and met her eyes. "Hallie, we need to keep you safe. That means we have to get through to your mom. But I don't think she'll listen to us."

Hallie couldn't deny that her grandmother had a point, but the idea of Owen knowing, of anyone else knowing, overwhelmed her with shame. A flood of tears ran down her cheeks. "Please ... please, don't tell him."

Her grandparents looked at each other, seeming to communicate without words. Then Granddad spoke up, "We still have some time before summer ends. You're safe for now. We'll see if we can think of another way." He put a hand on her shoulder. "But you don't need to fear having people know. You didn't do anything wrong."

His words pulled at the knot of fear inside of her and she flung herself into his arms as she broke into sobs. Granddad still loved her. He didn't see her differently now. But could anyone else do the same?

"We should talk to Maisy now," Howard said when he joined Marissa in their room.

Marissa looked down at Sylvie who was eating contentedly, then she brought her head up to meet her husband's eyes. "I know. It's just been such a good day. Maybe we should wait."

Howard sat down in the chair across from the bed. "Until when?" His eyebrows raised in challenge.

Marissa looked back at the baby in order to avoid Howard's gaze. She'd already convinced him to wait when they got home from church so the talk wouldn't ruin what remained of their weekend. He was right and she knew it. They shouldn't keep putting off the inevitable. But confronting Maisy was likely to bring a dark cloud into their sunny day. "Tomorrow?" she tried.

"And what if tomorrow is a good day? Should we keep putting it off? Would it be better to do it on a day when she's already unhappy?"

Marissa squirmed with all his questions. "All right. We'll talk to her today. Let me get Sylvie settled first."

He patted her knee and kissed the top of her head before leaving the room.

She let the baby finish eating, enjoying the serenity of time with her younger daughter. Why did parenthood have to keep getting more complicated? If only it could be blissfully simple forever.

Marissa sighed when Sylvie indicated she was done. It was time to face whatever was going on with Maisy. She laid the baby down in her bassinet and rocked it until Sylvie was asleep. Then, she left her bedroom and trudged down the hall to find her husband.

Howard stood in the kitchen, looking into the refrigerator. Marissa stepped up behind him and wound her arms around his waist. Turning to face her, he drew her into a hug. "I was just trying to figure out what to make for dinner," he said.

"Let's go talk to Maisy. Afterward, we can make dinner together."

"She's outside. I'll call her."

When Maisy came in, they all sat down in the living room.

"What's going on?" Maisy asked.

"We just need to talk to you about something," Marissa said.

Maisy sank back into the couch cushions, her brow furrowed. "What?"

Marissa looked at Howard pleadingly. She didn't know why talking to Maisy was so difficult for her, but it always had been. And when she did talk to her daughter, she usually said the wrong things. Maisy had always responded better to her father. And now, with Kevin gone, Marissa often relied on the bond that had formed between Maisy and Howard.

"Maisy, your mother and I have noticed you, on occasion, talking to someone when there's no one there," Howard said. Then he fell silent and waited for a response, but Maisy only stared at him. He tried again, "Yesterday when you were playing in Betty's yard, we saw you talking to the swing as if someone was sitting there. But no one was."

Maisy stayed silent and crossed her arms over her chest.

"Maisy, we're concerned about you," Marissa said. "We just want to talk to you about it."

"I don't *want* to talk about it," she said belligerently.

"If you don't want to talk to us about it, then maybe it's something you should talk about with Dr. Flanagan," Marissa said. Dr. Flanagan was the one and only child psychologist on the island and Maisy had been seeing him since they'd moved here. In the beginning, her time with him had been about dealing with the tragic death of her father and sister, and Marissa's subsequent suicide attempt. In more recent times, the visits were infrequent and mostly for the purpose of making sure Maisy was still doing okay. The talking to no one issue seemed like something he could help with, but Maisy's face darkened with the suggestion.

"I'm not crazy! There's nothing wrong with me." She jumped up from the couch and glared at Marissa. "Just leave me alone!" She turned on her heel and stormed off toward her room.

Maisy's bedroom door slammed and then the house fell silent.

Marissa looked at Howard with a miserable expression.

"Well, at least the door slamming didn't wake the baby," he said with a shrug.

"I shouldn't have brought up Dr. Flanagan. I always say the wrong thing to her."

Howard scooted closer to Marissa and put an arm around her. "Maybe it was the wrong thing and maybe not. Just because she blew up at us doesn't mean it was wrong. Give her some time. She was clearly unnerved by the fact that we've seen her talking to no one." He stopped in thought for a moment. "Maisy tends to be defensive when confronted. We may see a different side of her later when she's had some time."

Marissa appreciated the fact that Howard said Maisy had blown up at them both. Of course, it was really her Maisy blew up at.

Chapter 22

Monday morning, Owen poured the last sip of his coffee into his mouth just after dropping Hallie off with Howard. Disappointed, he set his travel mug down in the cup holder and blinked his eyes. He hadn't slept well the previous night, and he knew without a doubt he was going to need more caffeine. With a sigh, he turned onto Main Street and parked in front of the pharmacy. He was planning to drop by later to pick up a few things anyway. Instead, he'd go ahead and do that now, and he'd add a caffeinated soda to the list.

Sliding out of his truck, he headed through the store's door and heard the familiar jingle of the bell. He picked up one of the handheld shopping baskets and started down an aisle. Once he had collected all of the items he needed, he headed to the checkout counter hoping Marissa would be there. His steps slowed when he saw Carrie Ann standing in the front. Each time he saw her, it got harder to let her go. And yet, he hated the thought of not seeing her.

Owen continued to the counter and began to unload his selections. Without saying a word, Carrie Ann scanned each item. Her silence got Owen's attention. He studied her face and noticed how solemn her expression was. Concern for her made his heart sink. She was a naturally upbeat person, and the drawn expression she wore wasn't like her at all.

"Something wrong?" he asked.

Carrie Ann looked up and met his eyes. Hers were weary. She picked up another item and scanned it before answering. Then, looking down she said, "I'm quitting swing dance."

"What? Why? I thought you liked it," Owen said in surprise.

Carrie Ann sucked in a breath and let it out. "I love it, but it isn't working for me anymore."

"What do you mean? Do you have something else going on Wednesday nights?"

She met his eyes briefly, then turned hers away again. "No. It's just too hard, Owen."

His heart sank at her words. Though he knew deep down he was the reason going to swing dance was too hard, he wanted to believe there was another reason. "Because of Freddy?" he tried.

She shook her head. "I miss Freddy like crazy, but no. It's too hard to be around you." Her voice was low and forlorn.

A sense of shame washed through Owen. He hated being the reason she was so miserable. He found himself almost ready to tell her she didn't need to worry about quitting class or anything else because he wanted to marry her. He opened his mouth to say the words, but they wouldn't come out. Something inside him wouldn't let him do it.

Carrie Ann's eyes welled with tears as she looked up. "I'm searching for a job on the mainland. When I get one, I'll be leaving the island."

Owen went completely still, even holding his breath. Seconds ticked by until his lungs burned and he took another breath. "You can't."

She glared at him, a hint of anger in her eyes. "Yes, Owen, I can."

"But … this is your home. This island wouldn't be the same without you." Owen's heart hammered as he wracked his brain for ways to convince her to stay.

She raised an eyebrow at him. "I think the island will recover."

For several breaths, Owen stared at her, desperation strangling him. "But I might not," he whispered.

"You have a choice, Owen. Say the word and I'll stay, but I won't be strung along." She shoved his bag of purchases into his hands and stomped off.

"What in heaven's name did you do?" The words spilled from Marissa's lips the second her brother answered her call.

"Hello to you too," he responded in an irritated tone.

Marissa glanced around the store to be sure there were no customers in need of help. Only two people were shopping, and they appeared to be fine. "This is no time for pleasantries, Owen. Carrie Ann is so upset she won't come out of her office. So, I ask again, what did you do?"

He huffed, the sound of his exhale reverberating through the phone. "I didn't *do* anything."

"If you think playing innocent is going to work on me this time, you're wrong. I already wanted to wring your neck as it was. Do you know Carrie Ann is talking about moving to the mainland?" Marissa anxiously fiddled with a loose string from her shirt. She wasn't a confrontational person, but the situation had pushed her to it. She couldn't understand her brother's behavior. And the thought of seeing her boss, who was also her best friend, move away was killing her.

"I know." His words were abrupt and clipped.

"So, she told you and that's what this is about. What did you say to her?" Marissa tried to rein in her frustration. Screaming at him wouldn't help.

"I asked her to stay. I told her the island wouldn't be the same without her. That's all."

"Yeah, that's all and that's the problem," Marissa spoke in an angry whisper to keep herself from yelling. She wished Owen was there with her so she could smack him in the back of his head. *Is he really that dumb?* "The island won't be the same without her? She wants to hear that you won't be the same without her. She's leaving because she's in love with you, and you won't move forward. But I know you, Owen, and you love her just as much as she loves you. So, what is your problem? When did you decide marriage was something to avoid at all costs?"

"I'm just not ready," he insisted, but there was a slight waver in his voice.

"That's not it. I can hear it in your voice. And really, what more could you need in order to *be ready*? You two have dated for two years. At this point, it's either right or it isn't. Something else is holding you back."

Silence filled Marissa's ear as she waited for a response. Finally, Owen spoke, "I'm not sure what's holding me back. I just can't seem to do it. I can't say the words. I can't make the commitment." His voice held deep pain.

Marissa lowered her voice and softened her tone. "I don't remember you ever having that problem back when you were chasing after Casey." She knew bringing up Charlie's mother was a sore subject. Owen had been in love with her for years and she only gave him heartache in return.

He sighed heavily. "You're right." His voice held sadness and hurt, but there was more than that. He was holding something back, Marissa was sure of it.

"That's it, isn't it? Your issue now has something to do with Casey. What aren't you telling me?"

"No, Marissa. I'm not going there with you," he responded forcefully.

Marissa moved forward carefully. "Whatever it is, Owen, it's holding you back from the best relationship you've ever had. It might help you to talk about it. You know I love you, Owen, no matter what."

"I know you do. I love you too, sis."

"Then talk to me."

He let out a heavy breath. "I think it is because of Casey that I can't move forward."

Marissa waited a few seconds for him to continue.

"The first time she came to the island, I asked her to marry me. The next day she was gone. She didn't explain. She didn't leave a note. She was just gone, and I didn't see her again until she came back with Charlie and left him with me."

"And that's stopping you from marrying Carrie Ann?" Marissa asked. She wasn't sure she understood.

"I don't know if I can explain it. But every time I think about asking Carrie Ann to marry me, I feel sure she'll run away."

The urge to slap the back of his head, if she could, overtook Marissa again. "Well, she *is* going to leave if you don't ask."

"I know that and I still couldn't say the words. I'm really screwed up, aren't I?"

Marissa glanced around the store again. One of the customers had taken his items to the counter in the pharmacy to combine with a prescription pick up. The other was still shopping, but would likely head to the front soon.

"From my own experiences, I think we're all a little screwed up. But if you want Carrie Ann to stay on the island, you need to explain all this to her. And you need to work on getting past the fears Casey left you with. Carrie Ann may well understand and give you some time, but she isn't going to wait forever, and I can't blame her."

"Yeah, I guess I can't either." Owen's tone was despondent, and it made her heart ache for him. The anger she'd felt when she first called fizzled away.

"We'll talk more later. I need to take care of a customer now."

Rebecca L. Marsh

Chapter 23

Hallie lay on her bed at Owen's house reading a book. Just as she began to feel completely immersed in the story, Owen's voice called to her. "Hallie, your mother is on the phone."

Pulling herself from the fantasy world of her book, she set it down on her nightstand before sliding off the bed and heading downstairs. When she reached the bottom of the stairs, Owen handed her his cell phone.

"Thanks," she said. She put the phone to her ear and walked into the living room where she flopped onto the couch. "Hi, Mom."

"Hi sweetie. How're you doing?" Mom asked.

"Pretty good." She'd been feeling better, lighter, since talking to her grandparents. She only wished she could have the conversation with her mother and get the same result. "I'm having a good time on the island."

"That's good to hear. But we miss you at home." Mom's voice was upbeat, but it sounded forced.

Hallie wanted to say she was sorry for running away and explain herself, but she knew where that would lead. Still, she hated the wall it had created between herself and her mother.

"I've been spending more time at Grandma and Granddad's house. And I've been watching some old home movies they have," Hallie said.

When her mother didn't respond, Hallie continued, deciding to bring up another subject that was going to be hard. "I watched some that were made when Daddy was a little kid."

"And I'm sure he was cute," Mom said with a smile in her voice.

"He was." Hallie hesitated, uncertain how to say what she needed to say. "Mom, why did you tell me Daddy joined the Army because of Grandma and Granddad?"

"Because he did. Hallie, we've been through this. They pushed him to do it. He wouldn't have chosen that over us if he hadn't wanted so badly to please them."

Hallie pushed forward in a low voice, little more than a whisper. "That isn't true, Mom."

"It is true," Mom said with force. "I was there, you were not."

Hallie didn't argue her mother's point. "I saw a video of Daddy when he was a little boy. He said he wanted to join the Army. He did it because it was his dream. He wanted to get the bad guys."

"He was just a little kid then. He changed as he got older. But *they* wouldn't let him change. And he wanted to please them."

Hallie hesitated, wondering if there was any point in having this conversation with her mother. Mom had believed a lie for a long time. Hallie didn't know if it was possible for her to let go of it. But if she could, it would make life a lot easier. If she could let go of her anger at Grandma and Granddad, as Hallie had, then maybe they could all be a family again. Hallie wanted that more than anything. *I've got to try.*

"I don't believe that anymore. I've watched lots of home movies. He wanted to join the Army. It was his choice, not theirs," Hallie said. She kept her tone calm and even, but strong and sure.

"You believe he chose that over me ... over us?"

"Why does it have to be one thing over the other? He wanted to be a soldier, but he also wanted us." Hallie thought about the video of Daddy and her when she was little. She remembered the love in his eyes. "I saw that in the home movies too. He loved us."

"When you love someone, you don't choose to leave them. You don't risk your life when you know they need you." There was a waver in her mother's voice that told Hallie how upset she was getting.

"He didn't want to leave us, but it was part of the job he wanted to do. And he knew it had risks, but he didn't want to die. He didn't want to leave us." Hallie spoke with compassion. It was only a short time ago that she was expressing the same things. She'd been using her anger at Grandma and Granddad to cover the anger she felt toward her father. But seeing the videos changed that. Seeing how much he loved her untied the knot of hurt that fueled her anger. She hoped her mother could get to the same place. "I don't think he would want us to blame Grandma and Granddad. I think he would want us all to love each other and take care of each other."

Hallie heard her mother sniffling. "Even if they didn't make him do it, they didn't try to stop him."

"It was what he wanted to do and they wanted him to follow his dreams. Mom, please, forgive them … forgive Daddy. Being angry doesn't bring him back, it just makes it harder to remember the good stuff."

Mom was sobbing now. Hallie waited for her cries to subside.

"I do want to remember the good stuff about your dad," Mom said. "I loved him so much."

"Me too." She hesitated, pursing her lips. "Grandma and Granddad do too."

Several seconds of silence passed between them, then Mom said, "I know that."

"Then forgive them."

"I'll think about it," Mom said with a sigh.

Hallie smiled. This was a far better outcome than she'd expected. All that was left was to get Mom to believe her about Leon.

Standing at the end of her bed, Marissa folded a load of laundry while the baby slept in her bassinet. She turned when she heard a soft voice.

"Mom?" Maisy said.

"What is it, sweetie?"

Maisy took slow steps into the room and stopped a few feet from her mother. "I'm sorry for yelling at you when you and Howard tried to talk to me the other day."

Marissa raised her eyebrows in surprise. "Thank you for the apology." She turned back to the laundry and began to fold again, but Maisy didn't walk away. Instead, she stood still, twisting her hands.

"Maisy," Marissa stepped closer and placed a hand on her daughter's shoulder, "is there something else?"

"If I tell you who I was talking to, you might think I'm crazy. ... But I'm not." Maisy shook her head vigorously.

"Sweetie, why would you think that?"

Maisy tightened her lips and looked at the floor. "I was talking to Kyla," she whispered.

Hearing her dead daughter's name sent a pang through Marissa's heart. She took a deep breath and tried not to let the emotion show. "I see. Why would that make me think you're crazy?"

Maisy looked up at her. "It's not crazy to talk to someone who isn't there—someone who died?"

Marissa shrugged. "Come sit down with me." She led Maisy to the side of the bed where they could sit without disturbing the folded laundry. "You know, I still talk to your dad sometimes."

"You do?" Maisy asked with surprise.

"Well, not out loud, but yes."

"What do you talk to him about?"

Marissa smiled and pushed a lock of Maisy's hair behind her shoulder. "You, mostly. Sometimes I feel like I should tell him how you're doing. You know, in case he gets busy in Heaven and misses something."

"Do you ever talk to Kyla?"

The pang hit Marissa again. She didn't know why it was so much harder to talk about Kyla than Kevin, but it was. She forced herself to keep eye contact with Maisy. "Sometimes."

"Do you tell her what's going on?"

"Mostly, I just tell her that I love and miss her."

"Did you tell her about Sylvie?" Maisy asked.

"No. But I'm sure she knows a little bit about what's happening here. She'd want to check in on us. Look down on us. Don't you think?"

Maisy nodded. "Yeah, I guess."

"What do you talk to her about?" Marissa asked, rubbing Maisy's back.

"I tell her that she's still my sister. I tell her that no one can replace her."

"Of course she's still your sister, and no one can replace her. She knows that." Marissa met Maisy's eyes with concern.

"Well," Maisy's tone went soft again, "what if she does think Sylvie is replacing her?"

"That's what you're worried about?"

Maisy nodded.

"Sweetheart, is that why you didn't want to hold Sylvie for so long?"

Another nod.

"Why do you think Kyla would think that?"

"Well, I know it sounds silly, but Sylvie looks like Kyla. And she's another sister. I felt like I was …"

"Betraying Kyla?" Marissa said when Maisy couldn't find the right word.

"Yeah." Maisy folded her arms over her stomach and slumped.

"Oh, Maisy, you can love Sylvie and still love Kyla."

"I know that now. I talked it out with Hallie and she asked me how Kyla would want me to treat Sylvie. I thought about the way Kyla stood up for me when other kids teased me."

Marissa smiled, loving the fact that Maisy was thinking about that rather than all the times Kyla had done the teasing. She waited to see if her daughter had more to say.

"So, when you and Howard saw me talking to the swing the other day, I was telling Kyla about Sylvie. I wanted to tell her that I would always love her. And I also told her that I would try to be a good big sister ... like she was." A tear ran down Maisy's cheek, and Marissa brushed it away.

"I think that's wonderful. I'm sure Kyla and Daddy are both really proud of you."

Maisy searched her mother's face. "Thanks, Mom. I guess I should have talked to you about it sooner. I feel better now."

Marissa kissed Maisy's forehead. "I feel better too. I love you."

"I love you, too, Mom." Maisy slid her arms around Marissa's waist and squeezed. Marissa held her tight, enjoying the feel of her daughter in her arms.

Chapter 24

Owen hummed as he buttoned his shirt and combed his hair. He took another look at himself to make sure he looked his best. Then he walked to the bottom of the stairs and called out, "Charlie! Hallie! Come on, let's go!"

The children skipped down the stairs chattering to each other. "I'm telling you, I wouldn't eat that," Hallie said.

"If you were stuck out in the woods with no regular food you would," Charlie insisted.

"I wouldn't be stuck in the woods." Hallie raised her chin.

"What if you went hiking and got lost?"

Hallie shrugged. "I don't like hiking. But if I did, I'd take some snacks with me."

"What if you ran out?" Charlie continued.

Owen stopped him with a hand on the boy's head. "Enough son. We need to get going." He sauntered to the door and ushered the kids out.

"Dad, why are you so dressed up?" Charlie asked as they hopped into the car.

"I'm not," Owen said.

Charlie furrowed his brow. "You usually wear old t-shirts to swing dance." Charlie leaned closer and sniffed the air. "And you're wearing perfume."

"Men don't wear perfume," Hallie said. "They wear cologne."

"Yes, thank you, Hallie," Owen said, evading his son's questions.

"Whatever," Charlie said with an eye roll. "Why are you wearing it?"

"I wanted to. Let's stop the interrogation." Owen supposed he shouldn't be surprised by the questions. It was foolish to think his son wouldn't notice the differences in his appearance. But he had no intention of telling Charlie why he was wearing a button-down shirt and cologne.

Charlie shrugged and returned his attention to his previous conversation with Hallie as they drove. When they reached Cory and Doreen's house, the kids jumped out, shouted their goodbye, and hurried to the door.

Owen waited until the kids were inside before he headed on to the flower shop. He picked up an arrangement of lilies and jumped back in his truck. His stomach swirled with butterflies as excitement and anxiety mingled inside of him. He prayed he would be able to go through with his intentions without choking at the last minute. *I can do this. I have to!*

Pulling up in front of Carrie Ann's house, he stared at the front door and willed himself to move forward. "Come on, Owen, you can do this," he said aloud, trying to bolster his confidence. "She isn't Casey. She isn't going to rip your heart out. And you love her." He took a small velvet box from his pocket and opened it, glancing at the ring inside. He'd taken some time out from work and gone to the mainland earlier in the week to find just the right one. In the end, he chose a square-cut diamond with little emeralds on either side.

Snapping the box shut, he returned it to his pocket. Then he closed his eyes for a moment, gathered his courage, and grabbed the flowers. When he reached the door, he dragged a hand through his head of blond curls before ringing the bell. Then he waited … and waited.

When no answer came after a full minute passed, he rang the bell again. Still, there was no answer. He knocked and called out, "Carrie Ann! Come on, open up!" Still no answer.

Owen glanced around. Carrie Ann's car was in the driveway. *Why isn't she answering? Does she hate me now?* He knocked one more time and when she still didn't answer, he tried calling her, but she didn't answer her phone either.

Owen scowled at his phone for a moment, wondering if he'd ruined things with Carrie Ann so badly that there was no way to fix it. He decided to call Marissa.

"Hey, Owen," Marissa said when she picked up. "Aren't you supposed to be at swing dance tonight?"

"Yeah, but I decided to go talk to Carrie Ann instead."

"Oh," Marissa's tone told him she knew something.

"What's going on? Her car is here, but she isn't answering the door." Owen tried to keep the irritation from his voice. It wasn't Marissa's fault he was in the situation.

"She went to the mainland for an interview."

"It's a little late in the day for an interview. And why wouldn't she take her car?"

Owen heard his sister take a deep breath. "The interview is actually tomorrow morning. But she has to drive down the coast, almost to Charleston. And she didn't take her car because it broke down. She borrowed my van."

"She's considering a job that far away? And you helped her?"

"Well, yes, Owen," Marissa's voice dripped with sarcasm. "What would you expect me to do? Hold her hostage?"

"Of course not, but you didn't have to loan her a car." Owen's voice went high with agitation. He knew he sounded like a child, and hated himself for it. But the idea of her going so far away tore at his heart. It was his own fault, but knowing that didn't stop him from feeling ripped apart by it.

"Owen, she's my friend. If you want to change her mind, then you know what you have to do."

"I was going to. That's why I'm here."

Marissa's voice came back softer. "Call her."

"I tried. She didn't answer." Owen paced across Carrie Ann's front porch, his chest tight with the thought of losing her.

There was a short pause. "She might still be driving. My van is old. There's no Bluetooth. Try again in a little while."

Owen sighed. "Yeah, I will."

"Good." Another pause. "And Owen, I hope it all works out. I want her to stay too. And I want you two together. You belong with her."

He glanced at the bouquet in his hand and thought about the ring box in his pocket. "I think so too," he said, realizing he wasn't feeling jittery any longer about asking Carrie Ann to marry him. Instead, he felt disappointed at being unable to do it. He was ready. It had taken the jolt of her plan to move away to make him recognize that, but he was ready.

Forty minutes later, Owen still paced Carrie Ann's porch. He'd called her three times, leaving messages when she failed to answer, and he'd left her four text messages that she hadn't responded to. He ran a hand through his hair and had to resist the urge to pull some of it out in frustration. He had to get through to her. This could be his last chance.

He stopped pacing when a thought came to him. He knew what he needed to do. He dialed his sister's number again and waited a few seconds, each one stretching out and feeling much longer.

"Hello," Marissa said.

"Rissa, can you keep Charlie for the night?"

"Why, is something going on? Did you talk to Carrie Ann?"

"No, she still isn't answering." He left the porch and strode toward his truck. "That's why I'm driving to South Carolina to talk to her."

"Really?" Marissa's voice held surprise.

"I have to. And that means you need to tell me exactly where she's going." He hopped into his truck.

"That's gonna be a problem." Marissa's tone deflated.

"You don't know where she's going?" Panic rippled through Owen's chest. Now that he'd decided to go, determination surged through him, and he couldn't stomach the thought of anything standing in his way. "Rissa, I have to know."

"Calm down, I'll call her and see if she'll answer me. I'll make something up about needing to know in case there's an emergency at the store and I can't get her on her cell. And don't worry about Charlie. I'm happy to have him stay here." She paused. "What about Hallie?"

"I'm going to call Cory and Doreen and ask if she can stay there. I doubt it'll be a problem but, if it is, can she stay with you too?"

"Of course she can. ... Okay, you call Cory and I'll call Carrie Ann. I'll get back to you as soon as I know something," Marissa said.

"Perfect," Owen said, feeling energized and hopeful. He said goodbye to his sister and fired up his truck. Then, switching to Bluetooth, he dialed Cory's number.

"Owen, I hope everything is okay," Cory said when he picked up. His voice was laced with concern. Owen should still be at swing dance and Cory wouldn't expect a call.

"Everything is fine. But I need to make an unexpected trip out of town tonight and I was wondering if Hallie can just stay with you."

"Certainly," Cory said. "Are you coming by to pick Charlie up?"

"No, Marissa will come get him. He'll stay with her tonight."

Owen said goodbye to Cory and drove home as fast as he could to pack an overnight bag. He threw items into a duffle bag without worrying about how they were packed. He glanced at his watch. If he hurried, he could make the next ferry.

His bag packed, he threw it over his shoulder and sprinted to his truck. He drove as fast as he felt was safe and made it to the ferry dock just in time. With a sigh of relief, he parked his truck on the lower section of the large boat and headed up on deck.

Normally, he'd sit and relax for the ride, watching the dolphins and pelicans. But this time he found it impossible to sit still. Periodically, he glanced at his phone to make sure he hadn't missed Marissa's call. *What was taking her so long?*

Owen took a few deep breaths and reminded himself he had time before he'd have to know the exact location. If his sister didn't call before he got off the ferry, he'd simply head toward Charleston. Still, not knowing exactly where Carrie Ann was and the uncertainty of whether or not she'd tell Marissa, was making his stomach swirl with bile. What if he drove all the way down the South Carolina coast and then couldn't get to her? *No, that isn't going to happen. Why wouldn't she tell Marissa where she is?*

Owen jumped when his phone trilled. The ferry was nearly to shore and he was on his way back to his truck. "Hello? Rissa?" He covered his other ear to block out the sounds of other passengers talking around him.

"She's in Summerville," Marissa said. "She told me she's staying at the Holiday Inn, room 230. I looked up the address for you." She rattled off the address just after Owen reached his truck, and he scribbled it on a notepad he kept in his glove compartment.

"Did she believe your story about needing to know for the store?"

"I'm not sure. But she didn't ask if it had anything to do with you. Honestly, Owen, after the way you've been, I'm not sure she'd believe me if I told her what you're doing."

Owen sighed. That did not speak well of him, but he knew it was true. "Then she'll be surprised when I get there."

"No doubt. I still can't believe it." There was silence for a beat. "Good luck. And call me after you see her."

"Yeah, okay."

Owen stowed his phone, and when the ferry was docked, he started his truck and headed toward Summerville and the woman he loved.

Rebecca L. Marsh

Chapter 25

Hallie went to her room at her grandparents' house, perfectly happy to be spending the night. She had a nice evening with them, and now that Charlie had been picked up, she was looking forward to putting pajamas on and cuddling up on the couch for a movie. Granddad was making popcorn and the chocolate chip cookies Grandma made earlier were still warm.

Running a finger along the spines of her father's books on the shelf, Hallie looked for one to set out next to her bed. When the movie was over, she'd do a little reading. But as she looked through the books, the one that ended up calling out to her was one of her father's old yearbooks. She pulled it out and studied the cover. A golden eagle was embossed in the center. Hallie ran her fingers over it. She'd look through the pictures later and see if she could find all the shots of Daddy.

She set the book down on her nightstand, changed into her pajamas, and hurried downstairs. "I'm ready," she called out, throwing herself onto the sofa.

A moment later, Granddad sauntered in with a smile. "I've got the popcorn and the cookies are on the kitchen counter." He handed the popcorn bucket to Hallie and went to the DVD player to set up the movie.

Just as he got it started, Grandma wandered in with her knitting bag and sat down next to Hallie.

"Everyone ready for *Over the Hedge*?" Granddad asked, sitting on the other side of Hallie.

"Ready here." Grandma raised one of her knitting needles.

"I'm ready," Hallie said before shoving a handful of popcorn into her mouth.

A while later, when the popcorn was gone, Hallie snuggled against her grandmother. She breathed in the scent of lilac soap and felt completely content. She wished she hadn't let anger and blame keep her away from this for so long.

When the movie ended, Hallie kissed her grandparents goodnight, brushed her teeth, and crawled into bed. She picked up the yearbook and began to flip through the pages. Finding her father's picture, she smiled at his shy expression. He never did like having his picture taken. She traced the lines of his face and tried to memorize them before moving on to the next page.

Halfway through the book, an envelope fell out from between the pages and landed in Hallie's lap. She glanced down at it, then set the book aside, and scooped up the envelope, turning it over in her hands. It was addressed to Daddy during one of his deployments. He must have brought it home with him and put it in this yearbook. Then, when he died, Mom had given a bunch of his stuff to Grandma and Granddad. His yearbooks were obviously among the items she gave them.

Hallie squinted at the small writing on the envelope to see who it was from and saw her mother's name: Amanda Hobbs. *Should I read it?* It felt a little wrong. This letter was something personal between her parents. And besides, it could be a mushy love letter. She blushed at that idea.

No, I shouldn't read this.

But somehow, she couldn't not read it. She needed to know what it said. Carefully, she pulled the folded paper out of the envelope, opened it up, and began to read.

At first, the letter was exactly what you'd expect a wife to send to her deployed husband; lots of gushing about how much she loved and missed him, how she couldn't wait until he came home. Then it took an unexpected turn.

Your parents came to see me last weekend. I didn't tell them about the baby. I just can't do it, Daniel. I know they didn't want us to get married. I'm sure they'll be upset when they find out.

Hallie stared at the words. Her grandparents didn't want her mom and dad to get married? She'd never heard that before.

Then her mind settled on the other part. Her mother was so certain that her grandparents would be unhappy about *the baby.* She was that baby. Her heart sank at the thought. Was her mother right? Was it possible Grandma and Granddad hadn't wanted her? She let the paper drop from her fingers as the thoughts ran through her head. The warm and cozy feeling she'd had just a short time ago seemed far away. Now all she could feel was confusion and the prickle of hurt.

By the time Owen reached Summerville, it was nearly midnight. He stood outside the Holiday Inn wondering if it was a good idea to knock on Carrie Ann's door at such a late hour. If he woke her up, would she be in any frame of mind to hear him out, or would she slam the door in his face? Indecision and anxiety rippled through him, making his stomach lurch. *I came this far. I can't chicken out now.*

He jabbed a hand into his pocket and wrapped his fingers around the ring box. *I'm doing this. I have to.*

His stomach still rolling, he made his way to the door, found the stairs, and climbed to the second floor. He wandered down the hallway, searching for the right room. When he found it, he stood in front of the door, his hands sweating as he ran through ideas of what to say to her in his mind.

Deciding he needed to see himself, he glanced around and saw a mirror on the wall just a few steps away. He stood in front of it and checked his appearance. His shirt was rumpled from the drive. *Perhaps I should check into a room first and straighten myself up.*

Owen shook his head. *No, I might lose my nerve. It's now or never.* He tugged at his shirt, doing his best to straighten it with little effect. With a sigh, he tried to find the right words as he looked at his reflection.

I need you, Carrie Ann. I'm not complete without you—no, that's not it. He shook his head as if to throw the words away. *That makes me sound like a needy stalker.*

Fixing his eyes to his face in the mirror, he tried again.

I've been such an idiot. I'm sorry. Please come back home and marry me—ugh, that sounds pathetic. I came all this way to make a grand gesture. It has to be romantic. He scowled at his reflection. *I should have stopped for some roses when I got off the ferry.*

Maybe I should get down on one knee and hold the ring box in front of me before I knock. That would be romantic, wouldn't it? And perhaps if I do that while I practice what to say, I'll get into the amorous spirit and find the right words.

Glancing up and down the hall, he verified that no one was around. Then he went to Carrie Ann's door, knelt, and pulled the ring box out of his pocket. He opened the box, and the diamond caught the light and sparkled. On impulse, he pulled the ring from the box to look it over one more time. *It's perfect. She'll love it—I hope.*

Just as Owen was about to put the ring back in the box and practice what he'd say, he sneezed. The ring flew from his fingers. In a panic, he scanned the floor, but it had vanished. *How far could it have gone?* He grimaced at the carpet's geometric design. That would surely make it hard to spot something small. He got on his hands and knees and began crawling around, studying the floor with a careful eye. *Where did it go?*

He shivered as a dreadful thought came to him. *What if the ring skittered under one of the hotel room doors? Oh no, please don't let it be that!* He kept crawling around, putting his face closer to the floor.

When the sound of a door opening interrupted him, he froze.

"Owen? Is that you?"

His heart dropped at the sound of Carrie Ann's voice behind him. He came to make a grand romantic gesture, and instead, she found him crawling around on the floor outside her room late at night.

With a deflated sigh, he turned, and without looking up at her, picked himself up off the floor. He knew he should look at her and say something, but his mind was blank.

When he didn't say anything, she spoke up, "What are you doing here? Did Marissa tell you where to find me? I knew she didn't need to know for the store." She paused and looked him over with tired eyes. Her purple-streaked hair was mussed, signaling that he woke her. "Why did you come? And what were you doing on the floor?"

He looked at his feet, avoiding her eyes. "I came because I had to stop you from leaving the island—from leaving me."

She scoffed. "I didn't leave you, Owen. You were the one who refused to move forward. I'm sick of you blaming that on me. And I'm not coming back to the island to stay in a relationship that isn't going anywhere." A tear rolled down her cheek. "I deserve better than that, but I love you too much to move on when I still see you all the time."

Owen's chest tightened. *She still loves me, that's a start.* "But it *will* go somewhere. That's what I came to say. That's why I was on the floor." His words flew out so suddenly, he wasn't sure he was making sense.

When Carrie Ann's face scrunched up, he figured that he hadn't made sense. "You were on the floor because our relationship is going somewhere?"

"No." He shook his head. "I was on the floor looking for the ring."

Her eyebrows flew up. "The ring?"

His shoulders slumped. *That must be the least romantic way to propose in history. But there's no turning back now. I'll just have to roll with it.* Straightening himself back up, he met her eyes and said, "That's right, I got you a ring. I came here tonight so I could propose to you."

Carrie Ann's eyes widened and her mouth dropped open. Before she could say anything, Owen continued. "You're right, Carrie Ann, you deserve more." Tears prickled his eyes. "And I want more. I always did, but ... well, I was afraid to ask you."

She shook her head. "Why? Couldn't you tell I wanted you to? I'm not exactly the subtle type."

He looked at the floor. "Neither was Casey. I thought she wanted me to propose, back before she left the first time. But that's what happened—she left right after I asked her."

"You asked Casey to marry you? You never told me that."

"Yeah, well, it wasn't exactly a moment I wanted to remember. It was humiliating. She didn't even say no. She seemed happy and excited when I proposed. Then, the next day, I found the ring I gave her with a note telling me she needed to move on. Owen sucked in a deep breath. "When I thought about proposing to you, all I could think about was that you might leave too. But then you decided to leave anyway. So, I had to at least try."

"Owen," Carrie Ann stepped close to him and cupped his face in her hands, "I'm not her. Don't you know that by now? I want to marry you. And I'm many things, but fickle isn't one of them. I'm not playing with your emotions."

He met her eyes sheepishly. "After all my screwups, you still want to marry me?"

She cocked her head to the side. "The ring you brought ... it's not the same one you gave Casey, is it?"

"Absolutely not! I would never do that. I sold the other one a long time ago."

"Then I guess we better get looking for that ring so you can put it on my finger where it belongs." Her face broke in a wide grin. "We're getting married!"

Owen beamed. "Let's find that ring."

Rebecca L. Marsh

Chapter 26

Marissa was sound asleep when her phone rang. Rubbing the sleep from her eyes, she picked up her phone and glanced at the caller ID. She was expecting to see either Owen's name or Carrie Ann's. She couldn't wait to find out how Owen's proposal went. But, squinting at the screen, she saw Cory's number instead. She answered the call.

"Cory, what's going on? Is something wrong at the store?" She asked, wondering if Carrie Ann's absence was leading to some kind of issue. Tim was supposed to open the store today, but he was young. Maybe he hadn't shown up yet.

"I wouldn't know. I haven't made it there myself."

Marissa's forehead crinkled in confusion as she waited for him to say more.

"I was getting ready to leave for the store when I noticed the door open to Hallie's room. I peeked in and she wasn't there. I thought she'd gotten up early and was downstairs having breakfast, but she wasn't there either."

Marissa sat up in bed and pushed the covers back as worry began to flood through her. "Cory, what are you saying?"

"She's not here, Marissa. She's gone. Is she at your house?"

"I don't think so, but I was still sleeping. I'll check with Howard and look around. Hold on." Her heart raced as adrenaline poured into her. She couldn't help but be reminded of a time a couple of years ago when Maisy had gotten very upset with her and run off. She certainly hoped this incident was nothing like that.

Throwing on a bathrobe and rushing out of the bedroom, Marissa headed to the kitchen to find Howard. "Cory, was she upset?" she said into the phone as she went.

"Not as far as I know. Last night we watched a movie together and she was having a good time. I can't imagine what could have upset her between then and now." Marissa heard the stress in his voice.

Reaching the kitchen, she found Howard at the stove making scrambled eggs. Sylvie sat in her infant seat, her little arms waving around, but no one else was in the room. "Howard, Cory's on the phone. He's looking for Hallie. She's not there. Is she here? Have you seen her?"

He turned at the distress in her voice and shook his head. "No, I haven't seen her." He stepped closer to her and put a steadying hand on her arm. "But let's look around for her."

Marissa nodded and relayed the message to Cory while Howard took the pan of eggs off the heat. They went to Maisy's room first and knocked on the door.

A few minutes later, Maisy opened the door, still in her pajamas. "Is breakfast ready?" she asked.

"No." Howard stooped down, bringing himself face to face with Maisy. "Sweetheart, have you seen Hallie this morning?"

Her nose crinkled. "No. Isn't she at her grandparents' house?"

Howard stood back up. "She's supposed to be." He looked at Marissa. "Let's go ask Charlie."

She nodded and they knocked on the door of their guest room with Maisy trailing behind them. Charlie came to the door. He was dressed and had a comic book in hand.

"Charlie," Marissa said, "have you seen Hallie?"

He shook his head. "Why would I have seen her? She's at the Hobbs's house." His face changed, clouding with worry. "Isn't she?"

"It seems she isn't. Cory is on the phone and looking for her," Howard said.

Panic rose in Marissa's chest. She found herself once again remembering that day when Maisy ran away. They'd found her standing on the edge of a cliff. *This is different. Today won't be like that.* "Oh no, Howard, this can't be happening again."

Howard glanced at the phone that was in Marissa's hand, hanging at her side. "Don't panic. Let's check the rest of the house."

They walked around the whole house, but there was no sign of Hallie. Marissa lifted the phone and met her husband's eyes.

"Tell him she isn't here and we're going to go right over and check Owen's house in case she went there."

Marissa relayed the message and they rushed to Owen's house. Using a spare key they kept in case of emergency, they entered the house, split up, and checked the house from top to bottom. But Hallie was nowhere to be seen. With a heavy heart, Marissa reported back to Cory.

"Are there any places around the island that she likes to go to?" Marissa asked Cory the question, but she tipped her gaze to Howard as she did so. He'd been spending a lot of time with Hallie during the workdays over the course of the summer. He might have some ideas of places to check. Marissa's phone was set to speaker so they could all hear one another.

"She's enjoyed fishing with me. She may have gone to one of those spots," Cory said.

"She had fun the days we went to the park," Howard added.

"And the pond there is one of our fishing spots," Cory said.

"Okay, we'll go look there," Marissa said.

"Good. I'll go to the pier and Doreen can check around town in case she went there," Cory said.

Marissa and Howard hurried to the park. When they arrived, they jumped out of the car, and Marissa tucked

Sylvie into a strap-on baby carrier before turning to Howard to ask, "What do you think is the best way to search?"

"You and Maisy take the north side and the playground. Charlie and I will take the south side and the pond," he said. "We should be able to check the whole park pretty quickly that way."

Marissa nodded and headed off with Maisy close behind. As they walked, Marissa couldn't help but think about the strangeness of once again searching the island for a missing child, and by her side was the child that had been missing the last time.

"Maisy," she said. "Can you think of any other places she might have gone? I mean, you two are getting to be friends, maybe you would know where to look better than anyone and I didn't think to ask before now."

Maisy shrugged. "I can't think of anywhere else. I thought she was doing okay. I mean, I thought she was pretty happy lately. I don't know why she would run away."

Marissa made a quick study of her child's face and saw the worry there. "She didn't say anything to you then?"

"No. Last time we talked, she was feeling better, not worse."

Marissa put an arm around Maisy's shoulders. "Don't worry, we'll find her."

An hour later, Marissa and Howard met up with Cory and Doreen at a diner in town. They had searched everywhere they could think of and still didn't know where Hallie was. Since the kids were hungry, having never eaten breakfast, the diner seemed like a good place.

When everyone else was finished ordering food, Marissa looked at Doreen. She sat with her face in her hands.

"Doreen, do you want anything to eat?" Marissa asked gently.

Looking up, Doreen answered, "No. I can't eat right now. I'm too worried about Hallie."

"I understand." Marissa patted the other woman's back. "Is someone watching your house in case she shows back up?"

"Yes, our next-door neighbor has her eyes peeled. She hasn't seen a thing." Doreen took a deep breath. "I don't know what to do. I don't even know why she did this."

Cory reached across the table and squeezed his wife's hand. "I think it might be time to call Amanda."

Doreen looked up sharply. "You think it's come to that? She'll be crazy upset. She'll blame us." Her voice grew higher at the end with panic.

"Honey, unless you can think of some other places to look, we need to start taking the next steps. Hallie is only twelve and she's missing. Her mother needs to know." Cory's voice was tender but serious.

"It's an island. She can't have gone far," Doreen asserted.

"She came to the island by herself," Cory pointed out.

Doreen hung her head. They all knew Cory was right.

"Did you check and see if she's been on the ferry?" Howard asked. "Wouldn't they notice a kid getting on alone?"

"You'd think so," Cory said. "And you'd think they'd call the police and report something like that, but they didn't do that when she came here."

"I'm not so sure that would be the protocol. Sometimes parents do put kids that age on ferries and even planes to travel to places alone. They probably just thought that's what was going on. But you should contact them. They likely would notice a child traveling alone," Howard said.

With a nod, Cory whipped out his phone and made the call. When he hung up, he turned his attention to the group. "They haven't noticed a young girl on the ferry alone.

But they admit they could have missed her." His eyes met Doreen's. "I'm calling Amanda now, but I think I'll take the call outside."

Her eyes welling with tears, Doreen nodded.

As soon as Cory was gone, Marissa said, "I'm sure we'll find her, Doreen. By now, the whole island is probably on the lookout for her."

"I hope so." Doreen sniffed and wiped her eyes.

"I don't know if it's any comfort, but wherever Hallie is, I'm sure she's okay. She's a resourceful girl," Howard added.

The misery on Doreen's face told Marissa it wasn't any comfort.

After a moment of silent waiting, the food arrived, and the hungry kids dug in. Howard and Marissa picked at their food slowly while Doreen sat twisting her hands.

When Cory returned to the table, his face was solemn. "Amanda and Dustin are coming to the island on the next ferry."

Doreen's eyes fell to the table. "There must be some other places to check."

"What about the beach?" Maisy asked. "She likes the beach."

"I sent Millie to both of the public beaches. Hallie wasn't there," Cory said.

"If there's nowhere else to search right now, then what else can we do?" Doreen asked.

"There are the woods ... but would she go there?" Howard asked.

"She doesn't like the woods," Charlie piped up. "She told me so when I was reading my guidebook to her."

Howard sighed. "The woods cover a large area. If it isn't likely she would go there, then it's probably a waste of time at this point."

"We could check the rocky beaches, but that's a lot of ground to cover too," Cory said.

"Yeah, it might be more worthwhile than the woods though," Howard said. "When does the ferry arrive."

Doreen's eyes dropped back down to her hands at the mention of the ferry. Marissa reached over and grasped her hand, trying to reassure her.

"It'll be here in an hour and a half," Cory said.

"Then we've got time to check some of the rocky beach areas before it comes in. It's probably best to start at the two sandy beach areas and walk on from there. It would be hard for her to access the rocky beaches any other way," Howard said. "And it wouldn't be any easier for us."

All in agreement, they made a plan to split up. And when the kids were finished eating, they headed out.

Rebecca L. Marsh

Chapter 27

As she walked along the beach, Hallie ambled around the rocks while she listened to the sound of the seagull's cries from up above. She glanced up at them in the cloudless, blue expanse and noticed how high in the sky the sun was getting. *It must be close to lunchtime.* As she thought about it, her stomach grumbled. She'd left her grandparents' house without eating breakfast.

After tossing and turning all night, she had needed to get away and be in a peaceful place with her thoughts. She wanted to try and work out how she felt about everything and everyone in her life. This summer had been one of changing perceptions as she kept learning things weren't what she thought they were.

Hallie located a large rock in a nearby outcropping and sat down. She rubbed her empty stomach. She'd have to go back to the house if she wanted to eat. She didn't have money to buy anything. She hadn't even thought to bring her backpack or a snack. She'd pulled on a pair of shorts and a t-shirt, and left. The only thing she did bring with her was a bottle of water and it was a good thing she'd thought of that.

Maybe I should go back to the house. Grandma and Granddad will be worried. They must know I'm gone by now.

Hallie squinted as she looked up at the sky. It was getting hot and her water was nearly gone. The only thing saving her from the heat was the light breeze that blew through her loose, sweat-dampened hair. It was time to go back to her grandparents and talk to them about the letter. That was the only way she was going to find out if there was any truth to it. She'd also have to deal with them being angry with her for leaving the house alone.

With a sigh, she stood up and began to walk down the beach again. She was close to the ferry dock and there was a path there to get off the beach. She looked out at the ocean for a moment and watched a pelican swoop toward the water. *I guess he's looking for some lunch too.*

As Hallie approached the ferry dock, she heard voices and car engines. She looked up and saw that the ferry was docked and people were disembarking.

Then something caught her eye—a white SUV that looked just like her mother's. She stopped in her tracks and stared at the vehicle. Her jaw dropped when she caught sight of the sticker on the back bumper. She couldn't read the words from where she stood, but she didn't need to. She knew that sticker—the black background and the yellow smiley face. The words on it read, *my child is a fantastic student.* It had come from her school. That was her mother's car.

Standing still, practically holding her breath, she watched the car drive away toward the residential section of the island. *I stayed out here too long. Grandma and Granddad must have called Mom and told her.*

She watched the rest of the cars leave the ferry and drive away. Then she watched a new group drive onto the ferry. If her mother knew she'd left the house, then her grandparents were even more worried than she thought. And they wouldn't have called her mother unless they had looked for her themselves first. That meant everyone on the island probably knew she was missing.

She slumped down onto another large rock and bit her lower lip. *I should go to the house and deal with it. Mom isn't going to leave until I'm found and she'll probably blame Grandma and Granddad. She'll be mad at them again.*

Her stomach growled painfully. She rubbed it as she thought about what she should do. *If I go back to the house, is Mom going to make me go home? Leon will be there.* Hallie's breathing grew faster at the thought. *Grandma said she wouldn't let Mom take me home until she believed what I said about Leon. ... But can she really stop Mom from taking me home? Mom will be mad at Grandma because she lost me. She won't listen.*

Hallie glanced at the path from the beach into town. If she was really careful, she could climb up the path and take the long way around to the residential area. She didn't think anyone would see her if she went that way and she could make it to a good hiding place. Her stomach would stay empty, but she could get out of the sun and it would give her a little time to think things through.

Owen wore a goofy grin for the entire drive back from Summerville. He couldn't help it. Carrie Ann was going to marry him. He was so happy, he thought he might explode. And to think he could have gotten here so much sooner if he hadn't convinced himself not to try. *There's no need to linger on my mistakes and the pain I've put us both through. All that is over.* As he thought it, he found himself looking in the rearview mirror to verify she was still following him in Marissa's minivan.

Sighing at his foolishness, Owen thought, *old fears die hard.* It would take a little time to let go of his fear of losing her, but he would get there.

On the ferry, they both went above deck to enjoy the ride. As Carrie Ann held his hand, he rubbed his thumb over the diamond setting of the ring he'd given her. He felt joy in knowing she wanted it there and relief because they finally found it the previous night after searching every inch of the hallway carpet.

"It's a beautiful day," Carrie Ann said, tilting her face up toward the blue sky.

Owen barely noticed what the weather was like as he drank in the sight of the woman at his side, the outline of her face, her soft purple-streaked hair blowing in the breeze. "It sure is," he agreed. "Today would be a beautiful day if it was raining cats and dogs with gale-force winds. Today I have you."

She gave him that look, the one that said, *you could have had me all along, you idiot*. He held up a hand to stop her from saying it again. "I know it was my fault I lost you for a while. I know I was a fool. But today *I have you*. And I love you."

The look on her face softened and her eyes grew moist. "Today and for the rest of your life."

He grinned. "Today and for the rest of my life."

Leaning in, he kissed her lips gently. When she pulled back, she pointed a finger at him and raised her eyebrows. "And you better not even think about trying to get away from me again. I'll chase you down."

He saluted her and said, "Yes ma'am."

She laughed and slapped him playfully on the arm. "I can't wait to tell everyone. But I guess Marissa already knows."

"She does, but you can tell everyone else that I finally woke up and did the right thing."

When the ferry neared the dock, they went back to the cars and prepared to disembark, after which they drove straight to Marissa's house. It was too late in the day to get any work in, so they were going to drive over, give Howard and the kids the good news (Marissa would be at the store working), and pick up Charlie and Hallie. After that, Owen would take them all out to a celebratory dinner.

Owen's joy deflated into curiosity when they rang the bell at his sister's house and no one answered. He glanced at his watch. Marissa should definitely still be at work and she would have taken Howard's car since Carrie Ann still had hers. So where were Howard and the kids?

He looked at Carrie Ann and frowned. "They should be here."

She shrugged. "Maybe they went out for a walk. Why don't you call Howard and find out."

With a nod, he pulled out his phone and dialed.

"Owen, are you back on the island?" Howard's voice sounded tight.

"Yes, but where are you? I'm at your house." Owen's forehead creased in concern as a pause followed. "Howard?"

"There's some trouble." Howard sucked in an audible breath. "Hallie went missing this morning and we're still trying to find her."

"What?!" Owen's panicked response brought Carrie Ann's eyes up to him.

"What's wrong?" she asked, taking hold of his arm.

He met her eyes and touched her hand to let her know he heard her, but couldn't answer right away. Then he spoke to Howard. "What do you mean she's missing? Have you checked my house?"

"Of course, right after we searched ours. We checked the park and the beaches. No one's seen her."

"What if she left the island? Oh, my word, this is bad. What can Carrie Ann and I do? Where else is there to look?" Owen rattled the words off as quickly as he could.

"Right now, we're talking to her parents … and the police. But we don't think she's left the island. None of the ferry or dock workers remember seeing a young girl alone."

Owen stilled, unable to breathe. *They were talking to the police. This might be even worse than when Maisy ran away.* "Has anyone checked Tara's Pointe? Or any of the other cliffs?" He hated to even think about that possibility.

"Not all of them. But it's strange, Owen, Cory says she wasn't upset as far as he or Doreen know. They said she was happy last night before bed. Then, this morning, she was gone."

With his next question, dread rose up in Owen's chest. "How is Amanda taking it?"

There was a short pause and Owen wondered if Amanda was in earshot. "She's understandably upset. She's talking to the police right now."

"Where are you?"

"We're all at the Hobbs's house."

"We'll be right over." Owen turned worried eyes toward Carrie Ann as he slipped his phone into his pocket. "Hallie's missing."

"I gathered that. What happened?" Carrie Ann asked.

Owen shrugged. "No one knows. Apparently, she was happy last night and then gone this morning. Amanda and her husband are here. They called the police."

"Then we better get over there and see how we can help. I'll call the store and have them close up until we find Hallie. And I'll call everyone else I can think of. We'll get the whole island looking for her."

Owen responded with a weak smile. When Carrie Ann set her mind on a mission, nothing stopped her. She would have everyone searching the island within the next hour, with the possible exception of Mrs. Benson, one of the town's older widows and the only one with a sour disposition.

They left Marissa's minivan and jumped into Owen's truck. Moments later, they were knocking on the front door of the Hobbs' house. Marissa opened the door with the baby in her arms. She wore a drawn expression. *This must be waking up all kinds of bad memories for her.*

Owen reached out and hugged his sister. When he pulled back, there were tears on her cheeks.

"Thanks, I really needed that." She shook her head. "I can't believe this is happening." Marissa stepped back and allowed Owen and Carrie Ann into the house.

"I can't either. But we'll find her," Owen said with determination he didn't fully feel.

"That's right, we will," Carrie Ann said. "I've got everyone on it. Main street is shutting down until she's found. We'll scour the whole island if we have to."

Marissa's eyebrows went up. "Wow, everyone shut down?"

Carrie Ann met her eyes. "The benefit of small-town life. We pull together when we need to."

"We should tell the police about all the help that's coming. Did you tell them to come here so our efforts can be coordinated?" Marissa headed toward the living room with Owen and Carrie Ann close behind.

"I told them to go to the community center. No way will they all fit here," Carrie Ann answered.

Marissa tapped her forehead. "Of course. You're right."

As they stepped into the living room, Owen saw a lovely woman with light brown skin talking to a police officer and assumed it was Amanda. Then he caught sight of Doreen sobbing in Cory's arms. He ambled over to them and placed a hand on Doreen's shoulder. She looked up, her eyes red-rimmed and puffy.

"Owen, I'm glad you're here," Cory said. "Hallie's been staying in your house for a few weeks now. Can you think of any other place we should look?"

Owen exhaled and looked up for a moment. "I can't see her going there again, but someone did check my garage thoroughly, right?"

"I did," Marissa said from behind him.

"I don't know. You checked all the places I'd think she might go. I can't see her heading for the woods, but I guess they need to be checked anyway," Owen said.

"The police are going to arrange a search of the whole island." Cory kept his arm around his wife in a supportive gesture.

"Good. Carrie Ann's arranged for tons of help with that. Everyone is heading to the community center," Owen said. He looked up as Amanda stepped away from the officers and headed toward him. Her gaze was steely.

"Are you Owen?" she asked.

He nodded, feeling all the shame she appeared to be willing on him.

"I trusted you." Amanda's voice rumbled low like a growl. "And look what happened."

"I'm so sorry." Owen hung his head, his eyes on the floor.

"Don't you go blaming him." Doreen, who had just been weeping, sounded unexpectedly strong, bringing Owen's eyes back up. "As I recall, she ran away from your house too."

Amanda shrank back a little with the hit, but only for a moment. "Don't turn this around. Not when my child is missing."

Cory held his hands out toward his wife and Amanda. "Finding Hallie is the only thing that matters right now. We can sort the rest out later."

Doreen nodded her agreement, and Amanda grudgingly did the same. A moment later, one of the police officers stepped over to them. "I'm told there's a large group of people down at the community center waiting to help us search for Hallie."

Owen's eyes found Carrie Ann. She'd walked away from the argument and moved things along in a more helpful way. He smiled at her and mouthed the words, *thank you*.

"Listen up!" A stocky police officer named Ralph clapped his hands to get the attention of the crowd gathered at the community center. He was one of only six officers on the island. Normally, there were three officers on day shift and three on nights, but they had all come in to help with the search.

The crowd quieted down and Ralph began to speak to them. "Okay people, we've got a missing girl and we're going to find her. I'm going to have my officers split you into groups and they will direct you in searching different parts of the island." His thick, dark mustache twitched as he nodded to the other officers.

When the groups were formed, Marissa found herself with the group that was searching in town. Along with Howard, Maisy, and more than a dozen other islanders, Marissa scoured through and around every building on Main Street.

When Sylvie began to fuss, Marissa bounced and spoke to her softly, but it didn't soothe the baby.

"Maisy," Marissa said, "Let's find Howard. I'm going to have to take Sylvie home. She's hungry and I'm out of bottles. You can stay and help Howard search."

"I'm hungry too," Maisy said. "Can I go home with you for a while?"

Marissa nodded and scanned the street for her husband. When they found him, he told Marissa to take his car home and he'd get Owen to drop him off later.

After driving home, Marissa and Maisy walked inside. Sylvie was beside herself crying for milk. "Go see what you can find in the kitchen to eat. I've got to feed your sister. When she's done, I'll come help you."

"I can find something." Maisy headed off, and Marissa was grateful she was being so helpful and accommodating. It was only five o'clock, but she was exhausted from the searching and the emotional upheaval. She was terribly worried about Hallie and hated to leave the search, but it felt good to sink into the rocking chair in the baby's room.

When Sylvie was fed and sleeping, Marissa strode to the kitchen to see what Maisy was up to. However, when she walked into the room, her daughter wasn't there. With a scowl, she headed to Maisy's room. *Was I in the baby's room that long?*

She knocked on Maisy's bedroom door and waited, but no response came. Pushing the door open, Marissa glanced around. Chester poked his orange and white head out from under the bed and meowed at her. Maisy was nowhere to be seen.

"Maisy?" Marissa called out, worry sneaking into her mind. *You know Maisy is here somewhere. You're only worried because Hallie is missing and it's got you on edge,* she told herself. She hurried to the living room, but Maisy wasn't there either. "Maisy!" she yelled again.

When no answer came, she reached for her phone and dialed Howard's number. The moment he answered, before he could even get a word out, fearful words tumbled from Marissa's mouth, "I can't find Maisy."

There was a short pause. "What do you mean you can't find her?"

"She went to the kitchen to get something to eat while I took care of Sylvie. But when I was done feeding the baby, she wasn't in the kitchen. She's not in the living room or her bedroom either and she isn't answering me when I call for her."

"Calm down," Howard spoke in a soft but firm voice in response to her alarm. "She's there somewhere. You're scared because Hallie is missing and because … well, you know." He didn't say the words—that she was worried because Maisy ran away once a few years ago. "But Maisy wouldn't run away. You know that. She wants to find Hallie, not disappear herself."

"Then where is she?" Marissa knew he was right, but she couldn't fight the urge to panic.

"Did you check outside?"

Marissa squeezed her eyes shut and pinched the bridge of her nose. She should have thought of that. "No. I'll go do that now."

"Good. I'll stay on the line with you while you do."

Marissa stepped out onto the front porch and examined the yard. She didn't see Maisy and there was nowhere to hide out front. "Not here. I'll check the back." She went back through the house and out to the back patio. She didn't see Maisy, but there was one more place to look.

Rebecca L. Marsh

Chapter 28

Hallie stirred and groaned as someone shook her shoulder.

"Hallie, wake up," Maisy said close to her ear.

Rubbing her eyes and licking her parched lips with a tongue that was almost as dry, Hallie rolled over on the hard ground. She peered up at her friend's face.

"What are you doing here?" Maisy asked in an exasperated tone. "Everyone is looking for you—and I mean *everyone*."

"I know," Hallie mumbled.

Maisy stood up and towered over her. "And you're still hiding? Do you want us all freaking out?"

Hallie scowled at the harsh tone. "No, but I can't come out *now*."

There was silence for a moment while Maisy assessed her. Cocking her head to the side, Maisy asked, "Why not?"

Hallie sucked in a deep breath and released it slowly. "Because my mom is here. I saw her drive off the ferry."

"Yeah, I know she's here. She's worried about you. That's what happens when you run away."

Hallie heard the accusation in Maisy's voice and knew her mother wasn't the only one who had been worried. "I'm sorry I made everyone worry. I wasn't running away."

"You've been gone all day. What do you call it?" Maisy put a hand on her hip.

Shame washed through Hallie and she turned her eyes to the ground. "I said I'm sorry. I just wanted to walk on the beach. I needed to think. I was planning to be back before anyone noticed, but I guess time got away from me." All the confusion about the letter she found rolled back through her, making her empty stomach hurt. She rubbed it absently. It would have been handy if she could have remembered some of the edible plants Charlie told her about. She was hungry enough to try them.

Maisy's expression softened and she sat down next to Hallie. "What did you need to think about?"

Hallie shook her head, not wanting to tell anyone. But Maisy didn't let it go. "The whole town is out looking for you. If you've got something on your mind you need to work out, you better talk about it now. Pretty soon, my mother will be looking for me too," she added for emphasis.

Biting her lip, Hallie reluctantly nodded. "I was looking at one of my dad's old yearbooks and I found this letter. It was from my mom to my dad when he was overseas—back before I was born." She stopped as her throat tightened.

"What did it say?"

Hallie pursed her lips. "My mom said she didn't want to tell my grandparents she was pregnant because …" It hurt so much to think there was any chance it could be true. "Because she thought they wouldn't like it."

Maisy's face scrunched up. "That's crazy. Mr. and Mrs. Hobbs love you. Why did she think that?"

"I guess because she also thought they didn't like her and my dad being married." Hallie ran a finger through the dirt on the ground.

Maisy put a hand on Hallie's shoulder. "I don't know how they felt about your parents being married, but it isn't true about you. They love you like crazy. Anyone can see that."

"Now they do. But what if they didn't want me?"

Maisy shrugged. "That doesn't matter now."

Hallie's head whipped up and she met Maisy's eyes with a sharp look. "It *does* matter. How would you feel if you weren't wanted?"

"I didn't want Sylvie at first," Maisy whispered. "But I love her now. The way I feel now is what matters."

"So, you're saying it doesn't even matter if they didn't want me?"

"I'm saying, feelings can be complicated—that's what my psychologist says. Haven't you ever changed your mind about how you feel about someone?"

"Yeah, but this is different," Hallie insisted.

"Why? Do you think Sylvie should be mad at me because I had a hard time getting a new sister after my other sister died?"

"That's different too. It's not the same thing."

"You don't know what it is. You don't know what they were thinking or feeling. You don't even know if they really felt the way your mom thought."

Hallie considered that and she had to admit it was true. "I know. But if I come out and ask them, I'll have to deal with my mother wanting to take me home." She met Maisy's eyes with a pleading gaze. "I *can't* go home yet."

"If you're not going to come out and deal with your mom, then what are you going to do? What other choice is there?"

Hallie pulled her knees up against her chest and wrapped her arms around them. "I don't know ... if you helped me ..."

Maisy's head whipped side to side. "No way! I'm not hiding you in this fort." When Hallie stared at her, begging with her eyes, Maisy continued, "It would never work. You already did that with Charlie and Uncle Owen's garage. My parents will figure it out in no time and then we'll both be in trouble. Besides, you can't live out here. That's nuts!"

Hallie hung her head. Maisy was right. "Okay." She grabbed Maisy's hand. "You'll go with me?"

Before Maisy could answer, footsteps came across the yard and Marissa peered into the fort at them.

Relief washed through Marissa when she looked inside the backyard fort and saw not only Maisy but Hallie too. She put a hand over her heart and let a woosh of air out of her lungs. "There you are." She met her daughter's eyes to let her know she was talking to both of them, then she addressed Hallie. "The whole town is worried sick about you." She glanced around the haphazard structure, mentally slapping herself for not thinking to look here sooner. "Have you been here all day?"

Hallie shook her head and shrank back against the plywood wall. "I was out on the beach for a while."

Marissa released another breath, relieved that they hadn't alerted the whole town when all they really needed to do was check their backyard. Still, she should have thought about looking here. If Hallie was at the beach earlier, they must have missed her with their timing.

"She just needed to think," Maisy said.

Marissa glanced at her daughter. She could tell by the look in Maisy's eyes that she was trying to ease the judgment on her friend. "It's still not okay that she left her grandparents' house alone—without even telling anyone."

"She knows that …," Maisy began, but Hallie put a hand up to stop her.

"It's okay. I'm ready to go back to my grandparents' house now." She looked down at the dirt. "And I'm sorry I worried everyone."

Marissa nodded. "Good."

"Can I have some water first?" Hallie asked.

"Of course," Marissa said, concern etching her face. "Have you gone all day without water?"

"No, but I only took one bottle with me. I ran out a while ago."

Marissa nodded. "And I suppose you're pretty hungry too."

Hallie placed a hand on her empty stomach. "Yes, ma'am. I haven't eaten all day."

"Well then, I don't suppose there's any harm in feeding you before I take you to face the music."

Maisy smiled and patted her friend on the shoulder.

"Thank you," Hallie said before crawling out the door.

Once they were inside and Hallie was devouring the leftover spaghetti Marissa had heated for her, Marissa called Howard and told him she found their missing girl. "I'll bring her to the Hobbs's house as soon as she finishes eating."

"All right. I'll let everyone know the search is over." Howard clicked off and Marissa turned her attention back to the girls at the table.

"Slow down a little, Hallie. I don't want you to get a tummy ache," Marissa cautioned her.

Hallie nodded without looking up. Seeing little change in the rate at which the child shoveled food into her mouth, Marissa sighed and hoped she didn't make herself sick.

When the spaghetti was gone and Hallie had chugged down two cups of water, Marissa gathered the two girls and the baby and headed to Cory's house.

Hallie's stomach felt better when she finished eating, but when they pulled up in front of her grandparents' house, it came alive with a swarm of butterflies. *I should have eaten less.* She pressed a hand to her belly and slid out of the car as slowly as possible. *I wish I could talk to Grandma and Granddad before I have to see Mom.* But as she glanced at her mother's car, she knew that wasn't likely to happen. Mom took the time to drive here, the chances of her being put off were slim.

Hallie gladly waited, hiding on the far side of the minivan, while Marissa got the baby out of the car. Any excuse to wait a little longer was a good one. *Mom's gonna be so mad. She won't listen. She never listens.* Hallie's stomach rolled.

The door to the minivan closed. "Let's go," Marissa said, then her tone softened as she met Hallie's eyes. "Waiting won't make it any better."

Hallie's lips tightened and she dug her fingernails into her palms as she climbed the porch steps. Mom would make her go home and Leon would be there. *I'm so stupid! I should never have left the house.*

By the time she made it to the front door, it swung open and her mother rushed out and swept Hallie up in her arms. "You're okay. Thank God, you're okay!"

Burying her face in her mother's shoulder, Hallie enjoyed the moment of love pouring from her mother. She knew it wouldn't last.

When Mom pulled back and fixed a steely glare on her, Hallie sucked in a deep breath and dropped her chin. "What in the world were you thinking running off like that? Do you think you can just take off whenever you want? Don't you know how worried everyone was?" The questions tumbled out of Mom's mouth so fast they blended together.

"I'm sorry," Hallie mumbled.

"You're going to have to do a lot better than that, young lady." Her mother's voice flared with irritation. She took Hallie by the wrist and ushered her into the house and to the living room.

Hallie took a quick look at her grandparents and Dustin before answering her mother. "I know, but can I talk to Grandma and Granddad for a few minutes first?" It didn't hurt to ask.

"No, you can't talk to them first. You're going to answer me." Mom put both hands on her hips.

Hallie grimaced. Maybe it did hurt to ask. She avoided making eye contact so as not to see the anger and disappointment in them. "I know it was wrong to leave the house alone and not tell anyone. I didn't mean to worry everyone. I just wanted to walk on the beach and think for a while. I thought I would be back before anyone got up."

"That's no excuse. Sneaking out isn't okay even if no one is up to notice. You know better," Mom scolded.

"I know." Hallie hung her head. "I shouldn't have done it. I'm sorry." She didn't know what else to say. "I really need to talk to Grandma and Granddad now if that's okay."

"I'm not done with you …" Mom stopped as Dustin touched her shoulder.

"We can talk to her some more in a bit. It won't hurt anything to let her have a few minutes with her grandparents," he said. Hallie met his eyes gratefully.

Mom agreed grudgingly and left the room with him.

Hallie looked at her grandfather, then her grandmother. She licked her lips and tried to form the right words.

"How about we sit down and you can tell us what happened this morning," Granddad said. He led her to the couch and they all sat down.

Taking a deep breath, Hallie studied her fingernails as she began to speak. Her words came out slow at first and gained speed as she went along. "Last night, after I went upstairs, I was looking through one of Dad's old yearbooks and I found a letter. It was a letter Mom wrote to him when he was overseas before I was born. She said something about not wanting to tell you guys she was pregnant because she didn't think you would be happy about it. She said you didn't want them to get married." Hallie paused to catch her breath. Then she looked at Granddad first and then Grandma, making eye contact with each for a moment. "When I read the letter, I felt upset and confused. That's why I went to the beach to think." She paused and they stayed silent, waiting for her to finish what she needed to say. She swallowed. "Is it true … that you didn't want me?"

"Oh baby," Grandma said. She reached out to put her arms around Hallie, but Hallie pulled back from her. "I'm so sorry you would ever think that. Of course we wanted you."

"You were a gift, Hallie. We loved you from the first time we knew you existed," Granddad said.

Still not satisfied, Hallie frowned. "Then why did my mother think you would be upset?"

Grandma shook her head. "I don't know."

"Is it true that you didn't want them to get married?"

There was a short silence, then Granddad answered. "Not exactly …"

Before he could finish, Grandma interrupted, "It was never about your mother personally. They were so young, and Daniel was just beginning his career."

Granddad jumped in again, saying, "We were concerned a new military career and a new marriage would be too much all at once. We love your mother."

"We always have," Grandma finished. "For some reason, she's continually had a hard time seeing it."

Relief flooded through Hallie, and briefly, she felt better. Then she realized she'd run off and upset everyone for nothing. Heat rushed to her cheeks with the shame of it. "I'm sorry for leaving this morning. I should have just talked to you."

Granddad patted her knee. "We all make mistakes."

"Yes, we do. However, running away every time you get upset is a problem, Hallie." Grandma met her eyes with an expression that managed to be soft and yet stern at the same time.

Hallie's chin dropped to her chest. "I know."

"We need to talk to your mother about all this now," Grandma said.

Her head whipping up, Hallie spoke in an urgent tone, "She'll want me to go back home with her. Leon's there."

"Then it's time to talk to her about that," Granddad said. "But first we need to explain today to her."

Grandma took Hallie's hand. "We'll be right here with you for all of it."

Hallie whimpered at the thought of the conversation they were about to have, then she nodded. It was time.

Hallie waited on the couch while Granddad called her mother and Dustin to join them. As she sat there, she held her breath. *She'll make me go home. She won't listen about Leon.* By the time Mom and Dustin were seated across from her, Hallie had balled her hands into fists and her nails were digging into her flesh.

"Your grandfather says you have more to tell us about why you ran off," Mom said, trying to meet Hallie's eyes.

Hallie avoided allowing the eye contact. She nodded and told her mother and step-father the same thing she'd told her grandparents. "But Grandma and Granddad just told me that they did want me and that they love you too. They were just worried because you guys were young and Daddy was just starting out in the Army."

Her mother nodded curtly. *She still doesn't believe they love her.* Hallie frowned. She had hoped her mother was past all that.

"Well, now that we've made the trip here, let's get you packed up and go home. The boys are with Mrs. Thompson down the street and we need to get back and take them off her hands as soon as we can."

Hallie's breathing quickened and her head swung side to side furiously. "No! I can't go back home. Not until summer is over."

"Don't be silly, Hallie. There's no sense in us coming back in two weeks," Mom said. She didn't seem to notice Hallie's distress.

"I can't! Please!" Tears streamed down Hallie's cheeks. She pushed her body back into the couch as if she could anchor herself there.

"We need to talk about that, Amanda," Grandma said in a tone that was not to be ignored.

Mom looked over at her, dark eyes flashing in surprise. "She's my daughter, Doreen. I can take her home whenever I please."

"No one's arguing that," Granddad said. "But there's a reason she came here in the first place." He gestured toward Hallie and her tear-stained face. "Can't you see how upset she is?"

Mom looked at Hallie then and took everything in. She inhaled deeply. "Okay, tell me why you don't want to go home."

Hallie's mouth went dry. Mom was listening, and yet she wasn't. Hallie could tell by the look on her mother's face. Still, she had to try.

"I can't go home until summer is over because I can't stay home alone." Tears filled her eyes and her throat tightened at the thought of being alone with Leon lurking about. Her voice came back as little more than a squeak. "I can't—not ever. Please let me stay here."

Mom huffed out a breath and tried not to look annoyed. "Hallie, you're twelve now and we can't afford day camp when we're paying for the boys to be in daycare. Even if we let you stay for the rest of summer, this issue will come back up again the next time we need to leave you alone in the house, won't it?"

Hallie's eyebrows drew together at the question. Her mother wasn't wrong.

"Hallie, it's time to tell your mother what you told us," Granddad said gently.

After a long, deep breath, Hallie spoke. "It isn't just about being alone. I don't really care about being alone for a while. But I can't be there alone when Leon comes around."

There, it was out. Now they would see if Mom was willing to listen.

"Hallie, we've been through this. Leon is family. There's no reason to be afraid of him," Mom said. She was trying to sound understanding and soothing, but Hallie could hear the impatience. She still didn't believe.

"See, I knew you wouldn't listen! I told you what he tried to do, but you won't believe me. *That's* why I ran away. *That's* why I need to stay here." Hallie turned her head away and tried to rein in the emotions that rushed through her. Her breathing was heavy and ragged as she tried not to cry again.

"I did listen, but you're being—" Mom stopped talking abruptly when Dustin cut in.

"*What* did Leon try to do?" He asked. His voice was firm enough to keep Mom silent.

Hallie turned to face him and met his eyes, before dropping her gaze to the floor. It was hard to say the words—to keep telling people, but Dustin's eyes told her *he* was listening. "He tried to touch me ... in private places." Her voice fell to a whisper with the last few words.

"That's ridiculous," Mom began. "He's family. He wouldn't—" Mom's words were cut off again by Dustin.

"When?" he asked.

Hallie met his eyes in surprise. *Does he believe me?* "That day when I stayed home alone because there was a teacher work day and you and Mom had to take the boys to an appointment."

"He touched you?" Dustin's face went dark, and Hallie wasn't sure what that meant.

She shifted in her seat. "He was about to, but you and Mom came home, and he stopped."

"So, he didn't do anything. You're just guessing at his intentions," Mom said, dismissing Hallie just like she had before.

"I *do* know what he was trying to do! Why won't you believe me?" Hallie spewed the words as hot, angry tears coursed down her cheeks.

"Because he wouldn't do that. He's—"

"Amanda, stop it!" Dustin said firmly. "If Hallie says he tried to touch her, then we need to listen."

Hallie stared at him in wonder. *He believes me.*

"Why?" Mom said, turning her attention to Dustin. Her demeanor changed abruptly from dismissive to alert. "Do you know something I don't? Has Leon done something like that before?" Now there was true concern in her voice tinged with an edge of anger.

Dustin faced her, his brow drawn together. "No, of course not. But if Hallie says he tried to touch her, we need to believe her. Why would she lie?"

Mom shrank back with a shrug. "Kids do lie for attention sometimes."

"Has Hallie ever made false accusations to get attention before?"

"No." Mom shook her head. "But it was just the two of us before. Now she has to share me with you and the boys."

"Amanda, she ran away. And it wasn't just down the road or even to a friend's house. She got on a ferry and hid in a hot garage until she was found. She was that serious. I can't believe she did all that just to get attention," Dustin said.

Hallie watched as her mother sat staring at Dustin. Then her face changed again. It looked as if a wall fell down that had been blocking her ability to accept what Hallie told her. A look of shame washed over her and tears sprang to her eyes. Her lips tightened and she met Hallie's eyes. She wiped her tears away and turned her attention to Dustin. "You're right. That's more than just an attention grab." When her eyes turned to Hallie again, they were filled with sorrow and fresh tears. "I'm so sorry," she sobbed. "I ... I should have listened. I didn't want to believe it could be true."

Dustin put a hand on her back. "I hate to believe it too. He's *my* cousin." His eyes darted back to meet Hallie's. "But he will *never* be allowed at our home again."

"What if that doesn't stop him?" Hallie asked. "What if he still comes around when I'm alone?"

Dustin knelt in front of Hallie. "You will not be left home alone again. We'll find a way to make sure of that."

When Hallie looked past him, her mother was nodding in agreement. Tears continued down her cheeks and her forehead crinkled when she met Hallie's eyes. "Can you forgive me?"

Hallie nodded slowly. "But I'd still like to stay on the island until summer is over. I want to stay here with Grandma and Granddad for a little while."

Her grandparents beamed at her.

"Well, I guess for now it's the best solution to make sure you aren't left home alone," Mom agreed.

Grandma stepped forward. "You won't need to worry about making another trip to the island to pick her up. We can bring her home."

Mom turned and smiled wanly at Grandma. "That would be very helpful, Doreen."

"It's not a problem. We're happy to help out. And, you know, I might be able to work it out so I can be with Hallie when there are days off from school." Grandma shrugged. "If you don't mind me coming to stay with you."

Mom sniffed and wiped the tears off her face with the back of her hand. "You're welcome at our home, Doreen. Thank you."

Then something happened that made Hallie's mouth fall open in surprise. Mom reached out and wrapped Grandma up in her arms. "Thank you for helping me see," Mom said.

When she let go of Grandma, Mom ambled over to Hallie and knelt in front of her the same way Dustin had. Her eyes were full of pain. "I am so sorry, baby. Do you really forgive me? I promise I'll listen to you from now on."

Looking into her mother's eyes, Hallie could see how deeply she meant it. "I forgive you." She fell into Mom's arms and buried her face in her chest. Overcome with emotion, Hallie sobbed against the fabric of Mom's blouse.

She couldn't be sure how long she cried, but when a light knock sounded against the door frame, Hallie lifted her head.

"Is it okay to come in now?" Owen asked, glancing around the room. "Or do you need more time?"

Chapter 29

Owen let his gaze sweep around the room, taking in each face to determine if the conversation had gone well or not. No one looked angry. "So … is everyone okay?"

He watched as Hallie and Amanda wiped their faces. Then Hallie sat down at her mother's side, leaning in while Amanda wrapped an arm around her. Owen smiled, knowing the talk went well.

"We're all fine. I think we've got the situation all worked out," Cory said.

Owen stepped into the room leading Carrie Ann. Marissa and Howard followed with the kids. "That's good to hear."

Doreen grinned. "Hallie is going to stay with us until school starts. Then she'll be ready to go home."

"Good." Owen smiled, happy for Cory and Doreen. He'd enjoyed having Hallie around, but it was good to hear that she'd worked things out with both her parents and grandparents enough that she was ready to leave his house. He turned his head when Hallie gasped.

"What is that?" she asked, pointing.

Owen followed her gaze to Carrie Ann's left hand where her ring sparkled. Glancing at Carrie Ann's face, he saw an uncharacteristic blush on her cheeks. Owen smiled and turned to face the room. He opened his mouth but before he could say a word, Carrie Ann took over.

"We're getting married!" She let go of his hand and held hers out to show everyone the ring.

The room erupted in smiles and words of congratulation. "You finally did it," Cory said, coming forward and slapping Owen on the back.

"It's about time, huh?" Marissa said.

Rebecca L. Marsh

Owen raised an eyebrow at his sister.

"Well, it is," she responded.

"You bet it is," Carrie Ann agreed.

"That's great news," Doreen jumped in. "Have you picked a date?"

"We haven't had a chance to talk about it." Owen glanced at Carrie Ann.

She looked into his eyes. "Maybe sometime in the fall?"

"Well, that's coming right up," Doreen said, her eyebrows knit together. "Would you have time to plan a wedding that quick?"

Carrie Ann shrugged and searched out Owen's eyes. "I don't need anything fancy. A small wedding with our family and closest friends is fine for me."

Cory chuckled. "At least half of this town thinks of themselves as your close friends. You might cause a commotion if you exclude them."

Owen patted his fiancé's hand. "You know he's got a point."

She shook her head and tucked a purple tendril of hair behind her ear. "You finally asked me to marry you. I don't want to wait anymore."

"Then we'll all have to pull together to get things ready in time for whatever date you two decide on," Marissa said. "You might have to compromise on some things and not have everything you want, but we can make it happen."

"The only thing I want is Owen. I'd be happy with the justice of the peace," Carrie Ann said.

Owen frowned. "We can keep it simple, but let's have a real wedding. This is too important for a quick 'I do' at the courthouse."

"That's my brother." Marissa beamed at him. "Ever the romantic."

Carrie Ann searched his eyes and nodded. "You're right. This *is* too important." She glanced at Charlie and

Maisy and added. "Besides, I know a few important people who need to have a part in it."

"That's the answer," Marissa said. Everyone in the room looked at her with confused expressions. "I mean, that's how we make it all happen in a short amount of time. We call on all our island friends to help out—to have a part in it. Connie will be thrilled to make you a wedding cake, even if she has to force it into her schedule at the bakery."

"Yeah, she would do that," Carrie Ann said, with appreciation in her voice. "And I'm sure Lacy Rodgers will be happy to help us with the flowers."

"We'll talk to Harry at the print shop about getting some invitations. Those will need to be done right away," Marissa said.

"You'll need a date first though," Doreen added.

Owen turned to Carrie Ann, "Pick one. Any date you like this fall."

Carrie Ann beamed at him as a tear trickled down her cheek. This was the vulnerable side of her that was not often seen. "The last weekend in September. It will still be warm enough to have the wedding outside so long as it isn't raining."

"That's perfect," Owen said, wiping the tear from her face with a finger.

"Owen?" Hallie spoke up from her seat on the couch. "Will I be able to come to your wedding?"

Owen was about to tell her that, of course, she and her whole family would be invited. But before he could get a single word out, Carrie Ann rushed over to Hallie and took one of her hands.

"Sweetheart, I *need* you to be there. You and Maisy are going to be bridesmaids." Carrie Ann looked at Amanda. "If it's okay with your mom."

Amanda smiled and squeezed her daughter. "It's fine with me. What do you say, Hallie?"

Hallie's face lit up. "I say, yes! Do I get to wear a special dress?"

"Of course you do," Carrie Ann said.

"What about me?" Charlie asked. "What do I get to be?"

Owen turned to him. "You don't know?"

Charlie shook his head and gazed at Owen's face.

"I thought you'd know," Owen said. He stepped over to his son and placed his hands on Charlie's shoulders. "Because there's no way I'd pick anyone else to be my best man."

Charlie's eyes widened and his mouth fell open. "Really?"

"Who else would I pick?" Owen asked.

"Uncle Howard?" Charlie said with a shrug.

Owen nodded. "He's going to have an important job too, but you're my best man."

Charlie grinned with pride.

A moment later, Amanda stood up. "I'm so happy for the two of you. And thank you for including Hallie in your plans. I know she's going to love that. But Dustin and I need to leave if we're going to catch the next ferry."

Dustin glanced at his watch as if to confirm, then nodded his agreement.

Hallie grabbed her mother's hand. "Thank you, Mom."

Amanda met her daughter's gaze with her forehead crinkled. "For what? Letting you stay?"

Hallie cocked her head to the side. "Yeah, but mostly for listening."

A shadow of sadness came over Amanda's face and she stood silent for a moment. She shook her head. "I ... I'm sorry I didn't listen before. I should have trusted you." She turned and looked at her husband. "Dustin is the one you should thank."

Hallie smiled at him. "Thank you, Dustin." She looked down at her shoes, then said, "You're a good dad."

Dustin's mellow expression faltered in surprise. "Thank you, Hallie. That means a lot to me."

"Give us some hugs, sweetie," Amanda said. "We really do have to get going."

Hallie threw herself into her mother's arms and held on. When she let go, she reached for Dustin. With his face full of emotion, he wrapped his arms around her and held her close. His expression told Owen that this was the first time he felt like a father to Hallie. And watching them, he remembered the first moment he ever felt that way with Charlie.

Rebecca L. Marsh

Chapter 30

The last Saturday in September

Owen frowned at his reflection in the mirror as he worked at tying the bowtie around his neck. *I should have insisted on not having ties—or at least on getting clip-ons.* He concentrated and tried to follow the directions he'd looked up online. A groan escaped his lips as his fourth attempt ended in another failure.

Just as he was about to begin again, a knock sounded on the door. With a sigh, he let the tie fall loose around his neck and turned toward the door. "Come in," he called.

"Today's the big day," Marissa's voice sang out. "My baby brother is tying the knot."

"Yeah, well, first I've got to tie this." He gestured to the purple tie. "Tell me you know how to work these things."

Marissa giggled. "I know someone who does. And I'll go get him in a moment, but first, there's someone here who wants to see the groom."

He raised an eyebrow. "Tell her it's bad luck."

"It's not Carrie Ann." Marissa turned to the open door behind her. "Come on in, sweetie."

Hallie poked her head through the opening. Her face was alight with a smile.

"Hey, Hallie, come on in," Owen said.

She stepped into the room, her long purple dress swishing around her ankles and tiny purple flowers braided into her hair.

"Wow! You look beautiful," Owen told her.

"Doesn't she?" Marissa said. "I already told her and Maisy they were so lovely they might steal the show."

Hallie blushed. "No way! Carrie Ann is so pretty. Wait till you see her, Owen."

Owen's smile widened. "So, you're saying it'll be worth the fight I've had with this tie?"

She nodded emphatically. "She looks like a princess."

"I can't wait to see for myself."

"I'll let you two talk a minute while I go find Melvin Saunders to help with the tie," Marissa said before leaving the room. Owen was surprised he didn't think of Melvin himself. The man wore a bowtie every day of his life and he was just outside the door helping get the community center's sound system ready for the reception.

When the door closed behind Marissa, Hallie stepped closer. "I wanted to say thank you."

"For what?" Owen asked.

"For letting me stay with you over the summer."

Owen's forehead scrunched. "You've already thanked me for that."

She took a deep breath and let it out. "But that's not enough." A tear trickled down her cheek and dropped to the floor. "Everything is better now. Mom listens now, and Dustin is like ... well, he's like a real dad to me now." She looked down, then returned her gaze to Owen with fresh tears in her eyes. "And I have Grandma and Granddad again. I mean, I know the truth about them and my dad. I know they love me."

"Hallie," Owen said, taking one of her hands in his. "I didn't do all that. I just gave you a place to stay for a few weeks. You worked the rest out yourself."

She used a tissue to dry her face. "But I wouldn't have—not without you and Charlie. And Maisy too."

Owen sniffed, pushing back tears of his own, and pulled her into a hug. "I'm glad I could be a part of all that. And seeing your happiness is thanks enough."

As Hallie pulled back from him, another knock sounded on the door.

"Owen, is it okay to come in now? I've got Melvin," Marissa called.

"Come on in," he called back. Then he met Hallie's eyes. "And you better get back to the bride's room, young lady."

Hallie grinned and danced out of the room as Melvin entered. "We'll get that tie all fixed up," he said.

Twenty minutes later, Owen stood on a small gazebo he'd constructed himself as an altar for the occasion and waited for the start of his wedding. *My wedding*—those words tumbled through his mind, filling him with joy. *I'm getting married!* It all still felt a little surreal—too good to be true. But it was true. Carrie Ann would walk down the aisle any moment now and stand with him to take their vows.

He glanced over his shoulder at the clear, blue sky, alive with seagulls. Then his gaze traveled down below to the ocean that broke in crashing waves against the rocky wall of the cliff. This place—Tara's Pointe—had a history that was both joyous and heartbreaking. It was given its name after the young daughter of their town's founder fell from the edge. That event led to the construction of a guardrail to prevent it from happening again. Since then, it had been the site of their annual fireworks displays for both New Year's Eve and the Fourth of July. The lovely spot had hosted several other weddings but it had also been the site of a serious event in Owen's family. Two years ago, Maisy had run to this spot when she was feeling deeply hurt. The situation ended well, but they'd come dangerously close to a tragedy.

That was part of the reason Owen and Carrie Ann thought this was the perfect place to have their wedding.

Good memories of the place would help push aside the bad. And besides, the spot was the most beautiful on the island.

When the music started, Owen snapped to attention and watched as the bridal party proceeded down the aisle. First, Charlie grinned as he walked with his aunt, so proud to be best man. They were followed by Carter and Maisy, Howard and Hallie, then Cory and Millie. Alex was the last before the bride, holding the ring bearer's pillow with all the care a seven-year-old could muster.

There was a brief pause as the music changed to recognize the bride. As the guests stood and turned to watch Carrie Ann walk down the aisle, Owen whispered to Charlie, "You ready?"

Charlie looked at him with a serious expression. "*I* am. Are you ready, Dad?"

Owen watched Carrie Ann heading toward him, her white dress blowing with the breeze and her hair tied up in a twist with a white lily stuck into it. He glanced at his mother and his sister-in-law sitting in the front row. Everyone he cared about was here, and stepping closer to him with every beat of his heart was the woman he loved. She was about to tie her life to his for as long as they both shall live. He grinned as his heart surged with joy. "I sure am."

Summer's Runaway

ABOUT THE AUTHOR

Rebecca L. Marsh is an award-winning author of women's fiction and member of the Paulding County Writer's Guild. She grew up in the mountains of western North Carolina, and now lives in Dallas, Georgia with her husband.

She is a Christian, a mother to a beautiful daughter, and an animal lover. When she isn't writing, she enjoys spending time with her family (cats and dog included), reading a good book, watching a movie, or playing a game.

She is the author of six novels, *When the Storm Ends, The Rift Between Us, Where Hope is Found, Remember the Butterfly, Summer's Runaway, and Beyond the Broken Shore.*

Visit her website at rebeccalmarsh.com

Or follow her on Facebook at

Author: Rebecca L. Marsh

ACKNOWLEDGMENTS

A special thanks to those who took the time to help me in any way—all my beta readers. You are all wonderful and I'm grateful for your help. Many thanks to my friend, Angie Young, a nurse who is always willing to help me with the medical questions that crop up along the way. Thank you to the Paulding County Writer's Guild who are both friends and support group for me, and especially Heather Trim who did such a nice job designing the cover for this book. Most of all, I want to thank my family—all of them. I also want to give a very special thanks to Joe and Maegan for being my support all along the way.

NOTE FROM THE AUTHOR

Thank you for reading *Summer's Runaway*. I value all my readers, and hope you have enjoyed it. Independent authors depend on reader's support for their work. If you'd like to leave a review on Amazon or Goodreads, I would greatly appreciate it

Thanks for your support!